I0762879

PRAISE FOR
BAT EATER AND OTHER NAMES FOR CORA ZENG

"A compelling, gory, ghostly romp, and a righteous battle cry aimed into the racist heart of the pandemic hellscape."
—Paul Tremblay, *New York Times* bestselling author

"An important and timely tale about life as an 'other' in chaotic times."
—Gabino Iglesias, *New York Times Book Review*

"This is what it felt like to live in New York City during lockdown: haunted, absurd, terrifying, ridiculous, and full of hungry ghosts. This book shook me in all the best ways."
—Grady Hendrix, *New York Times* bestselling author

"An adult debut that frightens to the bone, deftly illustrating trauma and paranoia in aching prose and with perfectly timed grim humor."
—*Library Journal*, starred review

"Singular in every way, this book dug its claws into me and would not let go."
—Ling Ling Huang, author of *Natural Beauty*

"Essential reading from a new voice in horror."
—*Booklist*, starred review

"Equal parts incisive and relentless. . . . Kylie Lee Baker catapults readers back to the chaos of the early COVID-19 pandemic."
—*BookPage*, starred review

"*Bat Eater and Other Names for Cora Zeng* has everything I look for in a compelling horror novel—strangeness, sensitivity, and empathy. This is easily one of the most exciting and unique books I've read in years."
—Eric LaRocca, author of
Things Have Gotten Worse Since We Last Spoke

"Baker successfully uses fear, both supernatural and human, to shine a spotlight on anti-Asian hate. Fans of creepy ghost stories and social horror will want to snap this up."

—*Publishers Weekly*

"Body horror and female rage fiction combine in a powerful novel that will leave you quaking."

—Alma Katsu, author of *The Fervor*

"I smashed through *Bat Eater*—shocking, visceral and haunted by more than ghosts: trauma, rage, grief, racism, crime scene clean-ups and COVID paranoia."

—Alice Slater, *Sunday Times* bestselling author of *Death of a Bookseller*

"This story of hungry ghosts demanding redemption is in a word . . . magnificent."

—Veronica G. Henry, bestselling author of *The Canopy Keepers*

"A profound reminder of the true horrors that lurk in the world, the ones that cannot be dispelled by turning on a light or flipping the page."

—Tori Bovalino, author of *My Throat an Open Grave*

"*Bat Eater* is a serial killer mystery and a heartbreaking portrayal of grief and a brutal depiction of a Chinese woman's experience during COVID and a genuinely terrifying ghost story, all at once."

—Kirsty Logan, author of *Things We Say in the Dark*

"Stylish, propulsive, occasionally shocking, and fueled by a great big beating heart for its characters, *Bat Eater* is a ghost story that exists in its own glorious phylum."

—Nick Cutter, bestselling author of *The Troop* and *The Queen*

KYLIE LEE BAKER

BAT EATER AND OTHER NAMES FOR CORA ZENG

A Novel

HANOVER
SQUARE
PRESS

Recycling programs for this product may not exist in your area.

ISBN-13: 978-1-335-00152-8

Bat Eater and Other Names for Cora Zeng

First edition published in 2025. This edition published in 2026.

Copyright © 2025 by Kylie Lee Baker

All rights reserved. No part of this book may be used or reproduced in any manner whatsoever without written permission.

Without limiting the exclusive rights of any author, contributor or the publisher of this publication, any unauthorized use of this publication to train generative artificial intelligence (AI) technologies is expressly prohibited. Harlequin also exercises their rights under Article 4(3) of the Digital Single Market Directive 2019/790 and expressly reserves this publication from the text and data mining exception.

This is a work of fiction. Names, characters, places and incidents are either the product of the author's imagination or are used fictitiously. Any resemblance to actual persons, living or dead, businesses, companies, events or locales is entirely coincidental.

TM and ® are trademarks of Harlequin Enterprises ULC.

Hanover Square Press
22 Adelaide St. West, 41st Floor
Toronto, Ontario M5H 4E3, Canada
HanoverSqPress.com

HarperCollins Publishers
Macken House, 39/40 Mayor Street Upper,
Dublin 1, D01 C9W8, Ireland
www.HarperCollins.com

Printed in U.S.A.

26 27 28 29 30 LBC 6 5 4 3 2

To everyone we lost in the pandemic

ONE

April 2020

East Broadway station bleeds when it rains, water rushing down from cracks in the secret darkness of the ceiling. Someone should probably fix that, but it's the end of the world, and New York has bigger problems than a soggy train station that no one should be inside of anyway. No one takes the subway at the end of the world. No one except Cora and Delilah Zeng.

Delilah wanders too close to the edge of the platform and Cora grabs her arm, tugging her away from the abyss of the tracks that unlatches its jaws, waiting. But Delilah settles safely behind the yellow line and the darkness clenches its teeth.

Outside the wet mouth of the station, New York is empty. The China Virus, as they call it, has cleared the streets. News stations flash through footage of China—bodies in garbage bags, guards and tanks protecting the city lines, sobbing doctors waving their last goodbyes from packed trains, families who just want to fucking live but are trapped in the plague city for the Greater Good.

On the other side of the world, New York is so empty it echoes. You can scream and the ghost of your voice will carry for blocks and blocks. The sound of footsteps lasts forever, the low hum of streetlights a warm undercurrent that was always there, waiting, but no one could hear it until now. Delilah says it's unnerving, but Cora likes the quiet, likes how much bigger the city feels, likes that the little lights from people's apartment windows are the only hint of their existence, no one anything more than a bright little square in the sky.

What she doesn't like is that she can't find any toilet paper at the end of the world.

Apparently, people do strange things when they're scared of dying, and one of them is hoarding toilet paper. Cora and Delilah have been out for an hour trying to find some and finally managed to grab a four-pack of one-ply in Chinatown, which is better than nothing but not by much.

They had to walk in the rain because they couldn't get an Uber. No one wants Chinese girls in their car, and they're not the kind of Chinese that can afford their own car in a city where it isn't necessary. But now that they have the precious paper, they'd rather not walk home in the rain and end up with a sodden mess in their arms.

"The train isn't coming," Cora says. She feels certain of this. She feels certain about a lot of things she can't explain, the way some people are certain that God exists. Some thoughts just cross her mind and sink their teeth in. Besides, the screen overhead that's supposed to tell them when the next train arrives has said DELAYS for the last ten minutes.

"It's coming," Delilah says, checking her phone, then tucking it away when droplets from the leaky roof splatter onto the screen. Delilah is also certain about many things, but for different reasons. Delilah chooses the things she wants to believe, while Cora's thoughts are bear traps snapping closed around her ankles.

Sometimes Cora thinks Delilah is more of a dream than a sister, a camera flash of pretty lights in every color that you can never look at directly. She wraps herself up in pale pink and wispy silk and flower hair clips; she wears different rings on each finger that all have a special meaning; she is Alice in Wonderland who has stumbled out of a rabbit hole and somehow arrived in New York from a world much more kind and lovely than this one.

Cora hugs the toilet paper to her chest and peers into the silent train tunnel. She can't see even a whisper of light from the other side. The darkness closes in like a wall. The train cannot be coming because trains can't break through walls.

Or maybe Cora just doesn't want to go home, because going home with Delilah means remembering that there is a world outside of this leaky station.

There is their dad in China, just a province away from the epicenter of body bags. And there is the man who emptied his garbage over their heads from his window and called them Chinks on the walk here. And there is the big question of What Comes Next? Because another side effect of the end of the world is getting laid off.

Cora used to work the front desk at the Met, which wasn't exactly what an art history degree was designed for and certainly didn't justify the debt. But it was relevant enough to her studies that for a few months it stopped shame from creeping in like black mold and coating her lungs in her sleep. But no one needs museums at the end of the world, so no one needs Cora.

Delilah answered emails and scheduled photo shoots for a local fashion magazine that went belly-up as soon as someone whispered the word *pandemic*, and suddenly there were two art history majors, twenty-four and twenty-six, with work experience in dead industries and New York City rent to pay. Now the money is gone and there are no careers to show for it and the worst part is that they had a chance, they had a Nai Nai who paid for half their tuition because she thought America was for dreams. They didn't have to wait tables or strip or sell Adderall to pay for college but they somehow messed it up anyway, and Cora thinks that's worse than having no chance at all. She thinks a lot of other things about herself too, but she lets those thoughts go quickly, snaps her hands away from them like they're a hot pan that will burn her skin.

Cora thinks this is all Delilah's fault but won't say it out loud because that's another one of her thoughts that no one wants to hear. It's a little bit her own fault as well, for not having her own dreams. If there was anything Cora actually wanted besides existing comfortably, she would have known what to study in college, wouldn't have had to chase after Delilah.

But not everyone has dreams. Some people just *are*, the way that trees and rocks and rivers are just there without a reason, the rest of the world moving around them.

Cora thinks that the water dripping down the wall looks oddly dark, more so than the usual sludge of the city, and maybe it has a reddish tinge, like the city has slit its own wrists and is dying in this empty station. But she knows better than to say this out loud, because everything looks dirty to her, and Cora Zeng thinking something is dirty doesn't mean the average human agrees—at least, that's what everyone tells her.

"Maybe I'll work at a housekeeping company," Cora says, half to herself and half to the echoing tunnel, but Delilah answers anyway.

"You know that's a bad idea," she says.

Cora shrugs. Objectively, she understands that if you scrub

yourself raw with steel wool one singular time, no one likes it when you clean anything for the rest of your life. But things still need to be cleaned even if Delilah doesn't like it, and Cora thinks there are worse things than leaning a little bit into the crazy parts of you. Isn't that what artists do, after all? Isn't that the kind of person Delilah likes? The tortured artist types who smoke indoors and paint with their own blood and feces.

"Mama cleaned toilets for rich white people because she had no choice," Delilah says. "You have a college degree and that's what you want to do?"

Cora doesn't answer at first because *Mama* means Delilah's mom, so Cora doesn't see why her thoughts on Cora's life should matter. Cora doesn't have a Mama. She has a Mom, a white lady from Wisconsin who probably hired someone else's mama to clean her toilet.

Cora quite likes cleaning toilets, but this is another thing she knows she shouldn't say out loud. Instead, she says, "What I want is to make rent this month."

Legally, Cora's fairly certain they can't be evicted during the pandemic, but she doesn't want to piss off their landlord, the man who sniffs their mail and saves security camera footage of Delilah entering the building. He price-gouges them for a crappy fourth-floor walkup in the East Village with a radiator that vomits a gallon of brown water onto their floor in the winter and a marching band of pipes banging in the walls, but somehow Cora doubts they'll find anything better without jobs.

Delilah smiles with half her mouth, her gaze distant like Cora is telling her a fairy tale. "I've been burning lemongrass for money energy," Delilah says. "We'll be fine." This is another thing Delilah just *knows*.

Cora hates the smell of lemongrass. The scent coats her throat, wakes her up at night feeling like she's drowning in oil. But she doesn't know if the oils are a Chinese thing or just a Delilah thing, and she hates accidentally acting like a white girl around Delilah. Whenever she does, Delilah gives her this *look*, like she's remembered who Cora really is, and changes the subject.

"The train is late," Cora says instead of acknowledging the lemongrass. "I don't think it's coming."

"It's coming, Cee," Delilah says.

"I read that they reduced service since no one's taking the train these days," Cora says. "What if it doesn't stop here anymore?"

"It's coming," Delilah says. "It's not like we have a choice except waiting here anyway."

Cora's mind flashes with the image of both their skeletons standing at the station, waiting for a train that never comes, while the world crumbles around them. They could walk—they only live in the East Village—but Delilah is made of sugar and her makeup melts off in the rain and her umbrella is too small and she said no, so that's the end of it. Delilah is not Cora's boss, she's not physically intimidating, and she has no blackmail to hold over her, but Cora knows the only choice is to do what Delilah says. When you're drowning and someone grabs your hand, you don't ask them where they're taking you.

A quiet breeze sighs through the tunnel, a dying exhale. It blows back Delilah's bangs and Cora notices that Delilah has penciled in her eyebrows perfectly, even though it's raining and they only went out to the store to buy toilet paper. Something about the sharp arch of her left eyebrow in particular triggers a thought that Cora doesn't want to think, but it bites down all the same.

Sometimes, Cora thinks she hates her sister.

It's strange how hate and love can so quietly exist at the

same time. They are moon phases, one silently growing until one day all that's left is darkness. It's not something that Delilah says or does, really. Cora is used to her small annoyances.

It's that Delilah is a daydream and standing next to her makes Cora feel real.

Cora has pores full of sweat and oil, socks with stains on the bottom, a stomach that sloshes audibly after she eats. Delilah is a pretty arrangement of refracted light who doesn't have to worry about those things. Cora wanted to be like her for a very long time, because who doesn't want to transcend their disgusting body and become Delilah Zeng, incorporeal, eternal? But Cora's not so sure anymore.

Cora peers into the tunnel. *We are going to be stuck here forever,* Cora thinks, knows.

But then the sound begins, a rising symphony to Cora's ears. The ground begins to rumble, puddles shivering.

"Finally," Delilah says, pocketing her phone. "See? I told you."

Cora nods because Delilah did tell her and sometimes Delilah is right. The things Cora thinks she *knows* are too often just bad dreams bleeding into her waking hours.

Far away, the headlights become visible in the darkness. A tiny mouth of white light.

"Cee," Delilah says.

Her tone is too delicate, and it makes coldness curl around Cora's heart. Delilah tosses words out easily, dandelion parachutes carried about by the wind. But these words have weight.

Delilah toys with her bracelet—a jade bangle from their Auntie Zeng, the character for *hope* on the gold band. Cora has a matching one, shoved in a drawer somewhere, except the plate says *love*, at least that's what Cora thinks. She's not very good at reading Chinese.

"I'm thinking of going to see Dad," Delilah says.

The mouth of light at the end of the tunnel has expanded into a door of brilliant white, and Cora waits because this cannot be all. Dad lives in Changsha, has lived there ever since America became too much for him, except it's always been too much for Cora too and she has nowhere to run away to, her father hasn't given her the words she needs. Delilah has visited him twice in the last five years, so this news isn't enough to make Delilah's voice sound so tight, so nervous.

"I think I might stay there awhile," Delilah says, looking away. "Now that I'm out of work, it seems like a good time to get things settled before the pandemic blows over."

Cora stares at the side of Delilah's head because her sister won't meet her gaze. Cora isn't stupid, she knows what this is a "good time" for. Delilah started talking about being a model in China last year. Cora doesn't know if the odds are better in China and she doubts Delilah knows either. All she knows is that Delilah tried for all of three months to make a career of modeling in New York until that dream fizzled out, smoke spiraling from it, and Delilah stopped trying because everything is disposable to her, right down to her dreams.

Cora always thought this particular dream would be too expensive, too logistically complicated for Delilah to actually follow through on. Worst-case scenario, they'd plan a three-week vacation to China that would turn into a week and a half when Delilah lost interest and started fighting with Dad again. The idea of flying during a pandemic feels like a death sentence, but Cora has already resigned herself to hunting down some N95 respirators just so Delilah could give her modeling dream an honest try.

Because even if Delilah tends to extinguish her own dreams too fast, Cora believes in them for all of their brief, brilliant lives. If Cora ever found a dream of her own, she would nurture it in soft soil, measure out each drop of water, each sunbeam, give it a chance to become. So Cora will not squash her sister's dreams, not for anything.

"I'll just put my half of the rent on my credit card until I find work," Delilah says, "so you won't need a new roommate."

Then Cora understands, all at once, like a knife slipped between her ribs, that Delilah isn't inviting Cora to come with her.

Of course she isn't. Delilah has a mama who speaks Mandarin to her, so Delilah's Chinese is good enough to live in China. But Cora's isn't. Delilah would have to do everything for her, go everywhere with her because she knows Cora would cry just trying to check out at the supermarket. Delilah could do it for her, but she doesn't want to.

Cora suddenly feels like a child who has wandered too far into a cave. The echoes become ghosts and the darkness wraps in tight ribbons around your throat and you call for a mom who will never come.

Cora's hands shake, fingers pressing holes into the plastic wrap of the toilet paper, her whole body vibrating with the sheer unfairness of it all. You can't string someone along their whole life and then just leave them alone one day holding your toilet paper in a soggy train station.

"Or you could stay with your aunt?" Delilah says. "Then you wouldn't have to worry about rent. It would be better for both of us, I think."

Auntie Lois, she means. Mom's sister, whose house smells like a magazine, who makes Cora kneel in a confessional booth until she can name all her sins. Delilah has decided that this is Cora's life, and Delilah is the one who makes decisions.

Delilah keeps talking, but Cora can't hear her. The world rumbles as the train draws closer. The white light is too bright now, too sharp behind Delilah, and it illuminates her silhouette, carves her into the wet darkness. Delilah has a beautiful silhouette, the kind that men would have painted hundreds of years ago. Cora thinks about the *Girl with a Pearl Earring*, and the *Mona Lisa*, and all the beautiful women immortalized in oil paint, and wonders if they said cruel things too, if their words had mattered at all or just the roundness of their eyes and softness of their cheeks, if beautiful people are allowed to break your heart and get away with it.

The man appears in a flash of a black hoodie and blue surgical mask.

He says two words, and even though the train is rushing closer, a roaring wave about to knock them off their feet, those two words are perfectly clear, sharp as if carved into Cora's skin.

Bat eater.

Cora has heard those words a lot the past two months. The end of the world began at a wet market in Wuhan, they say, with a sick bat. Cora has never once eaten a bat, but it has somehow become common knowledge that Chinese people eat bats just to start plagues.

Cora only glances at the man's face for a moment before her gaze snaps to his pale hand clamped around Delilah's skinny arm like a white spider, crunching the polyester of her pink raincoat. Lots of men grab Delilah because she is the kind of girl that men want to devour. Cora thinks the man will try to kiss Delilah, or force her up the stairs and into a cab, or a thousand things better than what actually happens next.

Because he doesn't pull her close. He pushes her away.

Delilah stumbles over the yellow line, ankle twisting, and when she crashes down there's no ground to meet her, just the yawning chasm of the train tracks.

The first car hits her face.

All at once, Cora's skin is scorched with something viscous and salty. Brakes scream and blue sparks fly and the wind blasts her hair back, the liquid rushing across her throat, under her shirt. Her first thought is that the train has splashed her in some sort of track sludge, and for half a second that is the worst thought in the entire world. The toilet paper falls from Cora's arms and splashes into a puddle when it hits the ground and *There goes the whole point of the trip*, she thinks.

Delilah does not stand up. The train is a rushing blur of silver, a solid wall of hot air and screeching metal and Delilah is on the ground, her skirt pooling out around her. *Get up, Delilah*, Cora thinks, because train station floors are rainforests of bacteria tracked in from so many millions of shoes, because the puddle beneath her can't be just rainwater—it looks oddly dark, almost black, spreading fast like a hole opening up in the floor. Cora steps closer and it almost, *almost* looks like Delilah is leaning over the ledge, peering over the lip of the platform.

But Delilah ends just above her shoulders.

Her throat is a jagged line, torn flaps of skin and sharp bone and the pulsing O of her open trachea. Blood runs unstopped from her throat, swirling together with the rainwater of the rotting train station, and soon the whole platform is bleeding, weeping red water into the crack between the platform and the train, feeding the darkness.

Cora is screaming, a raw sound that begins somewhere deep inside her rib cage and tears its way up her throat and becomes a hurricane, a knife-sharp cry, the last sound that many women ever make.

But there's no one to hear it because New York is a dead body, because no one rides the subway at the end of the world. No one but Cora Zeng.

TWO

August 2020

There are skull fragments jammed in the grout of Yuxi He's bathroom. Cora pinches them between her gloved fingers, wiggles until the tiles release them, leaving tiny holes behind. Brains pool in the bathtub around her feet, but Cora is swaddled deep in the cocoon of her hazmat suit, and somehow she feels safer here than at home wearing only her own skin.

She drops the skull fragment in a biohazard bag and scans the wall, which is now full of thin marks where the pieces lodged themselves. Memories of the final gunshot. There is still all the hair, and the brains, and the skin flaps, but those things wash away easily.

Cora prefers bathroom cleanups. Fresh blood almost always scrubs out of tiles with enough bleach, but carpets are hardly ever salvageable. They have to cut out the bloody sections and leave gaping holes behind, so even though the families won't see the blood and guts anymore, they'll know exactly where it was. They can imagine it, and imagining is sometimes worse than seeing.

"There's some in the vents," says the voice of Harvey Chen from behind Cora. In his hazmat suit, he's just a lumpy yellow silhouette that could be anyone in the world. But his voice is undeniably Harvey, perpetually whining, a few decibels too loud to be polite—it's fine in the hazmat suit, but even when he takes it off, he always yells like he's forgotten he's no longer wrapped in plastic.

Harvey's uncle owns a dry-cleaning shop in Chinatown that expanded into crime scene cleanup, since hardly anyone needs their dry cleaning done during a pandemic, but a surprising number of people need brains scrubbed off their walls and even cheapskate families don't like doing that kind of thing themselves. Cora came for a job cleaning clothes and left with a job cleaning entrails.

Harvey fumbles with a screwdriver through his thick gloves and starts unscrewing the vent panel.

"We don't know how deep into the vents this shit went," he says.

"Probably not that far," Cora says. After all, it was a bullet to the head, not a grenade. She doesn't bother raising her voice, even though the hazmat suit will swallow her words, but for all of his loudness, Harvey has impeccable hearing.

"If we miss a piece, it'll get sucked into another apartment," Harvey says. "Hairy skull pieces raining down on unsuspecting families. Actually, that would be kind of hilarious. Maybe we shouldn't clean the vents."

Cora isn't sure which part of that is supposed to be hilarious. Harvey understands blood and gore in the way of people who play a lot of video games. Finds it exciting the way you only can when it's not yours. Cora knows it's not his fault—he's just a horror movie junkie trying to make rent, and there's no harm in finding what joy you can in a dirty and depressing job that *someone* has to do. Being around him makes it easier to pretend that this is all just special effects on a movie set, because he's so utterly unfazed by it all.

Cora once thought crime scene cleaners would be intimately familiar with death, but the truth is, they never actually see the bodies. The police take them out first and leave the mess behind. In her four months working as a crime scene cleaner, Cora has never once seen a corpse. She has only seen one corpse in her whole life.

"There are filters in the HVAC," Cora says. "Skull pieces won't fit through."

"And this whole building will smell like rotting flesh," Harvey says.

"You should move in. You'd feel right at home," Yifei says, pushing the wet vac into the room.

"All three of us smell like a hot garbage truck on a good day," Harvey says. "Don't throw stones in a glass house, Liu."

Yifei has already lost interest in Harvey and has started rifling through Yuxi He's medicine cabinet. It's easy to snatch things from crime scenes because people assume they were ruined from the blood and guts and the cleanup crew did them a favor by throwing them out. Yifei has collected sleeping pills and throw cushions and ceramic cats, and those are only the things Cora noticed. She decided early on not to question Yifei about it because it's the only strange thing about her, the only thing that hints at why she'd be working a job like this and not in an office with a water cooler and cubicle. Like a hairline crack in a porcelain teacup. Cora is afraid that if she picks at it too much, Yifei will start looking at *her* instead, asking questions.

And Cora won't have answers because Cora isn't a person, not really.

She's been thinking a lot about obituaries lately, how her own would be short and impersonal.

Coraline "Cora" Zeng, 24, of Manhattan, passed away on INSERT DATE AND PLACE OF DEATH. Preceded in death by her sister, Delilah Zeng.

That's all she can come up with, because if Cora died today, she would die being nothing more than Delilah's sister, the only fact that matters.

She's tried to metamorphosize herself into someone else—a box beneath her bed is stuffed with yarn from when she tried to be the kind of person who crochets, her bookshelf is mostly cookbooks from when she attempted to be the kind of person who likes cooking, and of course there was that night she watched intricate nail art videos until dawn. But everything sloughs off Cora like dead skin because she is not the kind of person who creates things, who makes a mark on the world. She is an echo, quieter and quieter until she's nothing at all.

"She's got trophies with wings," Yifei says.

"Who?"

"He Yuxi," Yifei says, in her perfect accent that puts Cora and Harvey to shame because Yifei isn't an ABC; she was actually born in China. She won't tell them what part, though. Every time Cora asks, she says a different place—sometimes it's Shanghai, other times Guangzhou, and sometimes it's just *a place so small you wouldn't recognize the name.*

"It's the caduceus," Cora says. When Harvey and Yifei don't answer, she continues. "The symbol for medicine. She was a doctor." Cora knows this because there was a pager on the bathroom counter beeping wildly. But it got covered in blood, and blood equals biohazard, so into the trash it went.

"She off herself?" Yifei says.

Cora shrugs because that's not the kind of information the police tell the cleanup crew. But Cora saw the broken lock on the front door, so she very much doubts it was suicide.

Then, of course, there's the other reason. The one Cora

doesn't want to let float around in her mind too long, lest it latch on. The one that Harvey and Yifei don't mention, so Cora won't either.

Yuxi He is the fifth Asian woman they've scraped off the walls this week, and it's only Wednesday.

It wasn't always this way. When Cora first joined the dry-cleaner-turned-corpse-cleaner, there was an even spread of motorcycle accidents on the highway and grandmas rotting for weeks in their attics and the occasional drug deal gone wrong in a warehouse. But lately it's nothing but Asian women in their apartments, so much blood that it looks like someone repainted the walls red. Cora hopes it just means Harvey's uncle has focused on customers in Chinatown who pay him under the table, that it's a shift in business and not in crime.

"I'll ask Paul," Harvey says, stripping off his gloves and digging around for his phone, which he definitely isn't supposed to have in a room full of biohazards, but he's already typing in his passcode. Harvey has an EMT friend who fills him in on all the gory details and sometimes even sends him photos. On more than one occasion, Harvey has slipped printouts of body parts into Cora's and Yifei's bags when they're not looking, impossibly convinced that they'll appreciate it as much as he would and are just too shy to admit it. Cora always tries to tear them up before she can see anything.

Harvey pockets his phone, turns on the shower, and angles the showerhead so blood drips down the walls and pools in the bathtub. He takes out a sponge and steps into the tub, but sighs at what he sees.

"The water's not draining," Harvey says. "There's too much fucking hair in the drain."

"Well, pull it out," Yifei says.

Harvey crosses his arms. "Gross."

"You're standing in a bath of brain slop and you think hair is gross?" Yifei says.

"Who the hell doesn't think that's gross?" Harvey says. "Girls always leave hair balls as big as hamsters in the shower."

"Don't say that like you've ever lived with a girl," Yifei says.

A strange ringing begins in Cora's ears. She wants Harvey and Yifei to stop arguing, so she squats down and sinks her glove into the murky swirl of blood water, pinching the hair ball. It's denser than she expected, squishy through the numbness of her gloves. She tugs, but it stays lodged.

"Cora is braver than you," Yifei says.

"Have I ever denied that?" Harvey says.

Cora pulls again, and the hair ball slides out a little but then catches again. A gush of fresh blood clouds the water, rushing from the drain. Cora readjusts her grip. The hair ball is much bigger than she thought, thick enough to wrap her hand around, like a cooked eggplant.

"Jesus, how much hair did that lady have?" Harvey says.

Cora tightens her hold and feels something crunch, even through her thick gloves. The realization that *this is not a hair ball* makes her freeze.

"Cora—" Yifei says.

But Cora needs to know now because the unknowing is worse than knowing, and she gives another firm tug and the hair ball dislodges. She pulls it above the surface of the water and it expands all at once, a black mass growing, unfolding in jagged edges, slack jaw, tiny teeth.

A bat.

Cora's hand goes limp and the bat drops, splashes bloody water onto the three of them. It sinks beneath the water for a moment, then bobs back to the surface, tiny mouth filled with scarlet.

"She has drain bats," Harvey says.

Yifei smacks the back of his head, leaving a bloody handprint on his hazmat suit. "Bats don't live in drains, dumbass," she says.

Harvey rubs the back of his head. "So, what, she put her own pet bat in the drain?" he says.

"Biohazard bag," Cora says, because the water is draining now and the bat is spinning, its beady black eyes staring at the ceiling, its wings carving lines into the water, and Cora feels the sudden urge to dispose of it the way people need to vomit—it has to happen *now*.

Yifei opens the bag and Cora pinches a wing, slinging the body into the bag where it splashes among the skull fragments. *Bat eater, bat eater,* the man says. Cora has never once felt sick at all the gore she's cleaned up—no corpse, no problem—but all at once nausea closes her throat and her stomach clenches and the sheer terror of puking inside a hazmat suit and not being able to escape from her own bile makes her want to die. She rushes out of the bathroom and rips off the face cover, tears off her goggles and face shield. The air tastes like blood, but it's cold, drying out the nauseous saliva pooling under her tongue.

"Yo," Harvey says, coming out behind her and offering Cora a bag of skull pieces. "Puke in here, not on the carpet. What's one more biohazard in the bag?"

"I'm not gonna puke," Cora says, hoping that saying it out loud will make it true.

She swallows and focuses on her surroundings, trying to scrape her mind of anything involving bats. She relaxes her fists, tries to focus on the lights and colors of the apartment that once belonged to Yuxi He.

It's smaller than what you'd expect for a doctor's place, though Cora has heard resident doctors don't make that much—one bedroom and a kitchen bursting with appliances.

There's a tiny nook in the window with a cushion that's thinner on one side, like someone sat there often, a stack of books forming a makeshift end table beside it. There's a mug shaped like a bear with a cookie pocket on the front, a half-eaten oatmeal cookie still sitting inside, tea gone cold. A jar of buttons on the windowsill. A sun-faded dream catcher tied around the window lock.

Cora has never seen Yuxi He, but somehow she feels that she has seen something infinitely more important than her corpse. This look into her last moments feels violently intimate. No one was ever supposed to see this. It doesn't matter that all Cora sees is normal and harmless—Yuxi He did not expect three unemployed millennials in hazmat suits in her apartment tonight, or her bathtub filled with her own brains.

"Want some ginger tea?" Yifei says, flicking on Yuxi He's electric kettle.

Cora shakes her head, cannot imagine consuming anything in this apartment. There is blood everywhere, even if Harvey and Yifei can't see it.

The reporters are waiting for them when they come outside.

The really desperate ones always stick around for the cleanup crew after the cops refuse to talk. But Harvey's uncle has one rule, which he said in Shanghainese so Cora had no idea what it actually was, but Yifei translated it as *Don't say shit to anyone about jobs.* Apparently the dry cleaner stayed afloat because Harvey's uncle was good about cleaning out bloodstains without asking questions, and people have come to respect that kind of discretion.

That doesn't stop the reporters from trying, though. It's always young ones, new in their careers, trying to prove they're worth their slim paychecks. They've offered Cora ten-course meals at Michelin-star restaurants, waved gift certificates at her, slipped cash into her hands. They're only slightly less persistent than the men who catcall Cora on the street at night, except instead of sex they want photographs of crime scenes.

Cora knows they always zero in on her because Harvey is six foot one and Yifei looks like she'll punch anyone who slows her down. They think Cora is the easiest one to crack. They like the way she hunches her shoulders and avoids eye contact and presses close to Harvey's back when she sees them; they smile because they know weakness when they see it and Cora can lie with her words but never with her eyes.

Cora wants nothing more than to rip her mask off and breathe, but with the crush of people on the sidewalk, she can't. The crime scene just had to be in the compacted heart of Chinatown, which Cora can hardly walk through on a good day, when she's not hauling a hazmat suit and a bag of cleaning chemicals. Old Asian ladies pulling carts manage to push through, but otherwise the reporters have cut off the sidewalk completely, forcing people into the oily puddles in the street.

The three of them still smell like sweat and inside-out human, so they force their way through the reporters with the power of stench alone. People shove microphones in Cora's face, amplifying her breathing. Someone else tries to cram a business card into her back pocket and their touch makes her jump, makes her feel like they've jammed a finger into the wetness of her mouth.

She grabs a fistful of the back of Harvey's shirt and presses closer to him as all of the reporters' questions blur together. Cora wants to tell them she doesn't have the details they want, but that would probably qualify as *saying shit to someone about the job*, so she ducks her head and holds tight to Harvey.

Just as they clear the crowd, a hand reaches out for Yifei's arm.

Thin, white fingers.

The hand closes around her and Cora stops short, hazmat bag slipping from her hands.

A roaring rises in her ears. There can't be a train here—they're aboveground, three blocks from the nearest train station, Cora knows because she had to walk here—but there's a high-pitched scream somewhere like brakes on metal, blasting through all her other thoughts, ripping away the colors of late morning, leaving her alone in the darkness of a train station.

More than four months have passed, but Cora remembers, with perfect clarity, the hand on Delilah's arm: a whisper of blue veins beneath the surface, tiny blond hairs, knuckles scorched pink from dryness, no wedding band, nails cut straight across.

In her dreams, the hand is a white spider. Its legs are translucent, its body the color of bones. It latches its fangs into Delilah and her arm falls from her body like a cut of meat. Delilah collapses into parts, a puzzle coming undone, and Cora wonders at what point a person stops being one singular person and becomes a collection of parts. An arm is not a person, so if Delilah is an arm underneath a train and a leg on a subway platform and a head lost in the crevices of the tracks, which part is the real Delilah?

Cora sees spiders in her apartment sometimes. There's a maintenance man who occasionally kills them for her, but more often than not she lies awake, curled under five blankets—her makeshift hazmat suit—and pretends she can't hear their little legs *tap tap tapping* on the walls.

Cora saw the man's eyes as well, but the memory is blurred by the rush of the train car and everything that came after. She saw his eyes between his hat and his surgical mask, but she can't remember them, and no one ever caught him. He could be the doorman at her apartment building, or a taxi driver, or her dentist, or even the fucking mayor, and she would never know.

"Fuck off," Yifei says in Chinese, yanking her arm away from the reporter.

"I'm sorry," the man says, also in Chinese, but the words are sticky, foreign. He's a white man with hair like a golden retriever. "Please, can we talk for just a few minutes?"

"I said *fuck off*," Yifei says in English.

Cora scrambles to gather her hazmat bag, afraid the man will try to grab her next, and pushes past Yifei and Harvey until they're outside the crowd, the truck in sight. Neither of them comment when she hurls her bag in the back and scrambles into her seat, arms crossed, grabbing onto her own forearms so no one else can.

Harvey slides into the driver's seat and rolls down the windows because all of them truly smell awful. Yifei sits in the back beside Cora and Harvey yells, "What am I, a taxi driver?" But Yifei pulls a flask out from the seat cushions and uncaps it, offering it to Cora.

It smells like brake fluid and will probably feel like it going down her throat and Cora doesn't think it will help, is a little bit afraid that it *will* and she'll have to start carrying her own flask around. Maybe Cora is destined to be the kind of person who drinks all the time, who blurs her problems with booze. Maybe she can go dancing at clubs and bring average-looking guys home and wake up on Saturday afternoons with a hangover headache and last night's makeup stinging her eyes like a normal twenty-four-year-old. That life sounds better than this one. Maybe Cora wouldn't be anyone remarkable, but at least she'd be *someone*.

But every life she can imagine building for herself just feels like throwing a tarp over a crime scene. It's just another way to carve out the chunk of her brain that still holds Delilah inside. Cora is only alive right now because the story of Delilah Zeng is behind aquarium glass in her mind. If there's going to be an After for Cora Zeng, she can never look back.

What was left of Delilah was buried. Her things are gone from Cora's apartment. The police closed the case because there were no leads. It's been months. It's over.

Yifei nudges the flask closer. She's trying to be nice, Cora knows that, but she doesn't want this olive branch. She wishes she was a mollusk, something with a hard shell, dark on the inside.

But if she has no friends, then one day she might end up like Yuxi He, brains splattered over her apartment walls, and no one will ever find her. If there is anything that Cora Zeng wants less than dying, it's dying and rotting until her body seeps into the carpet and drips through the ceiling of the apartment below. Bodies melt in the summer like cheese in a microwave, and a heat wave is coming next week. Cora will be damned if she makes a mess when she dies.

She takes the flask, knocks back a mouthful that tastes like fire, and wishes it would keep burning.

THREE

The shower is an act of unmaking, both the most wonderful and terrible hour of Cora's day. Cora isn't sure how the smell always bleeds through the hazmat suit, but without fail, she comes home smelling of decomposition.

Her clothes go straight in the wash with two capfuls of bleach, shoes and all. Cora stands naked in the kitchen and washes her hands twice with mechanic soap—the kind meant to strip your hands of car grease—then goes straight to the shower and turns the hot water all the way up until steam fills the bathroom and she can hardly breathe. First is the rinse and scrub to dislodge any chunks, like Cora is a piece of fruit. Then the salt scrub, because that's how you purge crawfish, how you make them vomit out all the garbage inside of them. Then comes the orange dish soap—regular bodywash always leaves a slick layer on the skin, doesn't cut through the greasy film that Cora knows is still there.

When it's done, Cora is wide-awake and raw and dizzy from the heat but it's the only time in the world she truly feels Fine—that moment when she steps out of the shower and hasn't touched anything at all.

It has always been this way. Even before the end of the world.

Cora has always moved through the world like a child in a fine art museum, afraid to touch. There are safe ways to touch her surroundings—her elbow jamming down a doorknob, the sole of her shoe on a toilet lever, her house key poking an elevator button. But Cora hates touching New York with her bare hands, because it is a city that sweats in the summer and oozes pizza grease from its pores and vomits sodden trash bags onto sidewalks. Once she turned eighteen, she only stayed here because Delilah said that's how you become an important person. But Cora doesn't feel important, she feels like she's trapped in the rotting corpse of a foreclosed house, and she never wanted to be important anyway. She just wanted to be Delilah.

A secret part of Cora likes the end of the world because it makes her strangeness feel quieter. The CDC says to wash your hands, so Cora is just being a Good American by washing her hands twice. If she empties her purse into a UV light box to sterilize everything inside, if she has three air purifiers for her tiny apartment, if she wears gloves on the subway—all of it is reasonable now.

There isn't one specific reason for the fear. Delilah said it was because Cora got pneumonia in third grade and had to go to the hospital and something about repressed trauma, but the thought of pneumonia does not scare Cora. Even COVID-19 does not particularly scare Cora. It is the dirtiness itself, not what comes after it.

And at the end of the world, Cora thinks, there are worse things than being too clean.

She rakes her fingers through her hair as she blow-dries

it, unwilling to sit down until all of her is dry because germs stick to wet skin better than dry skin. When she's dry and in her clean pajamas, she finally goes to her kitchen, pulls out a frozen oatmeal bar, and flicks on the convection oven, listening to its rhythmic clicking as it heats up and glows orange.

Cora never intended to live alone, not in New York. But she learned very quickly that most roommates do not take kindly to the constant smell of Clorox and all-night whirring of air purifiers. She lived with Delilah for so long that she'd forgotten what everyone else thought was normal. Auntie Zeng took it upon herself to ask her broker friend to find Cora an apartment, and he'd quickly shown her this Chinatown studio with no outward appearance of mold or pests, and Cora figured it was the best she could hope for. With monthly checks from her dad and Auntie Lois, plus a huge discount on rent (courtesy of COVID), Cora can afford to stay on her own for now. She lives just a breath too close to the subway and hears the trains running in her dreams, and when she opens her windows to her rusty fire escape the air always smells like weed, but that's the kind of discomfort Cora can live with. She's used to something always burrowing in her ear, prickling at her skin.

Her studio is small and white because bleach cannot strip a color that doesn't exist. It has two windows but only one that opens, one pot of English ivy because it supposedly cleans the air, one box of Delilah's possessions shoved into a corner, and a bookshelf full of books that Cora plans to read one day—books that will make her smarter or better-adjusted or more worldly. In truth, all Cora wants is an apartment with no flat surfaces, nowhere for dust to settle. But that would be an apartment with no floor, just a perpetual abyss, a dark and endless hole.

She opens the fridge and slides open the fruit drawer but

hesitates, the stark fridge light buzzing, the bright circle of light on the gray kitchen tiles.

An apple is missing.

Yesterday there were two apples, five clementines, one avocado. Cora was going to eat one apple with cinnamon tonight and one with peanut butter tomorrow; she remembers making this plan in the shower with all the certainty of a lawyer drafting their closing statement. She makes these plans so her fruit never goes bad, because once it starts to bruise, Cora refuses to eat it and into the trash it goes, wasted.

Cora squints because maybe her eyes are too tired, maybe she can no longer process colors correctly and apples look like oranges. She slides the drawer shut, closes the fridge, takes a deep breath. Then she opens the door again, opens the drawer. Still, there is only one apple.

This time, Cora slams the drawer shut. She closes the fridge and presses her back to it, sinking to the floor, as if something terrible is going to burst from inside and only Cora can hold it back.

Cora has been misremembering things lately.

She thought she bought a loaf of bread last Tuesday, but on Wednesday morning her bread box was empty. The week before, she gave a purpose to each and every one of her dozen eggs, but by nightfall, she was one short and her plans were ruined.

Delilah always said Cora was the good kind of crazy, the kind that didn't hurt anyone, that did good things but just too much of them. But now Cora has forgotten something, has gaps in her memory, empty holes in the grout of her brain where something used to be, and that doesn't feel like the good kind of crazy anymore.

She wonders, not for the first time, if she ripped out too much of her brain when she pulled Delilah out of it. Extricating Delilah Zeng from your mind is probably a lot more difficult than it seems, like pulling out a tumor that's grown into all of your brain's crevices—getting rid of it means ripping out healthy tissue too.

Cora's head thumps back against the fridge, rattling bottles inside.

It's so unfair.

Cora is doing all the right things. She has a new job. She speaks to her coworkers. She tries new hobbies. She is doing all the things normal people do.

Yet she still feels like a puppeteer dragging her wooden body through the motions, and maybe she always will. Maybe she can't exist without being her sister's parasite.

She checks the fridge one more time, the single apple rolling in its drawer as she throws the door open.

Something inside of Cora must be unraveling, and the thought makes her palms sweat, and even though she hates sweating she clings to the thought like a life raft because...

Because the alternative is that someone has been in her apartment.

She doesn't know which possibility is worse.

Cora suspects that her Auntie Zeng is a pyromaniac.

I have never set something on fire without a good reason is Auntie Zeng's response when Cora says this out loud, which isn't exactly a denial. Auntie Zeng is her dad's baby sister, the one who came to America as a sixteen-year-old and liked it enough to stay, unlike Cora's thirty-year-old father, who only stayed long enough to marry one and a half times and have two kids before deciding China was less of a shithole than America. Auntie Zeng married a mysterious man who died under even more mysterious circumstances, leaving her to live off a widow's pension at age forty-five.

They kneel in the living room of Auntie Zeng's apartment in Chinatown, an empty metal trash can full of joss paper in flames. Cora is fairly certain that joss paper is not meant to be burned inside. Not because she knows more about Chinese culture than Auntie Zeng, but because this is definitely a fire hazard. The room fills with smoke, but Auntie Zeng breathes it in like a drug. She quit smoking last year, and Cora wonders if this is her way of cheating.

"You still have skin?" Auntie Zeng says whenever Cora shows up at her door.

Cora rolls up her sleeves to show her that, yes, she still has skin and it's dry and too pale but it definitely exists and has not been sandpapered away, but Auntie Zeng never really looks. She knows just by looking at Cora's eyes.

Cora lived with Auntie Zeng on and off ever since middle school, when her mom started her cult initiation process. Those years were a mess of moving back and forth between the Midwest, Auntie Zeng's old place in Flushing, and Delilah and her mama's apartment in Chinatown. Their dad was long gone back to China, so Cora was pinballed around whenever her mom had a change of heart, or Delilah's mama decided she cost too much to feed, or Auntie Zeng's court case for her dead husband tied up all her money and she had to move into a studio. Cora would have preferred sleeping on Auntie Zeng's floor to living with Delilah's mama, who Cora knows speaks Mandarin but always spoke Fujianese so Cora wouldn't understand.

The official reason for Cora's visit today is the first day of Zhongyuan Jie, the hungry ghost festival. Auntie Zeng says it's when all the ghosts take a vacation from hell to visit earth for a month. The living are supposed to feed them and pray for them and make them offerings of things ghosts almost certainly don't need anymore, like clothes and jewelry. But that's only what Cora has seen from Auntie Zeng. Everything Cora knows about China has been filtered through her, so sometimes she's not sure if something is true or if it's just the way her aunt is. Cora imagines if she herself were someone's one and only source of American culture, how they would find it strange that Americans take such long showers and have such smelly jobs and cry so much.

The unofficial reason for her visit is that it's almost the third Friday of the month, which is when Cora's dad sends her money as soon as Auntie Zeng reminds him. It's been this way ever since she was a kid, and back then it was because no one trusted Cora's mom not to feed the money into her cult, so Auntie Zeng would make sure Cora still had shoes that fit and food in her lunch box before letting her brother send more.

These days, the money goes straight to Cora's bank account, just enough to pay for her utilities, but only if Auntie Zeng tells Cora's dad that she's fine living on her own, because no one trusts Cora's own words anymore. After Delilah, he pushed hard for Cora to move in with Auntie Zeng, convinced that New York wasn't a safe place for a woman to live alone, as if he actually cared. Cora thinks he just wants her alive because it's easier to toss her a couple hundred bucks every month than pay a lump sum for another funeral. He has a third wife and two sons in China so he doesn't need Cora anymore; she wasn't even his favorite American daughter. He just wants her quiet and far away from his new family.

Cora knows this, but she isn't above taking hush money, not in this economy. So all she has to do is convince her aunt that, yes, she is completely Fine, she doesn't need a babysitter. Cora loves her aunt—that doesn't mean she wants to live with her. She also loves having her own apartment to unfold herself in, loves not having to explain what she's eating or when she's sleeping or why her water bill is so high.

Auntie Zeng starts coughing from the smoke and mercifully opens a window. Cora's gaze drifts to the smoke detector, which has a strip of blue painter's tape over it.

"Okay, break time," Auntie Zeng says in slow Mandarin, the way you'd talk to a child because she knows that Cora won't understand otherwise. "I have something to show you."

As the smoke wafts out the window and the air begins to clear, Auntie Zeng disappears into her bedroom, leaving Cora kneeling alone in the hazy living room. A row of maneki-neko cats stare at her from the shelf across the room, painted black eyes shining even through the smoke, beckoning paws slowly swinging forward and backward, forward and backward. Auntie Zeng said she used to steal them from Chinese restaurants when she was a teenager because they reminded her of home, and Cora's not entirely sure she ever kicked the habit.

Auntie Zeng's apartment is full of trinkets like that, porcelain figures that make Cora feel watched whenever Auntie Zeng leaves the room. There are entire worlds crammed into every cabinet, key chains and cookies and pretty glass bottles rattling in every drawer. None of it fits because this place is half the size of her last place in Hell's Kitchen, but apparently that landlord thought Auntie Zeng didn't have a green card and tried to get her to pay for her utilities with sex and threatened to deport her if she refused.

Every few seconds, a koi fish *thumps* against the glass of its tank by the living room window. Cora thinks the tank is probably too small for a fish the size of a guinea pig, but it has been with Auntie Zeng longer than Cora has been alive, so she doubts anything will change now. Its name is Tom Hanks because Auntie Zeng thought that was a popular American name in the '90s, and Cora suspects that one day it will open its mouth and swallow the entire world like a black hole.

Auntie Zeng comes back with a reusable shopping bag and upends it on the floor, shiny plastic *thunking* against the trash can. Cora picks up a package, angles the light away so she can see what's inside.

It's a Gucci bag, complete with the golden G's for a buckle, the logo echoed in navy across the upper flap, the ugly green and red stripes. Cora is no expert in designer bags, but even she can tell this is a knockoff. It's too light to be leather, could probably float away if she tossed it at a strong breeze. The second closest package is a terrifying origami rendition of a Pomeranian with a pink bow around its neck. Beside the dog are bottles of vitamins, except Cora can see the creases on the bottom of the bottles too and knows those are also made of paper.

"I found a man who makes special joss paper," Auntie Zeng says. "You can ask for anything you want, and he can make a paper version that you can burn to send to the afterlife for your ancestors."

"Which of our ancestors requested a Pomeranian?" Cora says.

Auntie Zeng ignores her. "I'll put in an order for you. If you want to send anything, I'll pay," she says. Her gaze doesn't stray from Cora's face and Cora knows she isn't talking about ancestors anymore.

"I'm hungry," Cora says, knees cracking as she heads for the kitchen, away from the smoke, away from what she knows Auntie Zeng is trying to say.

It's hard to eat at someone else's house without imagining all the hands that grew the vegetables and cut the meat and packaged it, how long it was sitting out with stale air and spit droplets falling on it before it made its way to Cora's mouth.

Other people don't know how to scrub vegetables like Cora does, don't wash their hands enough after handling raw meat. But Cora knows if she doesn't eat, she will seem less Fine and she won't get her utility money. So she puts a dumpling in her mouth right when her aunt crosses into the kitchen, makes sure she sees her eat, reminds herself that Auntie Zeng's food has never once made her sick and it's statistically unlikely that today will be the first time.

Her aunt watches her for a moment—Cora can feel it even if she can't see it—then sighs and fills a bowl with soup from a pot on the stove, pops open the lid of the rice cooker on her makeshift counter—she has a bathtub in her kitchen with a wooden board thrown over it for more counter space, a remnant from her building's tenement days. Then she points at a chair with a pair of chopsticks.

"Sit," she says. She turns and drops a dumpling into Tom Hanks's fish tank. "Not there!" she says when Cora starts to sit down in front of the only place setting.

"Ghost chair," Auntie Zeng says. "For your uncle."

"You hated my uncle," Cora says, but she switches seats all the same.

"That's why I feed his ghost," Auntie Zeng says. "I had enough of him in one life. I don't need him haunting me in the afterlife." She drops some paper dumplings on the plate and strikes a match, setting them on fire in the middle of the table.

Cora coughs, waving away the smoke.

"And where is the bracelet I gave you?" Auntie Zeng says.

Cora nods toward her bag on the hook by the door. She always takes off her jade bracelet for work. If she wore it under her hazmat suit, it would be dirty, and she would never be able to wear it again because you can't bleach jade.

Auntie Zeng shakes her head. "You need it for protection. Especially this month."

But Delilah was wearing her jade bracelet when she was decapitated by a train, so Cora doesn't put much faith in its protection abilities.

"I'll send you home with the paper dog," Auntie Zeng says. "You can burn it."

Cora pictures flames eating the dog's face. "I don't want to get evicted for setting my building on fire," she says.

"Do it outside, then."

"I think starting trash can fires is illegal too."

Auntie Zeng sighs. "You need to burn something for your sister," she says.

Cora's grip tightens on her spoon.

Even if she believed in that sort of thing, if she were to burn something for Delilah it would be her stupid essential oils, not joss paper. Delilah only ever liked dogs in theory; she didn't like the hair on the couch or picking up poop or chewed-up shoes. Hurling a Pomeranian into the afterlife for her would probably guarantee a haunting.

Cora says nothing, but Auntie Zeng doesn't take the hint. "Violent deaths leave unsettled ghosts," she says quietly. "You don't want her to suffer, do you?"

"Don't," Cora says in English, the word a low warning. She does not want to talk about that. She has never once talked about it.

"Your sister's circumstances are unusual," Auntie Zeng says carefully. "You don't want to take chances. You could leave her ghost hungry."

A train rushes past the window, rattling the cats on the shelf. Auntie Zeng's apartment is a few blocks from the train station and the sound shouldn't carry this far, but still the floor hums and the water laps up to the edge of the fish tank and the soup ripples in her bowl and Cora is only a breath away from flipping the table over, shattering every dish, burning her aunt with soup—just one more word and Cora will do it.

She can stand to remember Delilah from before, in her pretty taffeta clothes and rhinestone nails, but Cora would sooner gouge her eardrums out with chopsticks than listen to her aunt talk about Delilah's "violent death." Delilah entered the train station and she never left, that is all that matters.

For months, Auntie Zeng hounded the police about it. While she cooked, she talked endlessly about how any day now they would catch the man who did it, how the trial would be swift and he would go to jail forever. Cora could only sit in the kitchen and stare at the black eyes of the maneki-neko cats and dissociate until she couldn't feel her fingers, because otherwise she would scream.

She knew Auntie Zeng believed in justice because it somehow worked out for her when her husband died, but Cora also knows that murderers are set free every day. She knows that even if the grainy MTA footage of the man's face could be used to find him, his lawyers would talk about how he was a good father and a responsible worker and was probably just having a bad day. Then they would comb through Delilah's diaries and Instagram and try to prove that she was the kind of girl who would throw herself in front of a train. And when that didn't work, they would turn to Cora, crack her open, learn all her secrets, and try to say that Cora pushed her.

Her sister's body has already been destroyed. All Cora has left are memories, and the lawyers would rip those apart too.

"Cora."

Cora looks down. She has rolled her sleeve up and started scratching at her inner wrist, the skin striped pink from her nails. She yanks her sleeve down.

There are many things Cora will do for her aunt. She will

sweep tombs for the Qingming Festival and clean her house for the New Year and help her make mooncakes even though Cora hates the texture of lotus paste on her hands. She'll pretend to read her aunt's cryptic Ghost Month Guide. She'll even pretend to pray to gods she doesn't believe in.

But she will not sit here and listen to her aunt talk about Delilah's death. She will not let her pretend that Delilah's soul is still here somehow.

Cora finishes her soup in silence, then drops the bowl into the sink.

"Cora—"

"Thank you for the meal," Cora says. "Can I go now?"

Auntie Zeng sighs. She looks at Cora, and Cora shivers with the sensation that her aunt is seeing all of her, all the thoughts that hum in her ears at night, the sticky lies that glue her bones together and keep her from being a collection of parts like Delilah.

"You're not a prisoner, Cora," her aunt says at last, and that's all the permission Cora needs before she grabs her bag and leaves.

Except, maybe Cora wants to be a prisoner.

Maybe she wants someone to teach her how to be a human the correct way, the way she never learned. Someone to wake her up and tell her what to eat, what to dream about, what to cry about, who to pray to. Because Cora somehow feels that every choice she's made has been wrong, that every choice she will ever make will lead her deeper and deeper into a life that feels like a dark, airless box, and when she peers through the slats in the wood she'll see the pale light of who she might have been, so bright that it blinds her.

But you can't teach someone how to be a person. Cora was never real, she was only an echo of Delilah, and with her gone, she is no one at all.

She gets home and unzips her bag only to find a package of joss paper stuffed inside. Auntie Zeng must have slipped it in when she wasn't looking.

Cora takes it out, deposits it directly into the trash can, and closes the lid.

A Guide to Ghost Month and Other Unfortunate Realities that American Girls Like to Ignore

I know that you two don't want to hear this, that these aren't the kinds of things American girls worry about. But none of us will be around forever, and I want you to have this information in case you need it one day after I'm gone.

I pray that you'll never need it.

At the very least, consider this practice reading Chinese. You could certainly use it (looking at you, Cora).

When it comes to ghost month, here is what you need to understand:

On the fifteenth day of the seventh month, a door opens.

The starving dead crawl out, mouths full of dust, and reach for a home that has already forgotten them.

Their stomachs scream for food, but their tongues are heavy and dry, their necks as thin as needles. They lick the tears of the living from the dirt, and sometimes, it is enough to sate them.

But sometimes, the hunger only yawns wider.

Auntie Z

FOUR

Sunday is the day of Auntie Lois's God, the kind that asks for Cora's money in a golden dish but won't let her drink wine because she was never baptized and she's embarrassingly old to be baptized now. *All are welcome in God's house*, Auntie Lois says, but she always emphasizes the *all*, as if God is especially generous for letting someone like Cora in, like there's something about her that's inherently unholy.

Cora thinks a church is not the best place to go during a deadly pandemic, that surely God would understand the extenuating circumstances. But Auntie Lois is more of a god to Cora than the one in heaven because she pays half of her student loans every month, and when God calls, you have to answer. Auntie Lois writes the check exactly at noon, after Cora has confessed.

Cora wears two surgical masks and Delilah's blue silk dress and kneels in her pew before a wooden Jesus, staked through with nails, painted with blood and tears. He hangs before stained glass windows that backlight his suffering in kaleidoscopic colors. The church is supposedly at 25 percent capacity—that's what anyone will say if you ask—but the pews seem at least half-full, and Cora doesn't think anyone is actually counting heads.

Cora knows her aunt thinks she's a heathen, but she does feel bad for Jesus, who had to suffer in front of so many people. The worst part probably wasn't bones splintering to make way for nails, or the constant tugging from his own body weight, or the hunger or thirst or hot sun over Palestine. It was probably having all his pain forced to the outside, the clean cage of his skin torn open and agony bleeding out, so many eyes and no way to hide from them. Cora cannot imagine how terrible it would feel if the typhoons in her mind were visible on the outside.

Of all the people she might become, Cora thinks that a Good Christian Girl isn't the worst choice. She imagines going on church trips to pumpkin patches and praying around an apple tree, baking little cupcakes for coffee hour, going to choir practice on Thursday nights, meeting a Good Christian Boy who will marry her and say things about "honoring thy wife," but the pandemic threw a wrench in those plans. Cora would take that life in a heartbeat, if God could hear her.

But, as Cora kneels in the pew and tries to pray, she knows no one is there. Cora is good at telling when people aren't listening to her—like Auntie Lois, who hears her voice and nods and hums in all the right places but the words never seem to sink in—and Cora knows that her thoughts don't reach anyone at all. Cora only sees darkness behind her eyelids, a black wall where God is supposed to be, a locked door in a tiny room. God is not listening to her, but she can't really blame him. It is so, so loud inside of her mind. It's the same when she prays to Auntie Zeng's gods, but at least there's less pressure when it's only Auntie Zeng and a burning trash can instead of hundreds of people who God actually listens to.

I'm ready, Cora wants to scream, *I'll let you make me someone.* But God doesn't want her, no one does. Auntie Lois says one day, if she keeps praying, He will come.

So Cora steadies her breath and asks God to make her normal. She opens herself to be God's parasite instead of Delilah's, and like always, no one answers.

She looks around because the only people who will see her are the other heathens who open their eyes while praying. But Cora is the only sinner today. All around her, Auntie Lois's friends kneel, pale hands clasped together. Some of their lips move, speaking silently.

Something glimmers in the corner of her vision and Cora looks up, toward God perhaps, but also toward the arch where the organ pipes touch the ceiling.

A clear drop of water runs down the gold-painted archway above the pulpit, capturing the candlelight and dragging it down to the floor. Another follows it, then another. Just like a body, the cathedral sweats in the summer, reeks of salt and caustic paint. Cora remembers the story of "Jonah and the Whale" that her aunt made her study, thinks that the beams in the ceiling look an awful lot like ribs, that maybe the whole congregation has been swallowed by a giant sea beast like Jonah was, that the low hum of pipes beneath their feet are the clockwork murmurs of its organs.

A tiny brown spider makes its way across the pew in front of Cora. She watches it tickle its way across the wood, climbing over the great mountain of a rain jacket slung over the back of a pew until it crosses in front of the light from the doorway that leads to the reception hall.

There is a shadow in the hall.

Someone is standing in the doorway, but from Cora's seat, she can only see their silhouette cast crooked on the wall, speared through with swirls of gold embossing in the wallpaper. The silhouette shivers along with the flickering candles, swaying back and forth. It stretches, warping as it rolls up the curved ceiling, the neck growing longer, head swallowed by the darkness of the ceiling, throat wearing thinner and thinner and thinner until it's only a needle-thin whisper.

"And the Lord said," says the priest, and Cora's gaze snaps back to the pulpit, "'I will be merciful to their unrighteousness, and their sins and their iniquities will I remember no more.'"

Auntie Lois slides back into her seat, and Cora copies her. When she looks back at the hallway, the shadow is gone.

"His forgiveness is one of His greatest gifts to us," the priest continues. "No matter how the people of Israel disobeyed, God's patience and forgiveness for them was infinite, for His love has no bounds. No matter your failures, your betrayals, you need only open your heart to God and He will forgive you, for you are His beloved child."

Cora grips the edge of the pew, her hands locking the way they sometimes do when she's breathing just a little too fast and her limbs don't get enough oxygen, her flesh as rigid as bone.

Three months ago, Auntie Lois stood up in church and told the congregation that after much thought and prayer, she had finally forgiven the man who killed her niece, and she loved him as God loved him.

Cora sat in her pew and memorized the sharp edges of the stained glass, needing to cling to something other than her aunt's words. The priest had praised her aunt, and the congregation looked on with a mix of sympathy and admiration and talked about how strong her faith was, and Cora had stared at the sunlight through the stained glass until her vision went blurry, had contemplated the sharpness of each cut piece, how easily they could split skin, how she could slice the whole congregation into hunks of meat just like Delilah and see how easy it would be for them to forgive her then, and why did everyone want to *talk* about it, to tell her what happened and what it means and what should come next, when Cora was the only one who was there. Auntie Lois hardly even knew Delilah; technically she wasn't even her niece and Auntie Lois never called her that until she was dead.

Cora doesn't even think her aunt loves *her* that much, yet she loves Delilah's murderer.

Cora has tried to forgive him because Auntie Lois says it will make her feel better, but Cora doesn't even know where to begin. She tries to imagine him, because you can't forgive someone who doesn't exist, but he bursts into a thousand white spiders in her mind, crawls into her mouth and ears. She thinks of only his hand and tries to forgive a single finger, even a fingernail on his body. She calls for feelings of love and grace like hauling an anchor to the surface of her mind, but it is far too heavy. All Cora can feel is that first hot splash of blood, the sharpness of it, the way it burned her eyes, the taste of its salt. If God cannot love Cora unless she forgives, then Cora will die without His love.

After the service, Cora kneels in a small dark box and whispers her sins through the lattice of stars.

Bless me, Father, for I have sinned is what you're supposed to say. Cora once asked Auntie Lois what to say if she hadn't sinned, but her aunt only shook her head and said, *You have.*

But, in the shadows of the box, with nothing but weak light in the shape of little stars on her lap, a strange universe inside itself, all Cora manages to say is "Hi."

She looks down at her cheat sheet. Auntie Lois typed up a list of all the sins she could think of, in alphabetical order, and gave Cora a pen to circle the ones she'd done. It starts with "abortion" and ends with "unfair wagers." Cora has circled three words in the middle.

Sacrilege because she's pretty sure she's done that accidentally, even if she can't name exactly how.

Doubt of faith because she thinks praying to Auntie Zeng's gods probably counts.

Fearfulness, circled twice, so hard that her pen carved through the paper and left a scratch on the hymnal, which Cora quickly hid in the pew. Defacing hymnals is probably another sin, but Auntie Lois didn't write that on the list.

Cora asked once why fear is a sin. Auntie Lois said that it shows distrust in God, that one should not fear men and only fear God. But Auntie Lois lives in Staten Island, on a quiet street where cops have nothing to do but stop teens from making out in cars. She may think she's met fear, when walking alone in a parking lot at night, or when a car swerves too close to her on the highway. But Cora knows that the face of fear is not an abstract what-if. Fear is born in the after, when the world peels back its skin and shows you its raw, pulsing innards, when it forces you to remember its name. Anyone who has seen the face of fear knows you should damn well be afraid.

Cora feels it now, in the closed space of the confessional booth. She thinks the darkness and tight walls are supposed to feel safe and private. But the darkness expands outward in all directions. It listens.

"What have you come to confess?" the silhouette says.

Cora's mouth is sticky. She hasn't had much to drink today, had to wake up early and brush her hair and get on a train to make it in time for the sermon. She rolls her cheat sheet into a tiny tube and slips it through the lattice instead of answering.

She hears the paper unrolling, then a silence that feels tight, like a spring pressed down. Cora doesn't know why she worries. People have probably confessed to murder in this booth before. In the grand scheme of sinners, surely Cora is not the worst this priest has ever spoken to.

"What is this?" the priest whispers. His words are clipped, his voice a careful quiet, but there is something underneath the words themselves, a low fire that Cora doesn't understand.

"My aunt gave me a list," Cora says.

On the other side of the booth, Cora hears paper crumpling.

"Why would you give me this?" the priest says. "Is this a joke to you?"

Cora grows smaller at the tone of his voice. She is six years old and Dad is yelling at her for reorganizing his pantry. This man is not her father, has no power over her, yet the tone of his voice rattles her bones in a way that feels instinctual, like Cora was born to fear loud men.

Cora tugs at the paper in her trembling hands, nearly tearing it apart. Then she realizes, breathless, that her cheat sheet is still in her hands.

What did she give the priest?

A door bursts open, clattering against the side of the booth. A moment later, her own door is torn open and light blasts into the tiny box. The priest closes his hand around her wrist and she screams, white spiders crawling behind her eyes, and the sound is so tortured and it echoes up to the golden arched ceilings and the priest jerks away from her like her voice has cut him, like she is the violent one. She slides to the floor and stays there because the marble is cool on her burning palms, because her hair shields her eyes and she can't see the rage on the priest's face. A few people linger at the pews in the back of the church, waiting for their turns at the confessional. All eyes are focused on her as her scream repeats itself up to the ceiling, floating up to God.

"Cora?" her aunt says, rising from her seat at the nearest pew, gripping a Bible against her chest.

"Don't bring this girl back here until she's ready to repent!" the priest says, and Cora's aunt flinches, knuckles white around the Bible.

"Father, I don't understand," she says, bowing her head, making herself smaller too.

Then the priest unfolds the paper crumpled in his fist and shoves it at Auntie Lois. She gasps, the sound cut off when she cups a hand over her mouth, forgetting that she's wearing a mask. The priest casts the paper to the floor and storms off, a door slamming somewhere distant. The paper flutters back and forth until it settles on the ground near Cora, face up.

It is a picture printed on cheap paper, streaked through with low toner, so Cora's eyes can't decipher it at first. Then, all at once, she sees it: there is half a beautiful face, a bathroom splashed with brains, a leaking eye socket with soupy white eye goo, scattered teeth. It takes her a moment to recognize the photo, and when she does it's from the pattern of the bathroom tiles. This is Yuxi He. Another one of Harvey's photos, courtesy of his first responder friend Paul.

Cora must have grabbed it from her backpack this morning in her groggy haze and shoved it into her church bag by accident. But Cora always cleans out her backpack, always shreds Harvey's "surprises" before she can get more than a quick glance at them. She can remember the sound of the paper shredder gnawing through it yesterday, its mechanical crunch. Had she shredded something else by accident? No matter how she thinks about it, nothing adds up.

Yuxi He's single dead eye stares up at her as if saying, *Of course nothing adds up, your mind is a labyrinth and you are lost inside.*

A pointed black shoe steps into Cora's line of vision, right on top of Yuxi's face. Cora looks up at her aunt, whose eyes are monstrous. Before the pandemic, Cora never realized how many secrets eyes could tell. She'd thought that with everyone wearing masks, it would be hard to read people's expressions. But Cora can imagine the tight line of her aunt's lips without seeing them, the clenched teeth, the frown lines carved around her mouth.

"Coraline," she says, "we're leaving."

Auntie Lois shoves through the heavy doors, walks faster and faster as they approach the train station, as if she can fast-walk away from Cora and forget that she exists. Whenever she's in Manhattan, she speed-walks or half jogs instead of walking at a normal pace, clutching her purse as if she thinks she'll be mugged in broad daylight in Nolita. She relaxes a bit on the Upper East Side, where she says people are more "civilized," but normally only drives in for church and heads straight back home.

"I told Lyla to put you in Sunday school earlier," she says, mostly to herself.

Cora remembers that conversation. She was eight, and her mom was crying in the pantry, sitting on top of spilled cornflakes and telling Auntie Lois how being a mom was so hard, and together they brainstormed ways to get Cora out of the house. Church was basically free day care, after all. Auntie Lois said she could drop Cora off at the public library on Saturdays, and even though technically you're not supposed to leave kids under twelve there by themselves, Cora was quiet enough that no one would notice. *There are lots of places Cora could probably wander around and entertain herself without an adult,* said Auntie Lois. *An aquarium, an art museum, a mall. It's not like she plays with anyone anyway. Just give her things to do, Lyla, you'll only have to see her from dinner until bedtime.*

Now Cora's mom is in what she calls an "alt religious commune" on Michigan farmlands that Cora is pretty sure is a cult, but she always gets sad when Cora says that. She pays her rent in homegrown kale and sleeps twice a week on the graves of the cult founders and talks to God by climbing tall trees and singing into the sunrise. Cora truly couldn't care less how her mom wants to worship, if it weren't for the fact that she gave the cult all her money instead of paying Cora's college tuition. NYU was entirely unsympathetic to the fact that, yes, technically Cora's mom could afford to pay more, but all her inheritance was wrapped up in kale farming for God. Auntie Lois picked up the slack on that front a bit, because it's very un-Christian to let your niece live in low-income housing when you have a four-bedroom three-bathroom house all to yourself.

Cora thinks her Auntie Lois maybe loved her when she was small enough to be dressed up in tulle skirts and giant hair bows, when she called Cora her Little China Doll. There are lots of pictures of Auntie Lois and Cora's mom when Cora was a baby, but fewer and fewer as she gets older. Things took a turn when Cora's dad decided he was moving back to China with or without Cora's mom, a twenty-four-year-old white lady who had never left Wisconsin and didn't even like Chinese food. After that, Auntie Lois decided Cora's dad was her baby sister's evil ex and Cora was a raggedy sweater he'd left behind, a curse of single motherhood she'd never asked for.

In a strange way, Cora can't blame her aunt. Because if—God forbid—Cora ever had a kid and the dad ditched her, she likes to think Delilah would have cursed him out in front of her kid, made up stories about his monstrousness—one day he's an opium kingpin, the next he's an enemy government's spy, the next he's a convicted serial killer on the run—because hurting her little sister makes him just as bad.

But she knows Delilah never would have done that. She

was a very reap-what-you-sow, karma-comes-for-us-all kind of person. She thought the starry sky was symmetrical and that every wrong would be righted in turn and that none of them could understand the cosmic timing of justice but that it would come one day. Around her, all of Cora's emotions felt as dirty as her hands, something that didn't afflict people like Delilah. No, Delilah would never be angry on Cora's behalf. If Cora were the one beheaded by a train, Delilah would probably have shrugged and said something like, *It was meant to be.*

Auntie Lois walks too fast, melting into an unmasked crowd that Cora doesn't want to force her way through. The distance between them grows wider, and Cora wants to ask about her check but is worried her aunt won't give it to her now even though she sat through the service.

A delivery bike flashes past her and Cora jumps to the left, nearly bruising her ribs on a parking meter. Someone bumps into her from behind and she falls forward, hands on the sidewalk, grease and gum and footprints that you can't see but can feel. Someone else falls behind her, making a sound of pain as they hit the pavement. She pulls herself up, wet palms clinging to a parked car. The alarm rips through the street, wailing in Cora's ears.

Behind her, a white man with cropped brown hair pulls himself up, brushing off his jogging pants. Cora opens her mouth to apologize, but the moment they lock eyes, something changes. His gaze sharpens, his eyebrows arch down, his shoulders square as he straightens up.

Cora presses back against the car even as the alarm screams, its vibrations pulsing up her spine. The man takes a step forward and Cora tries to apologize but she can barely hear her own voice over the car alarm, is sure the man can't hear it.

He reaches for her face.

Cora chokes on a breath, backed against the car. *He is going to rip my face off*, she thinks. She's read about dogs and chimps ripping people's faces off. Surely angry white men could find a way.

But his fingers hook over the edge of her masks, brushing her lips, the gesture so horrifyingly intimate that Cora's mind grinds to a halt, every thought gone except the scratch of his rough knuckles on her lips. He pulls down her masks, casts them to the ground, and spits in her face.

Cora clamps her mouth shut.

Her whole body goes on lockdown, jaw clenched and lips pressed together, *Don't let anything in*. She stays perfectly still as warm saliva tracks down her chin, her throat, pooling in her collarbone.

I need a COVID test, Cora thinks, even though she's pretty sure she needs to wait a few days before it would be useful, but she cannot wait that long. She needs to know immediately.

She can't say any of this with her mouth closed, so she makes a pained moaning sound inside of herself. She sinks down to the ground and now the back of her head is against the car, the alarm blaring against her skull. The man tells her to go home to China, but China is not her home—if it was then maybe she could have gone with Delilah, maybe they would both be there right now, alive, and she wouldn't have another person's burning wet saliva on her face.

Then the man is gone and Cora can feel the liquid filling in the crevice where her lips press together, trying to leak inside of her. Some of it is definitely in her eyes. She wishes the man had just peeled her face off like she thought he would. Down the street she can still see the church steeple, the cross in the gray sky, the home of the God who does not want her. She came here for God, to be normal, to be Good, and now there's someone else's spit in her mouth and God's door is still shut in her face.

People are asking if she's okay, drawn by the car alarm, but Cora can't answer without opening her mouth, so she just cries and scrubs her mouth with her sleeve and hopes that the tears will wash her eyes out even though she knows you can't sterilize eyes without blinding yourself. Cora will always have to live with the knowledge that she can never wash this man away, not completely.

At the corner of her vision, the crowd parts and she hears her Auntie Lois. "She's fine," she hears her say. Someone recounts what happened and Auntie Lois sighs at the great inconvenience.

She grabs Cora's wrist and pulls her away from the crowd. Cora's legs feel wooden, hardly responding as she stumbles down the sidewalk. Cora remembers her bag and tears through it, pulling out her hand sanitizer, pouring it into her palm, rubbing it into her lips and chin.

"Cora, stop!" her aunt says, but it's too late, Cora is already smearing the hand sanitizer into her collarbone. The smell of alcohol knifes up her nostrils and clears her mind a bit, and after a moment Cora dares to open her mouth and spit on the sidewalk.

"Cora," her aunt says, but Cora doesn't have time for her right now, is busy scrubbing the seam of her lips with more hand sanitizer. "Cora, stop," she says, grabbing Cora's hands. When Cora goes still, she releases her, pulls a few tissues out of her bag and hands them to Cora, as if something like this can just be wiped away with a Kleenex, as if it's not already inside of her. Cora crumples the tissues in her hands, stares back at her aunt, waiting for a reprimand.

Her aunt looks at her, and Cora sees a great many thoughts in her eyes, a thousand unholy things she probably wishes she could say to Cora. Maybe she thinks she's being kind by not saying them out loud, but Cora already knows.

"God wants us to forgive," Auntie Lois says at last, and Cora doesn't know if she's talking about forgiving the man who spit on her, or forgiving Cora for being the way she is. The car alarm is still going, but Cora can hardly hear it now because inside her mind, everything is much, much louder.

FIVE

By Monday, Cora is scrubbing blood from the wall of Zihan Huang's apartment, Yifei is berating the broken wet vac, and Harvey is eating Oreos and playing *League of Legends* on his phone because there isn't much to be done until the wet vac can be resuscitated.

"Go easy with the steel wool, Zeng," Harvey says. "You're gonna scrub a new window into the wall."

"At least Cora is actually cleaning," Yifei says.

"I'm not the one who broke the wet vac," Harvey says, then swears when he messes up his game.

Cora scrubs harder, wishes she could scrub their voices away too, scraping the steel wool across the wall until the blood finally starts to flake away, peeling up color with it. All that's left is raw wood, rough and unpolished, but that's what the landlord wants, isn't it? All traces gone. No memory of Zihan Huang left. A bare apartment to resell.

Cora has been tracking her symptoms in the Notes app on her phone since the church incident. The only new symptom is a lingering nausea clamping at her throat sometimes, but that happens on bad days even when she isn't exposed to other people's spit.

When Cora got home after the service, she scrubbed her lips with a toothbrush, rinsed her mouth with rubbing alcohol, scraped her tongue with the blunt end of a butter knife. But all she can think about is the warmth of the saliva on her lips, warm because it came from inside someone else's body. Cora wishes her body was sealed tight like a snow globe, that nothing could ever penetrate the inside.

She scheduled a COVID test but has to wait five days, and now all she can do is stick her face in a bag of coffee beans every few hours to make sure she still has a sense of smell. She goes to work and says nothing about it even though her body feels foreign, a ship that she can no longer steer.

The steel wool snags on something and Cora is forced to stop to avoid unraveling it. Her arms feel warm from exertion, momentum lost as she unhooks the wool and traces her gloved hand over the splintered holes in the wall.

Axe marks.

No one tells the cleanup crew the details, but this is not the first axe murder Cora has seen. She knows the scars that axes leave in walls, the way they bite down and rip the insulation around them when yanked out. She wonders what part of Zihan Huang got axed first. Hopefully her throat so it was over fast. But there are two axe marks in the wall and at least ten on the floor, so whoever did this needed—maybe just wanted—more than one swing.

Cora thinks it must take an incredible amount of anger to kill someone with an axe in 2020.

Axes don't just slide in and out of skulls like knives into butter. They splinter bones and get stuck, have to be wrenched out, hefted back overhead, and plunged back in again. You can't hack someone to death gently, there needs to be force behind it, and that force—not the blade—is what tears the bodies apart, leaving messes for people like Cora to clean up.

More people use guns. Guns are easy and impersonal, a quiet click from across a room, and you can explode someone's brains without even touching them. In a way, Cora doesn't think that should be allowed. If you want someone dead, you should have to sink your fingers into their eyes, feel their trachea collapse under your hands, let them scratch your arms and pull your hair and cry and beg. Because if you kill someone, you should want it more than anything you've ever wanted before. It shouldn't be easy.

Whoever killed Zihan Huang *wanted* it.

There are stray ribs and intestines and even a lock of hair floating in all the blood. There's so much of it—the downstairs neighbors called in a mysterious stain on their ceiling, and that was how the police found her.

Yifei kicks the wet vac and it whirs to life.

"Fucking finally," Yifei says, descending on the red slurry of brain matter.

"Wait, there's ribs," Cora says, dropping her steel wool. "You're going to clog it again."

"I'm not turning it off until I'm done," Yifei says. "Who knows if it will turn on again?"

So Cora abandons the wall and squats down over the slurry, starts removing the ribs and tossing them in the bag while Yifei calls her a hero. She finds a broken bracelet, little charms matted together by tendons. Half a cell phone, the screen in sparkling shards. Something soft and round, like a meatball, but with a sharp edge that tries to prick at her finger even through her gloves. She holds it in her palm, staring at the red mass the size of a golf ball.

"Cora?" Yifei says over the whirring of the wet vac.

Cora swallows, swiping a thumb across the ball. Her hand clenches involuntarily, a nervous muscle contraction like when she's about to fall asleep and her foot jerks awake. Her fingers press down, tightening around it.

"What is it?" Yifei says, impatient now. She reaches out and Cora wants to tell her to stop, that Cora has been struck with the sudden nausea of touching something that she absolutely shouldn't, something that was hidden and meant to stay that way. But Yifei plucks the meatball from Cora's hands and polishes it against the front of her hazmat suit, then reexamines it.

White eyes stare back at her.

"Wait, what the fuck, that's my Sonic key chain!" Harvey says, hurrying to put his glove on, snatching it from Yifei.

"Harvey, leave your shit outside!" Yifei shouts. "It's a biohazard now!"

"I can wash it!" Harvey says, shaking it so some of the blood and skin sloughs off, splatters against the wall. No one will know the difference, but they're really not supposed to make the mess worse than it already was.

"Biohazard!" Yifei says, pointing the wet vac nozzle at Harvey, jabbing it at the key chain.

"Fuck off, Liu!" Harvey says, tucking the ball against his chest, and the wet vac sucks a section of his hazmat suit instead.

"Get that off my nipple, are you insane?" Harvey says, hurling the key chain at Yifei's head. She tries to pull the nozzle away, but it yanks Harvey with it. He lets out a strangled sound and tries to step back, slips in the blood and falls back against the wall, rattling the picture frames.

Something *thumps* inside the wall vent.

All three of them freeze, turning to the small metal grill beside the TV stand, where a sheet of plexiglass has been duct-taped over the air vent. In a normal living room—one not covered in entrails—the strangeness of it might have been louder, maybe even the first thing Cora noticed.

The wet vac chokes and shuts off again, the silence cold as the three of them stare at the vent. Cora squints through the steel grill, can barely make out a black shape but not much else.

"The fuck?" Yifei says, pounding her fist against the wall.

Two more thumps, a wet splash. Something makes a high-pitched trill from within, like a fire alarm somewhere far away.

"She had something trapped in the vents," Yifei says, kneeling down. She plucks at the corner of the plexiglass and begins to remove the tape.

"Wait," Cora says. Because whatever is inside that vent, Zihan Huang wanted to keep it inside.

But the hazmat suit swallows Cora's voice, and Yifei pulls off the tape in one clean *rip* and shoves the screen aside, the grill clattering to the floor along with it.

Something rushes down the vent and crashes into Yifei in a spray of dust. She trips backward over the wet vac and hits her head on the coffee table and the air is a gray cloud that Cora can't see through at all. Something hits her shins and she stumbles, slipping in the puddle of blood, catching herself on the edge of the couch. Harvey shouts something that doesn't even sound like a language, then runs into the kitchen and returns with a cast-iron skillet. The shadow bounces toward the vent, clattering against the plexiglass and jostling the grill before flashing back toward the overturned coffee table.

Harvey slams the skillet into the ground.

Something bursts underneath, then a high-pitched hiss, like a deflating balloon.

Yifei sits up and all three stare at the pool of fresh blood yawning wider from under the skillet. The cloud of dust begins to settle, coating the room in a gray haze.

"Shit," Harvey whispers, backing away.

"Jesus, Harvey," Yifei says, leaning forward and trying to shove the skillet aside. It sticks, and she has to shake it loose.

The creature is flat. Cora is reminded of popped balloons and how little they resemble their perfect round forms, all jagged at the edges. The creature's skull is smashed into a crooked oval shape, a crown of mushy brains spilled around it. But even as warped as it is, Cora can make out its black wings.

Bat eater.

"What is it with bat infestations this week?" Harvey says.

Neither Cora nor Yifei respond. Cora knows this isn't an infestation but doesn't say it out loud.

She knows because the wings are ripped like old cheesecloth, tattered sails, flightless birds. This bat has been shredded by something. It was never meant to fly again. It was supposed to starve to death, trapped in Zihan Huang's vents until the smell of rot filled her house. Cora turns to the vent, where there are several other bat corpses, some already melting into the metal.

"You killed a bat," Yifei says.

"I didn't mean to!" Harvey says, holding his hands up. "I panicked! I couldn't see what it was!"

In a strange way, Cora feels bad for Harvey. Most people don't know how easy it is to end a life. In video games, you can swallow rounds of bullets before going down. But in real life, bodies are delicate. Skulls pop open like biscuits, bones shatter beyond repair, torrents of blood rush from a small wound.

Harvey's hands twitch as he casts his gaze around. After a moment, he pops open a small biohazard bag and starts peeling the bat off the floor.

"I'll bury it," he says.

"Yeah, do that," Yifei says. "Then a raccoon will dig it up and eat it and we'll have COVID 2.0."

"Cremate it?" Harvey says. "Viking funeral? I feel like shit, okay?"

"You're not the one who put bats in a vent," Yifei says.

"You think someone put them in there?" Cora says. Something about her tone makes Harvey and Yifei stop and look at her. Cora goes still because sometimes her desperation leaks out through her words. Cora wants Yifei to be the one who says it because Cora can't trust her own sense of impending doom. If someone else says it, it becomes real.

Yifei jerks a gloved finger toward the bat's wings. "All I know is they couldn't fly through a vent in the roof with wings like that," she says.

Cora looks to the discarded tape on the floor. Clearly, Zihan Huang had known something was inside and desperately wanted to keep it in there. Maybe she heard them dying before Yifei jostled them, heard their cries echoing down across the cold metal and shadows, the constant *drip drip drip* of their decay splashing down. Maybe she was too scared to stick her head inside and peer up into the darkness, so she did what Cora would do and tried to make it quieter, tried to forget about it. After enough time passes, the lying always becomes easier.

The funeral for Zubat (named after Harvey's favorite Pokémon) takes place on a stretch of abandoned train tracks and soft earth in Long Island City. The corner store cashier looked at them strangely when Yifei dropped nothing but a garden shovel and a bottle of Everclear on the conveyor belt. Harvey called her a sadist and added a six-pack of beer and some fake flowers.

It's late, but summer days stretch long and the sky is still orange as Harvey digs a hole while Cora and Yifei drink.

Cora doesn't drink often. Drinking makes the world cloudy, makes her bones soft and blood heavy like treacle, her mind one foot in a dream. It feels like being buried under a great invisible weight, and Cora *likes* it, wishes she were always so calm, and that is why she almost never drinks.

But it's the only way she can stomach sitting on train tracks. Harvey suggested it and Cora couldn't explain why the idea made her want to peel her skin off. It's not something she talks about with her coworkers. Harvey and Yifei are her designated corpse-finders, not her friends. So she took a swig of Yifei's Everclear and by the time she was stumbling over the train tracks, it was almost survivable, being here. She has to do it, because she apparently cannot be a Good Christian Girl, so maybe she can be a Fun Socialite who casually drinks and does fun things after work, whatever those are. Burying dead bats is probably missing the mark, but this is a practice run of saying yes to things she doesn't strictly have to do. Maybe she will be the kind of person people like to hang out with.

"Is that deep enough?" Harvey says. He drops the shovel and it clatters against the train tracks. Lord Google told them to bury dogs at least three feet deep to stop raccoons from digging them up, so they decided the rule must be similar for bats.

"Do I look like a yardstick to you?" Yifei says.

Harvey sighs and gestures for Yifei to hand him a beer, which she pointedly ignores. He grumbles and grabs one himself, taking a swig before handing it to Cora, then grabs the biohazard bag of Zubat's remains and upends it into the hole.

"Anyone want to say a few words?" he says, picking up the shovel again.

"Rest in peace, and sorry you had to look at Harvey Chen in your last moments," Yifei says.

"Fuck you," Harvey says before turning to Cora.

"Um." Cora's mouth feels dry. She takes another swig of Everclear, which only seems to dry her mouth out even more. Harvey is clearly taking this very seriously while Yifei thinks it's a complete joke, and Cora isn't sure which side she's supposed to be on. "I hope the bat afterlife is better than this," Cora says at last.

Yifei snorts, but Harvey seems pleased enough. He pats the dirt down, pulls the fake daisies out of his pocket, and stakes them into the ground.

"I'm sorry," he says to the dirt, smoothing it down around the flowers. "I didn't mean to, and I know that doesn't change anything but I feel like you should know. I hope it was fast."

He stares at the dirt for a moment longer, and Cora wonders what, exactly, he's looking at. Then he drops the shovel and approaches Cora, and for a horrific moment she thinks he wants to touch her with his hands that just buried a bat. He only touched the outside of the bag, but the outside probably wasn't that clean since it came from the crime scene. But Harvey reaches for his beer in Cora's left hand and she hands it to him all too quickly, careful to avoid his fingers. He sits between Cora and Yifei and raises his bottle.

"To Zubat," he says. "May he fly in a world better than this shitty one."

Yifei lifts her glass and Cora lifts the bottle of Everclear to the orange sky. They all take a drink, but Harvey drains the last half of his beer and tosses the bottle aside, putting one arm around Yifei and the other around Cora.

Yifei grumbles but doesn't protest, and Cora remembers that she's been working with Harvey a lot longer than

Cora has. Cora goes rigid, glancing down at where his hand clutches her bare shoulder.

"Thanks," he says, the word tight, quiet.

"You're lucky I have nothing better to do," Yifei says. "You can release us from your grubby paws now."

"Nah," Harvey says, squishing them both to his sides. "I look like a baller. I've got two hot girls who agreed to bury a flattened bat with me."

Cora flushes red—which isn't hard after all the Everclear—but Yifei only scoffs and shoves Harvey away, pushing him against Cora, who barely holds herself up.

"You don't *have* either of us," Yifei says.

Harvey sighs and releases Cora, taking another swig. "Life is long."

Yifei gives Harvey a deeply unimpressed look. Beer drools out the side of his mouth.

"Not to ruin our friendship or anything," he says. "I mean this in the most objective, nonromantic way possible. Purely transactional. We can fuck but we can't date."

"We can't do either of those things unless you wear a bag over your head," Yifei says. "And yes, I'm speaking for Cora too."

"Hey, Cora gets a vote. She's a living, breathing citizen of this world," Harvey says, leaning back to look at her.

"No thank you," Cora says into the rim of the Everclear bottle, hiding her expression by taking another sip. She thinks that, in another lifetime, maybe she could be attracted to someone like Harvey. His face is inoffensive. His smile is kind of nice. But she cannot, in this world, imagine Harvey in a romantic context after seeing him finger-paint with blood and spilled bowels.

"Life is long," Harvey says again, shrugging. He cracks open another beer and leans back on his elbows. "Man, how the hell did we end up here?" Harvey says. "What kind of fucked-up job is this?"

"It doesn't feel fucked-up when you're doing it," Cora whispers into the rim of her bottle. "Just afterward."

"I just like gore," Harvey says. "Does that make me a psychopath?"

"Yes," Yifei says. "You're not supposed to like it."

Harvey hums and takes another sip. "Maybe *like* isn't the right word. I guess I just… I know it scares other people, but not me. It feels like some sort of superpower. Even when I was a kid and saw roadkill—raccoons with bugs in their brains or squirrels who fell out of trees and broke their skulls on the ground and bled out—it felt the same as everything else. There's trees that get sticky with sap and grass that needs to be cut and beehives under the porch and squirrel blood on the sidewalk, and it's all part of the world, you know? It wasn't shocking, it just *was*."

"That's because video games had already rotted your brain," Yifei says.

Harvey hums, doesn't deny it. "I don't think I always know the difference," he says.

"The difference?" Cora asks.

Harvey nods. "My dad bought me lots of games when I had to stay downstairs," he says. "The basement had no windows, and the light bulbs had all burned out. It was always wet—my dad threw a bunch of those dehumidifier boxes down there, but they filled up so fast and spilled over, and it was still so damn wet, like being inside someone's mouth. And it was crawling with silverfish. They reflected the light from the TV, so I saw all these glimmers on the walls, but when I tried to get close it was too dark to see them, and they slithered back into the cracks in the walls, so I was never totally sure if they were there. One crawled into my ear once, and after that I felt like they were all over me as soon as I went down the stairs. Everything itched, but not from my skin, from inside me, like their little legs were tickling my brain. I sat on my beanbag and played *Mortal Kombat* and tried to imagine that I was there, not in the basement, and that's the only way I could forget about the silverfish and the dark. I felt like I spent years down there sometimes. Then the basement door would open and the light would come down the stairs and all the silverfish would run away and I'd remember who I really was, but I wanted to go back. It didn't feel fair. Sometimes, when it's really bright outside, it feels like I'm still in one of my games, like I have unlimited lives, everything is scripted, and I'm just pushing buttons and it's okay if I fuck up—I can go back to my last save. Except I know that's not true. I only have one life, and that's fucking terrifying. I burned through so many lives in video games, died so many times. No one would ever make a game where you only have one chance. But that's all any of us get. And the worst part is I know I'm losing. You get a sense for it in games when things aren't going your way, when it's better to just start over. But this is my only life and I'm losing already, and I don't know how to make it stop."

Cora and Yifei are staring at Harvey, not drinking anymore. Cars rush by across the distant overpass, trees shivering together in the murmuring breeze.

"What do you mean, you 'had to' stay downstairs?" Yifei says. "You weren't allowed to go upstairs?"

Harvey hesitates before bringing the bottle back to his lips. His gaze jumps back and forth between Cora and Yifei, his face flushed from alcohol. He turns away and finishes the bottle, and Cora watches his Adam's apple move slowly as he swallows. He sighs and casts the bottle at the tracks. It bursts, the streetlight reflecting its shattered pieces.

"I don't live with my dad anymore," he says at last, with

finality. "Not since my uncle came over from Shanghai." He turns to Yifei. "Okay, I said too much. What about you, Liu? Spill your secrets."

"I'll need more than a few beers to talk about my family," Yifei says. "Harvey, you're a fucking lightweight." But her voice sounds clipped, like she wants to change the subject, and Cora knows too well what it sounds like when you have a secret, how much of it spills out in the words you don't say.

"Damn," Harvey says, turning to Cora. "Zeng, are you drunk enough to spill?" he says.

Cora shakes her head. She isn't drunk, not really, not anymore.

That's why she feels uneasy when the darkness of the distant train tracks converges into a silhouette, a black hole of a girl in a dress, standing as if waiting for a train that will never come.

SIX

Ever since that night on the tracks, Cora has begun to see spots of darkness.

Every day there are more of them, a swarm of tiny specks at the corners of her vision that disperse when she looks in their direction, hovering just beyond her gaze. They are almost indistinguishable from the fruit flies that swarm the crime scenes Cora cleans up. Fruit flies won't eat bodies, but corpses that have rotted long enough to make a mess usually have kitchens full of rotting fruit and bread. Cora finds herself swatting at bugs that don't exist, and even though Cora can't see Yifei's or Harvey's expressions behind their face shields, she can feel them watching her, wondering.

She spends an hour researching, but an hour wormholes into three hours when she learns that you can have a parasite called toxoplasma in the back of your eye that causes "necrotizing." Cora isn't a doctor but she knows that means something is dying inside you. You can get the parasite from raw meat, and it eats your eyeball until you go blind. So either the dots are completely harmless floaters or her retina has detached and she's going blind, and only a doctor can tell her which it is. Cora worries until she's dry heaving over a trash can and finally decides to call an optometrist.

Most doctors are closed for all but emergency appointments, but she finds a doctor on the Lower East Side who wants to see her right away, doesn't even offer a telehealth appointment, which only makes Cora feel sicker. An hour later, she sits in a waiting room, each breath sucking the double layer of masks against her face like a moist second skin.

The eyeball diagrams plastered on every wall leer down at her. Cora hates the cross section of the optic nerve the most, a rope that anchors the lens into the eye jelly like a bathtub plug and chain. Cora doesn't like thinking of all the parts that make her up, all the glands and sacks and tendons and flaps. She wants to exist like a Lego person, with one singular body that exists in and of itself, solid, no room for anything inside.

The doctor has a name tag that says *Dr. Robinson* and eyes the lightest blue Cora has ever seen, like he stared at the sun for too long and it bleached away all but a whisper of their color.

"It's nice to meet you, Caroline," he says, and Cora doesn't correct him as she sits in a chair that squeaks and sticks to the backs of her legs. The room smells like alcohol wipes and the sharpness of the scent calms Cora a fraction.

"We'll test your vision first, then I'll take a look inside your eyes, see what's happening with your floaters," he says.

Cora nods even though she knows her vision is fine—if anything, it's too sharp. She hates seeing the world in stark clarity, the pores on other people's faces, the dead skin on their shoulders, the stains on their teeth.

The doctor pulls up the chart of letters, the big *E* staring back at Cora. She names off the random letters like a ritual, feels like she's failing when she can name them all easily. She lets the doctor pull a machine in front of her face and presses her chin into it as he makes her world go blurry and sharp again. He leads her out of the room and starts adjusting another machine. From here, more eyeball posters loom above Cora.

"Why eyes?" Cora finds herself asking.

"Sorry?" the doctor says, turning around.

Cora wants to take her question back, realizing at once how childish it sounds. But Cora just wants to understand how people find their dreams, how those dreams could possibly revolve around eyeballs. She's never grasped how doctors choose a specialty, how they want to understand one body part so intimately that they spend a decade studying it. How can anyone want anything that badly? What is it about eyeballs that called to this man? Why doesn't anything in the world call to Cora?

"What made you want to be an optometrist?" she says. "I don't know anyone who's that excited about eyeballs."

Dr. Robinson laughs. "Eyes are beautiful organs," he says. "There's nowhere else in the human body that you can see a part of the central nervous system without cutting anything open."

Cora almost asks him if he's ever seen a squashed eyeball, wonders if he would still think eyes are beautiful then. But her gaze catches on his ripped glove, a tiny crescent of white skin peeking through. The doctor follows her gaze, then sighs.

"Just a moment," Dr. Robinson says, stripping his gloves off.

Cora freezes, feels like he's just peeled off his flesh, baring his exposed muscle and pulsing veins to her. She forces herself not to look at his bare hands, because even she knows that this is only her fear and not something real. She knows that her optometrist doesn't push girls in front of trains in his spare time—it's an absurd idea, too coincidental. Cora will probably never meet the White Spider. Most people don't cross paths with the same murderer twice. Unless he's looking for them.

Cora has started to wonder how much of those hands are actually her memory and how much of them are a dream. She knows that memories are not like turning pages in a photo album until you find the right one—every time you recall something, your brain rebuilds it from scratch, and every time it's just a little bit different. It has to be, because brains are not video cameras; they don't have that much empty space for unnecessary details. Someday, Cora will remember the hands and they will be completely divorced from reality, the hands of a stranger who never once touched her sister.

Cora hears cardboard tearing and thinks it's safe, chances a glance, but Dr. Robinson's hands are still bare. He pulls a new box of gloves from a shelf, runs his finger under the perforated edge to tear off the cardboard seal, and at this new angle, there are no similarities at all—his fingers are too short, bulge too much at each knuckle. Maybe that's just what Cora needs to believe, but her heartbeat slows as she convinces herself of it. Mercifully, he puts a new pair of gloves on.

Cora thinks that her new hand phobia might be her most annoying symptom of all. Most people can at least vaguely understand why she wants things to be clean, consider it reasonable to some degree. Flinching at bare hands is a bit harder to explain.

"Now," he says, wiggling his fingers and tugging the gloves down, "for this test, you'll feel a quick puff of air on your eye." He sits on a stool on the other side of the machine. "You'll see a picture of a barn in the distance. Try to keep your eye open as best as you can and stare directly at it."

Cora leans forward, settles her chin in the cup, angles her

face until she sees the bright green field, the red barn, the blue sky, like she is at the bottom of the well looking up at the world through a tiny hole.

Night eclipses the farm scene, and Cora thinks at first that this is the test.

But the darkness sparkles, and Cora realizes that this is just her floaters scattered across her vision again. Here, concentrated in the tiny lens of the machine, they form a frothing pool of black, so deep and alive that she can almost see beyond it, if she looks a bit closer…

"Try to look at the barn," Dr. Robinson says.

But there is no barn. There is nothing but the endless night, which has started to coagulate into shapes. Faces stretched down into screams, jaws wrenched open, glistening black teeth—

A burst of air in her eye makes her tense. She blinks, and there is the green field, red barn, blue sky.

"All done with your right eye," Dr. Robinson says, and Cora quickly sits back. The doctor smiles, but Cora doesn't smile back, takes too long to respond. She can tell because the smile falls off his face.

"I…" Cora falters, swallows the dryness in her mouth. "Sorry," she says, which isn't an explanation, but it's all she can manage.

"It's all right," he says, but his voice seems quieter now, like he has only just begun to realize that Cora is not the kind of patient he wants. "Do you want to continue?"

There isn't a polite way to say no, and Cora still needs answers, so she leans forward again, forces her chin back onto the ledge. She stares at the little circle of a bright summer farm scene and keeps her eye wide-open until another gust of air makes her flinch back.

Dr. Robinson leads her back to the first room, dilates her

eyes with stinging eye drops, tears sliding under her masks where she can't wipe them away. He leaves her alone with the eyeball posters for a while and gives the drops time to work, and soon the overhead light begins to ache at the edge of her vision, the letters blurring at the far end of the room.

The doctor returns and shines sharp lights at her and tells her to follow his finger. Cora fights the urge to slam her eyes shut, sure that one of his delicate tools is going to lodge itself into her eye jelly, through the lens, pulling on the optic nerve, ripping it out like hair from a bathtub drain. Most people don't know how delicate the human body is, how easily things can pop and crush and break. Surely Dr. Robinson doesn't know, because Cora is almost certain he's never gouged someone's eyeball out. But all it takes is a single moment to cross into the broken reality, the bad one.

At last, he clicks off his penlight, sits back.

"You don't have any floaters," he says. "Your eyes look perfectly healthy to me."

"Oh," Cora says. She knows this is supposed to be good news, but the specks are in the upper right corner of the room now, hovering, a nest of bees.

"Do you ever get migraines?" the doctor says.

Cora shakes her head. "I don't think so."

"If you ever had a migraine, you would know," the doctor says, and Cora feels like she's answered incorrectly, sinks down in her chair. "It's possible to have migraine auras without migraines," he continues. "They can cause visual disturbances. Do the dots ever go away?"

But Cora isn't sure how to answer anymore, because she doesn't know if the dots fade or if she just stops noticing them, and she doesn't want to answer incorrectly again.

"Sometimes," she says to her lap.

The doctor nods, like this is the right answer, the one he

expected. "You should go to your PCP," he says, "ask if they want to refer you to a neurologist."

His tone is kind, but Cora hears everything he's not saying: *The problem is not in your eyes. It's in your brain.*

And Cora doesn't want anyone digging around in her brain, not anymore. She already knows there are too many frayed wires up there, too many broken circuits. She knows that all organs are nothing but meat, and she knows a brain doctor isn't any more shameful to see than an eye doctor, but she doesn't think she can survive another medical professional telling her that her mind is a web they cannot untangle.

None of them can help her because she can't tell them the truth. Whenever anyone gets a glimpse of what Cora's mind is truly like, they always have one hand hovering above the panic button, ready to send her away, make her someone else's liability. No one wants to help her untangle her mind; they want her to disappear.

The problem can't be in her brain. There must be some hidden corner of her eyeball the doctor hasn't seen. Cora doesn't think she'll be satisfied until the doctor has removed her eyeball and mapped out its contents, memorized every vein and nerve. There is a darkness in there somewhere that he hasn't found yet. Cora thinks of the toxoplasma, the parasite that slowly dies without its host to devour, withering into nothingness over months and months.

"Okay, I will," Cora lies, "but can you do any other tests?"

"There are no other tests for floaters," the doctor says.

"Not for floaters," Cora says. "For anything."

The doctor frowns. "Are you having any other symptoms?"

Cora shakes her head. "I just want to be very thorough, since I'm here anyway."

She knows she's talking too fast, her words rolling downhill the way they sometimes do when she lies, and she can see the hesitance in the doctor's eyes.

"There is nothing else to test for," he says. "I don't doubt that you're having symptoms, but I can assure you that your eyes are not the problem."

Cora nods and sinks back in her chair because she knows when to stop pushing. She pays, puts it all on her credit card to deal with later because state marketplace insurance inexplicably doesn't cover eyeballs. The doctor fumbles through the payment software since his secretary isn't there, and then Cora is finally outside, ripping off her masks like dead skin. The dots are mockingly absent from her vision, as if confirming that Dr. Robinson is right.

Cora stops at a bodega that at least keeps its door open for reasonable airflow, buys a bottle of ginger ale because she's getting nauseous but already knows it's the kind of sickness that starts in her brain and not her stomach. A bottle of ginger ale and some of the emergency Pepto-Bismol in her purse can placebo her brain into not making her puke.

The parks are all a war zone of overgrown grass tangled with crushed red Solo cups, empty chip bags, garbage cans bursting with take-out containers, but Cora needs to drink something or she'll puke before she makes it home, so she presses her back to a tree, pulls down her mask and drinks small sips that taste like garbage because of the smell. She counts the dots as they reappear in her vision, one by one, like stars coming out at night. They bother her a little less now that she knows she isn't going blind. She already knew someone had poked holes in her brain, after all.

Neon orange posters flutter on the trees around her as she drinks, moving in tandem with the wind like the whole park is breathing around her. They're waterlogged graphics advertising a protest that's already happened, and now the faded text looks like the ghost of a dream because Cora knows nothing has changed. News of the mayor's increased police budget broke the week after a cop shot an unarmed man in Florida, and the protests have only increased as Mayor Webb uttered the words "running for reelection." Cora should feel angry—she knows that more police wouldn't have saved Delilah, but all she feels is that the sky is a dome sinking lower and lower, trapping her in a world that she hates but can never escape.

She finishes the bottle and feels light, full of air. She imagines Delilah sitting here with her, telling her she doesn't need a neurologist, that she can be fixed by burning the right oils, holding the right gemstones. And Cora doesn't believe in that kind of thing the way Delilah did, but Delilah always solved her problems eventually, one way or another, even if it was just through the passage of time. For a minute, Cora entertains the thought of buying some of Delilah's silly oils, becoming the kind of person who believes in aromatherapy and crystal healing and energy exorcisms because Delilah always seemed calm enough—but no, the whole point of After is to build something without Delilah.

Cora walks home, clutching her empty ginger ale bottle because the trash cans are all full, crinkling it in her left hand. She makes it to her lobby, to the staircase, jams her keys in the lock, slips inside and bolts the door and slides down the back of it, and only then does she feel like she can breathe. She lets out a wounded sound and feels her way back up to her feet by her end table, slides her shoes off, falls onto the couch.

But her finger catches on a loose thread. She brushes her hand across it and finds a handful of hair beneath her palm.

Cora screams, jerks her hand away, backing into the coffee table.

It's only loose stuffing, spilling out from the arm of the couch.

But it wasn't there this morning, Cora is sure of it. And as she sits down on the coffee table because her legs can't hold her anymore, her fingers ghost over the hardwood and she feels a dip that she knows wasn't there before either. Her fingers trace the half-moon shape and she knows even before she looks down what it will be.

Her table has bite marks.

The crescent shape of a human mouth has bitten through the varnish of her table, split the wood.

Cora goes very still. A strange calmness washes over her, and she is deep in a sea so cold that she can't feel her body at all, the way she prefers.

You should go to your PCP, Dr. Robinson said. *Ask if they want to refer you to a neurologist.*

But Cora has already been to the place that they put you when you become a liability. Where they want your mouth loose and drooling from sedatives, release you when you're quiet and learn the answers that they like, even when they know you're lying but don't care. Her world focuses in on the singular determination to never, ever, go there again.

She looks down at the bite marks and slides her phone out of her pocket.

She could call her Auntie Zeng, or even Auntie Lois, but both of them already see Cora as something volatile, a rescue dog that needs to be carefully coddled or it will bite and scream and pee all over the floor.

She pulls up the contact for Coworker #1 and hits Call.

SEVEN

Yifei's apartment is a tower.

She lives in Confucius Plaza, the redbrick beast growing out of Chinatown's spine, guarded by a bronze Confucius statue that must be at least fifteen feet tall but somehow looks like a tiny pawn before the great behemoth of the apartment complex.

The elevator is out, and Yifei lives on the twenty-first floor, so Cora ascends the stairs in meditative silence, likes the way her legs start to burn after the fourth floor and keep burning until she can hardly feel them at all. Her footsteps echo up, and Cora realizes she doesn't know just how high the apartment building goes, if it ever ends. A few unmasked people come into the stairway arguing in Cantonese and Cora backs against the wall, holds her breath until they pass.

Yifei offered to meet at a park, but the smell of hot garbage is still burned into Cora's memory and this isn't the kind of thing she wants to talk about in public, not knowing who's listening. So instead, she's gloved and double-masked as she heads to Yifei's apartment, sweating into both as she ascends the staircase.

Cora knocks on the door and hears shouting, takes a step back until the door flies open and Yifei appears, smiling. She isn't wearing a mask, but then, of course she isn't, she's in her own apartment.

Cora usually sees Yifei in a hazmat suit, or just after she's been stewing in one for hours. She's unused to seeing her in daylight, the way her hair curls just past her shoulders when it hasn't been tied back tight, the gentle brown of her eyes when they aren't ringed with goggle lines. The way she might look if she were a normal person working a normal office job. Yifei could pass as normal in a way that Cora knows she herself never could.

Yifei smells like a magazine perfume sample as she comes closer, her hair still damp like she's just showered, and that makes Cora slightly less tense when Yifei leans in to hug her because at least she's clean. Everything in Cora screams that she shouldn't be this close to someone who's unmasked, but she supposes that she already spends well over eight hours with Yifei every day at work, so if Yifei has COVID, she'll give it to Cora regardless.

Yifei pulls Cora to her and whispers in her ear, "My roommate is here, so just follow my lead."

Cora doesn't have the chance to ask what she means before Yifei takes her hand and pulls her into the apartment.

She steps into a living room that feels more like an Ikea showroom than a home, much less a place that Yifei Liu lives. It is the quintessential American home, matching white plywood chairs and a table with a fruit basket with unbruised bananas. A coffee maker, gold soap dispenser, and sponge shaped like a hedgehog sit on the clean granite counter.

Across the open space, a blonde woman and man are lying on the couch, watching a sitcom Cora has never seen before.

"Ryan, Paisley, this is my friend," Yifei shouts at them, but her accent is stronger than Cora has ever heard before. Yifei usually only has a trace of an accent on certain words, but now she's tripping over syllables like she's just learning English. She turns to Cora. "Don't speak English," she says in Mandarin.

The blonde girl hangs her head over the edge of the couch and waves, giving a half smile. The man doesn't even turn from the TV.

"Hey, I'm Paisley," she says.

Cora freezes up, looking to Yifei in a panic because *why can't she speak English?* But the terror in her face is apparently unsurprising to Paisley, who drops her hand and turns back to the man. "Does she really not have any American friends?" she says.

"No one in this whole building is American," Ryan mumbles.

Yifei ignores them, opening the fridge. "She thinks I can't speak English," she says, still in Mandarin, and it takes Cora a moment to process it, so unused to hearing anything but Auntie Zeng's slow speech. "My old coworker who sublets me this place set us up as roommates. She assumed I didn't speak English when we first met, so I just went along with it and now I don't have to talk to her. It's a great arrangement."

Cora stands speechless as Yifei pulls out two cans of White Claw and slams them on the counter. Cora stares at the cans, not sure how Yifei expects her to drink without taking her mask off. Yifei studies her for a moment, frowning. "Wait, you do speak Mandarin, right?" Then she says something else in Cantonese and Cora shakes her head.

"I understand Mandarin, but I'm bad at it," she mumbles in Chinese.

Yifei only shrugs, popping open the tab of her drink. "It's not like those two know the difference," she says, jerking her head toward the couple. "Watch." Then she raises her voice a fraction, looking at Cora earnestly. "My ears are full of bees," she says. "I lick all the silverware before putting it away and I squeeze my roommate's pears so they bruise and go bad faster. I also play Chinese opera music when they have sex."

Cora glances at Ryan and Paisley, who only turn the volume up on the TV. She wonders how much of that is true. Knowing Yifei, probably most of it.

"Say something back, or it doesn't sound like a conversation," Yifei says.

"Um." But *um* isn't Mandarin, and Cora clamps her mouth shut, scrambling for words to cover up her mistake. She notices a butter dish on the counter and somehow, to her embarrassment, "I like butter," are the only Chinese words that come out of her mouth.

"Perfect," Yifei says. "Come on, you poor thing, let's go to my room." She tugs Cora's wrist and shouts, "See you later, Paisley!" in English before pulling Cora away. Cora clutches the White Claw in both hands and lets herself be dragged.

Cora hesitates in the doorway to Yifei's room. The walls are covered in shelves so full of ceramic figures and vitamin bottles and old books and pencil jars that Cora can't see the paint color. The shelves slant forward from the weight and Cora is sure she'll be crushed when everything slides to the floor. Cora recognizes an acorn-shaped cookie jar from a cleanup scene and realizes that the random assortment of things is probably not random at all—these are the things Yifei has taken from crime scenes. The room is such an antithesis to Cora's own apartment that she feels like it will reject her existence, force her back out like a key jammed into the wrong hole.

But Yifei tugs her over the threshold and Cora hovers just past the door while Yifei takes her phone out and starts playing Chinese opera music on her speaker, waving for Cora to close the door.

"Just so Paisley can't hear," Yifei says, turning the volume up. "You can sit."

Before Cora can ask where, Yifei drags a beanbag out from under her bed and kicks it toward Cora, and Cora isn't sure she wants to interact with anything in the room but forces herself to sit down before any thoughts can take hold. The beanbag crunches under her, like it's full of crumpled paper instead of beans, all the filling dispersing until she's left with only two thin layers of leathery beanbag fabric between her butt and the floor.

"So what's up?" Yifei says, sitting cross-legged on her bed. "Weird of you to call me. I mean, you can always come over, but I never thought you wanted to."

Cora can't quite meet Yifei's gaze, stuck staring at the Newton's cradle, the bottles of herbal medicine, the jars of bottle caps. Her room is like one of Cora's old I Spy books, secrets and visual overstimulation. Cora also isn't sure how to begin to translate her thoughts to someone who doesn't live inside her head, isn't privy to the carousel of worries constantly blurring together.

"Do I seem weird to you?" Cora says, finally looking at Yifei.

Yifei blinks, takes a long sip of White Claw without breaking eye contact. "We're crime scene cleaners."

Cora shakes her head. "I mean…" Cora trails off because what, exactly, does she mean? Cora has always seen things that weren't normal, in one way or another. And for the most part, it's been survivable.

But she wonders now if she's been splintering ever since that day, if one night she quietly crossed over an invisible line and now it's not a problem she can stuff under her bed any longer. Cora is used to terror, a worry that wrings your organs out and carves holes in you like termites in wooden furniture, but if enough of you is devoured, soon there's nothing left of you but what *was*, and Cora is starting to feel full of holes, like Yifei can look straight through her.

She almost unstops the faucet of her mind, almost lets her words pour out and hopes that Yifei can make sense of them, but then her gaze falls on a shiny plastic package on Yifei's desk next to a box of matches. Cora's jaw clamps shut and the words won't come.

Yifei follows her gaze, then pulls the joss paper off her desk.

"You need any?" she says. "I already burned a bunch."

"You actually believe in that?" Cora says. It's a rude thing to say, but it's the only thing Cora can manage.

"Hell yes," Yifei says, frowning. "I don't want to be haunted by hungry ghosts. I have enough problems as it is."

Hungry.

Cora remembers the teeth marks on her table, the missing apples. "What could ghosts possibly be hungry for?" she asks.

Yifei's frown carves deeper into her face. "It's not a need, it's a punishment. Their families neglect them, so they starve." She waves the papers in front of Cora's face. "I say better safe than sorry. There's too many people who would haunt me if they had the chance."

Something about her expression is too sharp, and the overhead lamp casts a light on something in the deep chasm of her pupils that Cora feels she shouldn't have seen. She recrosses her legs and the light shifts and whatever Cora saw is gone.

"Have you ever seen one?" Cora whispers. It feels like a question she isn't allowed to ask, and the way Yifei goes still only confirms this.

"Can you keep a secret?" Yifei says.

Cora's stomach clenches. Her skin is taut, a dried canvas. She nods.

Yifei grabs the hem of her T-shirt and lifts it up. Before Cora can ask what she's doing, her gaze drifts to a purple scar across the whispers of Yifei's ribs, just below her bra. It's a deep crater, the empty rivers of the dark side of the moon, glossy with scar tissue. The edges are a jagged pattern, the same half-moon on each side, and Cora realizes all at once what they are.

Teeth marks.

"I know Americans don't like to think about this kind of thing," Yifei says, and Cora knows that "Americans" includes her. "Frankly, I didn't really care much about it when I was a kid. But the thing about hungry ghosts is they don't care if you believe in them."

She drops her shirt, but the memory of her scar is carved into Cora's mind. She reminds herself that a living, breathing human could just as easily have given her the scar, that ghosts are not real just because Yifei Liu the kleptomaniac crime scene cleaner says so.

"Show me again," Cora says. Her words come out smooth, confident in a way that Cora doesn't feel, but she needs to see.

Yifei hesitates, then lifts her shirt again. Cora leans forward and ghosts a finger across the scar tissue, rippled beneath her skin. It doesn't feel like she's touching the memory of a hungry ghost. There's no electric shock or bolt of ghostly energy rushing through her bones. Just gnarled flesh, a rough porridge of it beneath her fingertips.

And Cora knows that Yifei believes she is telling the truth. But that doesn't mean her story is true.

Delilah is *gone*, not in the soft quiet way of her grandparents fading into starched white hospital sheets. From the moment of impact, Delilah was so definitively gone that the paramedics wouldn't touch her, wouldn't even try. She was so very much gone that an open casket funeral was not an option because they couldn't find enough pieces of her face on the train tracks. Her mama came and took all of her things that Cora hadn't already hidden, ripped down her posters, threw her toothbrush in the trash, shut off her cell phone so Cora can't even listen to her voicemail message. There is no religion in the world that can bring her back.

There's no such thing as a hungry ghost, not in Cora's life, because someone that deeply and irrevocably gone can never come back.

Yifei hisses as Cora presses too hard. Cora pulls her hand back and mumbles an apology. Yifei looks at Cora expectantly and it crashes over Cora all at once how ridiculous her situation would sound if she said it out loud.

I don't have as many eggs as I thought. I think the floaters in my eyes are evil.

Yifei drops her shirt. "You can come over whenever, you know," she says. "You can call me anytime. I don't have a life, so I don't mind."

Cora forces her mouth into something resembling a smile. She must do a bad job of it, because Yifei grimaces in response. "You want to get out of here? Get a real drink or something?"

Cora shakes her head. The floaters in her eyes converge, a haze around Yifei, a dark silhouette like a living shadow behind her, dispersing when Cora tries to look at it because it's not really there. It's only a trick of the light.

EIGHT

On Saturday, Auntie Lois calls and tells Cora that she and Father Thomas have found a way for her to repent, and to Cora's delight, it involves cleaning.

"He needs part of the cathedral swept tomorrow," Auntie Lois says, "and he wants to have a talk with you. If you listen to him and help clean up, you can come back to the service next week."

If the price of Auntie Lois's financial support is missing a week of church and sweeping, Cora won't question it.

Cora meets Father Thomas on Sunday evening on the front steps of the church, just before the iron gates. The stained glass windows look oddly gray at this hour, all the colors wine-deep, the painted faces of angels stoic in the darkness. The church feels like a sleeping beast as Cora approaches. She is sure that if her footsteps are too loud, the bells will clamor and the doors will fly open and God will force Cora to her knees.

Father Thomas waves as Cora turns the corner, as if she might not recognize the wraith of a man in a clerical collar standing alone in front of a church. He's one of the ministers in training, much younger than the one Cora accidentally flashed a crime scene photo to. He has dark hair and amber eyes and looks more like a shadow that stands behind a person than a man himself, so tall and willowy in his black cassock. His eyes are the only bright spots on his body, like he himself is a pale marble cathedral, his eyes two golden stained glass windows. He always seems nervous when he gives his sermons, but Cora prefers it that way—he seems more human somehow. Because something about the immense gilded ceilings of the cathedral commands fear, and Cora doesn't like being the only one who feels it. Maybe he can be the one who shows her how to be a Good Christian Girl, since the other ministers think she's a lost cause. Maybe God's heart is just a locked door that someone has to open for you, and maybe he can be that person. She stops walking, stands an awkward distance from him because he's not wearing a mask.

"Cora," he says, smiling. "Thank you for coming."

"I'm happy to," Cora says, because that is what a Good Christian Girl would say. Her smile feels thin, but Father Thomas seems pleased.

"And *I'm* happy to get a chance to talk with you," he says, pulling out a ring of keys. But rather than turning to the iron gates of the church, he keeps walking down the sidewalk, and Cora has no choice but to follow him.

Cora cannot fathom why he has so many keys, or how he tells them apart. He flips through them, feeling the teeth as he walks. They stop at a small redbrick building beside the cathedral—Cora had always assumed it was some kind of storage shed. Father Thomas jams a key into the lock. It *thunks*, teeth slotting in, but when Father Thomas tries the handle, the black door groans but doesn't give. He presses a palm flat against the door and shoves, hard. With a clunk, it swings inward.

The smell of mildew hits Cora in a hot wave. It's the kind of rotting wetness that she can taste, like she's swimming through a bog and the mossy water is filling her mouth.

Father Thomas enters, waving for Cora to follow. Her mind spins through a few hundred kinds of deadly mold that she might breathe in, but she prefers any of them to church service, so she follows him in.

They enter a room with a low ceiling, forcing Father Thomas to duck slightly. It's a tight hallway lit only by the streetlights spilling inside. Father Thomas pulls a flashlight from a hook on the wall, then hands it to Cora and takes another for himself. He clicks it on and casts a sharp beam of light, too weak to see the end of the hallway. Cora catches a glimpse of a smaller door to the right.

"As you can see, this place is in need of repairs," he says. "That's part of why we haven't cleaned it. It's perfectly safe, though, just a bit dark."

"This place?" Cora echoes, but Father Thomas doesn't pick up on her question. He unlocks the door to the right and pulls out a broom and dustpan, handing them both to Cora, who tucks the flashlight under her armpit.

They keep walking until Father Thomas's flashlight suddenly floods a white brick wall, another wooden door.

"A bit of extra security," Father Thomas says, smiling, feeling for another key. "We don't want teenagers running around down here. They never find their way out."

Then he opens the next door, and red light spills across the floor.

The ceilings open up to wide arches, white walls painted red from the emergency lights. There are five identical doors on each side of the hall, wood so dark that they almost look like holes, knocked-out teeth. At the end of the hall, there is one door, larger than the rest.

Father Thomas turns off his flashlight and smiles at Cora. "It's a family vault," he says. "You thought Manhattan was expensive to live in? You don't even want to know how expensive it is to be buried here."

He laughs, the sound echoing up to the swooping arches, growing softer, sadder as it rises. Cora realizes she was also supposed to laugh and does so too quietly, too late.

"This is a crypt?" Cora says to cover up the awkward echo of her laugh. "I didn't know they had those in New York."

"It does feel a bit European, doesn't it?" Father Thomas says. "There are eight or so in the city. We were considering opening to the public before all the..." He gestures vaguely to Cora's mask. "You know. People don't like to think about death as much anymore. But I suppose that's not true for you, Cora?"

"What?" Cora says. How does Father Thomas know what's in her mind?

"Your job," Father Thomas says, his voice lower, eyes gentle, like he's reminding her of something terrible. "Your aunt mentioned your profession to me. She said this would be a good job for you because you're used to much worse. Was she mistaken?"

"I... No, she's right," Cora says, not liking that her aunt talks about her job as if she has any idea what Cora sees, what Cora can handle. "I won't actually see any dead bodies down here, will I?"

Father Thomas laughs again. He is perhaps the only person who thinks Cora is funny. Even if Cora doesn't agree, at least she's said something right, isn't accidentally being a heathen again.

"No, don't worry about that," he says.

He starts walking again, stepping into the hallway, dousing himself in red light. His eyes look bright gold in the crimson glow. "Let me show you around," he says, opening the first door on the right.

He ducks under cobwebs like they're inconsequential, but Cora freezes at the sight of a large spider hanging from the doorway. The light casts it in searing red, electrifying its web, but then it scurries up a fine thread and Cora can see that it's only a black spider. She holds her breath and hurries after Father Thomas into the small room, its walls lined with large, horizontal doors. Cora tilts her head to the side, as if the arrangement will make sense if she only contorts herself.

"The Holloway family," Father Thomas says, gesturing to the doors, and that's when Cora understands—behind each door is a corpse. They are packed into marble bunk beds. On the far wall a limestone cross is mounted, carved with names that Cora can't discern in the dim light. Father Thomas points to several empty spaces in the walls, where there is only gaping darkness instead of doors.

"For the children they never had," Father Thomas says, his voice low. "Imagine if all of us built crypts for our dreams. You're too young to worry about that now, but someday maybe you'll think about it."

"That's…poetic," Cora says, the words like Styrofoam in her mouth, but Father Thomas smiles like this was the right answer and Cora feels like he's put a gold star sticker on her term paper.

He points to the green tiles crisscrossing the walls, which look vaguely familiar even before he says, "These were some of the first tiles used in Grand Central Station. Fitting, isn't it? All the dead are going on a journey."

"I hope when I die, I won't have to take the subway to heaven," Cora says, and Father Thomas laughs again. It's presumptuous of Cora to think she'll make it to heaven, but as far as Father Thomas knows, she's just a good, God-fearing girl.

"Yes, hopefully there are no rats on the way to heaven," he says. Then he slides past her quickly, like a shadow rolling across the wall, and slips back into the hall, opening the next door.

A man is standing in the crypt.

The hallway light carves out the lines of his ribs in red, grips the muscles of his bare shoulders, his arms stretched out as if taking flight.

Father Thomas shines the flashlight on him, his cream-white skin, and Cora realizes all at once that he's made of marble. This is not a man; it's a large crucifix.

"I promised you no bodies, didn't I?" Father Thomas says, grinning over his shoulder. "Don't worry, Cora, you're safe here."

Cora swallows and follows wordlessly into the crypt. This one is slightly larger than the last. It's a small white hallway of doors that seem sealed shut, no seams to them at all, nothing but painted crosses and names fading into the paint.

"You do know that, don't you, Cora?" Father Thomas says, walking slower now. "That you're always safe and welcome here?"

"Here?"

"At mass, I mean," Father Thomas says. "God loves you as you are."

And how am I? Cora wants to ask, but doesn't. Her throat feels sore already from the mold, and something about the shrill shade of red in the hall is giving her a headache.

"You are always welcome here, I want you to know that," Father Thomas says, his voice soft, velvety. "No matter how many complaints we get, you may always come to God's house."

"Complaints?" Cora says, the echo slipping from her lips before she can stop it.

Father Thomas waves his hand as if it's inconsequential. "People afraid of getting COVID."

"But I don't have COVID," Cora says.

"No, but…" Father Thomas looks away, and the shadows hide his expression. "You know how people are."

But Cora's silence says more than her words could, and Father Thomas grimaces, considering his next words carefully. "These are times of fear," he says. "Even good people succumb to fear sometimes. Not everyone is as brave as you, coming down to a crypt." He lets out a small laugh, as if he's made a joke, but Cora doesn't even smile politely this time.

"Fear of what?" Cora says. "Of me?"

Father Thomas sighs, and that is enough of an answer. Cora drops her gaze to the dusty floor, an odd heat churning in her stomach.

Cora Zeng does not get angry. Not because Auntie Lois says anger is a sin, or because Delilah could never be bothered with such an emotion, or because Cora is sage enough to understand that it is a pointless, destructive feeling. Cora Zeng does not get angry because anger always melts through her fingers until it's a pool of anguish under her feet. There is not enough oxygen inside Cora to keep anger burning. No matter how hard she tries, she can only wield her sharpest thoughts against her own flesh. She knows, on some level, that most of the problems in her life are her own fault in one way or another. Anger is just one of those thoughts that can never quite sink its teeth into her—she is not solid enough, and its jaws close around nothing at all.

At least, that's what she used to think.

But now, in this dark, moldy crypt, Father Thomas is telling her that there are people in his congregation who fear her. There are thousands of monsters in the world—not just the ones in folktales, but the ones in real life who push girls in front of trains—and yet, there are still people who think Cora Zeng is the most fearsome of all.

A sharp laugh forces its way out of Cora's throat. Those people should see what fear truly is. Let them taste their sister's blood, watch her headless body twitch, hear her throat still wheezing for breaths that won't come, gurgling as the blood drowns down the wrong pipe. Let them remember it every time they close their eyes, whenever they hear the sound of a train, whenever salt stings their lips. Remind them that the same thing could happen to them any day, and then let them talk about what fear really means.

"I'm not saying they're right," Father Thomas says, expression soft. "I don't agree with them, Cora."

"I know," Cora says stiffly, and it's not a lie. She knows Father Thomas thinks of himself as a good person, that he would never turn Cora away for being Chinese.

But he forgives the people who would, even though it's not his place to dole out forgiveness on Cora's behalf. He loves the people who would never love her.

"You want me to sweep this hallway?" Cora says, because she doesn't want to talk anymore.

Father Thomas doesn't respond for a moment, perhaps sensing that the conversation hasn't gone as planned. After a breath, he nods, shoulders drooping, and Cora almost feels bad for him.

"Yes," he says. "I have some work I need to finish, but I can be back in an hour or so. Will you be all right down here?"

"I clean up entrails for a living," Cora says. "I'll be fine."

She knows her words weren't what a Good Christian Girl would say, can tell from the look on Father Thomas's face that she shouldn't have said it—everyone thinks her job is interesting in theory, but no one actually wants to hear about it. But the words have their intended effect because Father Thomas nods and finally leaves, and somehow in the space of a few minutes she has failed once more at becoming someone.

The crypt door shuts and Cora hears murmurs, the tiny *tap tap tapping* of spiders running across the walls. Cora didn't realize how loud Father Thomas's presence was until he left. The whispered sounds of moisture and bugs and settling stone itch at her ears, so she does the only thing she can and starts sweeping up the dust and dirt inside the Holloway family tomb.

It comes away in thick layers, like matted wool coming off an overgrown sheep, and Cora thinks her dustpan won't hold it all, but she concentrates on the stiff bristles of the broom scraping it from the floor, revealing the brown tiles below. It is all too easy to sink into a trance of peeling away the layers, because this is the part of cleaning that Cora likes the most—the part where you rip off the skin and what's left is unrecognizable, transformed. She ducks around the cobwebs, scrapes the dust ball into the hallway just as a door closes.

The sound echoes, coming from the opposite end of the hall, farthest from where Cora and Father Thomas entered. Cora goes still, waiting for Father Thomas's voice, but no other sound follows and the ghost of the echo fades away.

Cora steadies her grip on her broom, takes a tentative step into the red hallway.

There are footprints in the dust.

Bare feet, beginning from the tomb door opposite Cora, leading down the hallway, ending in front of the large door opposite the entrance. Tiny flecks of dust drift in a pale snowfall as if just disturbed.

Cora drops her broom and heads for the entrance.

It's not real, she thinks. Cora's own eyes are filled with holes, unreliable, and all of this is a trick of red light. But the knowledge doesn't comfort her. Cora knows all too well that the mangled clockwork of her mind doesn't always respond to logical arguments, that the fact that something is objectively safe doesn't mean her mind won't short-circuit anyway, make her hyperventilate until her limbs lose so much oxygen she can't stand up.

She grabs the doorknob. It twists back and forth in her hands but doesn't have any effect on the door, solid wood so unmoving that it almost seems painted into the wall. She remembers Father Thomas shouldering the front door open—the wood is old and warped and uncooperative, the crypt so rarely visited. A spider descends on a thin string in front of her face and she jumps back, its eyes cast red in the emergency light. The air now tastes like dust from all the sweeping and Cora holds her breath, not wanting to be heard.

This is just like at Dr. Robinson's office, Cora thinks. *All you have to do is look somewhere else and it will disappear.* So Cora takes a steadying breath and does the only thing she can: she sweeps the footprints away.

The dust in the main hallway is thicker, a dense coat caked with a layer of grease on the bottom, peeling away in gray-brown clumps. Cora wonders too late if there are rats down here, if part of the stickiness is animal droppings. She scrapes the ball of brown muck and dust towards the door, and finally sweeps away the final footprints at the far end.

The door looks identical to the one Cora and Father Thomas entered through. Her hand drifts toward the handle, but it only ghosts over the cool metal, not daring to apply any force. Why would anyone walk here? Is it another family tomb? She scrubs the door with her sleeve, then presses her ear against the wood.

Her mind takes a moment to adjust to the loudness of pipes echoing through the walls, the warm hum of the furnace. She holds her breath to hear better, but her own heartbeat is so loud. Her fingers tighten around the doorknob, almost begin to turn it, but her hand falls away and she takes a step back. Sometimes the unknowing is worse than the knowing. But other times, Cora cannot bridge the distance between the two.

When Cora turns around, there are more footprints.

Bare feet walking the space beside the path that Cora scraped away, coming to a stop right before her.

Cora goes very still, staring at that empty space where someone—*something*—should be, the falling dust sparkling through the glare of red light, the faraway glimmer of spider strings dangling from the ceiling.

She holds her breath, certain that something is about to happen, but the dust settles and Cora is still alone in the dark.

Slowly, she kneels down, sinks her bare finger into the footprint to test its realness. Her fingertip brushes the sticky floor in the center of the footprint. It doesn't mean anything, of course—brains control touch as much as they control sight, and Cora could be imagining the sensation of bare floor under her finger—but something about the cool tiles on her skin feels the same way as touching Yifei's scar. It feels like the truth, whatever that's worth.

Cora remembers the look in Yifei's eyes when she talked about hungry ghosts. Cora turns the thought over, considers it for a long moment, then crushes it.

Footprints or not, there is nothing in front of her. There is no one there.

Cora tightens her grip on the broom and sweeps those footprints away too, scrapes the grimy coating from the entire hallway until the perimeter is lined with dust balls and the brown tiles are laid bare. When it's done, she's covered in sweat, feels as if the red lights are baking her. The doors on both sides of the hallway look identical, and she can no longer remember which is the one she came out of and which one leads into an unspecified beyond, a place that Father Thomas didn't describe.

She slumps down against one of the doors to a family tomb. Cora has no idea how long it's been, how much longer she has to sit here before Father Thomas returns, but it feels like it's been days. She wonders what will happen if Father Thomas has a heart attack in his office and dies and tells no one where he's left her. Even if her aunt knows where she is, she probably doesn't know where Father Thomas keeps his keys.

We don't want teenagers running around down here. They never find their way out, Father Thomas said, as if a teenager had gotten trapped down here before, had been left here long enough to rot.

Cora remembers her phone is in her pocket, pulls it out, but of course there's no service down here—dead people don't need to make phone calls.

She's missed another call from Auntie Zeng. Cora knows she's overdue for a visit, but she can't quite bring herself to talk because Auntie Zeng sees everything, knows everything. She'll know that something is wrong with Cora the minute she hears her voice.

"Cora?"

She turns. Father Thomas is standing in the doorway.

"Are you all right?" he says.

Cora stands up. "The door was jammed," she says, brushing the dust off her pants.

He winces. "I'm so sorry, I didn't even think about that. This place is so old, things tend to stick. It looks like you've made progress, though?" He surveys the floor scraped raw, the overflowing dustpan and gray tumbleweeds. "I should have given you trash bags." Then he gestures toward the open door, into the pale hallway. "Come on, I think you've done enough."

Cora starts to follow him, but another voice stops her in her tracks.

"Cora."

She turns, looks over her shoulder.

Another Father Thomas is standing in the opposite doorway, a mirror image of the one she's walking toward.

"Cora," the second Father Thomas says, eyes locked on the far end of the hall. If there is one look Cora knows intimately, it is fear. That is what she sees in the bright glare of Father Thomas's eyes. "Cora, whatever you do, don't go through that door," he says. "That's not me."

She turns back to the first Father Thomas. He lets out a slow breath and crosses himself, closing his eyes for a moment. "Cora," he says, "you need to come here, right now."

"Cora, that's the wrong door," the other Father Thomas says, gripping the doorway. "This is the way we came in, this is the way we'll leave."

But Cora stands rooted in the middle. One Father Thomas is from the world she entered, and the other is from the world where the invisible footsteps led, but of course Cora has swept them away, so now she has no idea which is which. Would she even know if she made the wrong choice? She backs against the door of the nearest tomb, looks back and forth between the two men, the darkness behind them. They both call for her, and Cora has never hated her name as much as she does in this moment.

"Cora, you have to decide," one of them says, but Cora can't do that; she needs someone else to decide for her because her choices are always wrong. Whichever door she picks will lead her somewhere terrible, she is certain of that.

She cups her hands over her ears, closes her eyes. She tries to conjure Delilah in her mind, tries to picture her standing in this dusty hallway in her pink taffeta dress even though Delilah would never be caught dead here, tries to imagine what Delilah would do.

In her mind, Delilah stands before her, pink tennis shoes on the sticky floor, pale pink dress searing crimson under the emergency lights. The Delilah of Cora's imagination has no face, just an egg-smooth expanse of pale skin because faces are the hardest to remember, and Delilah has long been rotting in Cora's mind.

This Delilah looks at the Father Thomas to her left, then her right, then back at Cora. She lifts a finger and turns away, about to point, and Cora could cry with relief. Some part of Delilah is still alive in her mind, can still show her the right path.

But Delilah doesn't point to either doorway. She points straight ahead, at the cold stone door of another tomb.

"Cora."

She flinches awake. Father Thomas is kneeling in front of her. Her gaze snaps to the doorway at the end of the hallway, hanging open. She can hear cars passing by, footsteps on the pavement. A breathing, pulsing, real world. The door to her right is still closed.

"Are you all right?" he says. His hand is on her shoulder and she's pretty certain priests aren't supposed to do that, but it was probably alarming to see her limp on the floor in a room full of corpses.

Cora swallows. "Sorry," she says. "It's hot down here, I must have fallen asleep."

"It *is* getting hot," he says, stepping back. "You've done a good job with the main hallway. Let's leave it at that. This isn't worth passing out over."

He offers her a hand and she takes it only because she's not sure she could stand up otherwise. He starts toward the entrance, but Cora lingers, looking at the door across from her, the one Delilah pointed to.

"What's in there?" she says quietly, nodding toward the door.

Father Thomas follows her gaze. "Not much," he says.

"Can I see?"

He hesitates. "If you want," he says, crossing the room, sorting through his keys. He jams a key into the lock, and Cora holds her breath for one terrible second before the door swings open. Cora sees an old coal-burning furnace in a tiny closet, a couple of spare mops, tiny white propane tanks, an overturned bucket. Cora doesn't know exactly what she expected, doesn't understand why she suddenly feels heartbroken, like she's been dumped and shoved out of a car in the rain. Delilah had led her nowhere.

"Probably the least interesting room down here," Father Thomas says, smiling and shutting the door.

Cora says nothing, picks up her broom, takes a steadying breath.

Dream Delilah is not real, she reminds herself. She's a part of Cora's mind, a chopped salad of her subconscious. Delilah did not lead her astray, because Delilah is gone. Cora led herself into a dirty janitor's closet because she always picks the wrong door.

"Consider yourself officially forgiven," Father Thomas says, smiling as he leads her back out into the night. But Cora doesn't feel forgiven, renewed, or reborn the way Auntie Lois says she should feel. God cannot forgive someone whose name he does not know.

Cora walks home, the tiny pinpricks of darkness in her vision hardly noticeable when she turns her gaze to the night sky.

NINE

Yifei says something in Cantonese to the waitstaff while Cora lingers behind her. The restaurant has plexiglass screens forming a clear wall between the customers and the counter, but she can smell meat and spices even through both of her masks and she wonders if that means they're not actually all that effective—if hot pork can break through, surely a supervirus can. But waiting outside seems like a conspicuously awkward thing to do, so Cora stands close behind Yifei and Harvey and tries to breathe as little as possible.

Yifei asked what Cora wanted to eat, but Cora was too embarrassed to say that she doesn't know the name of many Chinese foods, that she just eats what's put in front of her when her aunt cooks, so she told Yifei to choose because she'll eat anything.

It's not a complete lie—Chinese food is easier for Cora to stomach than American food because it has never once made her sick. She remembers her mom serving her undercooked chicken breast covered in Shake 'n Bake, speckled hot dogs bathed in ketchup, meatball subs that looked gray on the inside when Cora took a bite. Auntie Lois said Cora's mom never really learned how to cook and only tried it for Cora, knowing that she should serve her kid something other than the bowl of Froot Loops and toast that she usually ate. Sometimes Cora would hide her mom's food in her backpack and throw it away at school, would stand in the "no lunch money" line in the cafeteria to get a cheese sandwich.

Yifei pays, waving away Cora's credit card, and carries their Styrofoam boxes outside, plops them down on a table in the section of the sidewalk reserved for outdoor dining, caged in with orange plastic barriers. Cora peels off her masks, conscious of the lines that must be branded under her eyes, and scoots close to Yifei so the cars don't pass too close to her. She imagines the side mirror of a pickup truck clipping the back of her head and making a crater in her skull.

Today was a rare free day, when no one died so messily that they had to call Harvey's uncle for a cleanup crew. Their on-call shifts end at six, so by five thirty, Yifei announced that they were getting dinner because Paisley and Ryan were annoying her. Cora prefers workdays to on-call days, because then at least she isn't waiting by the phone all day, afraid to start doing anything real in case a call comes. Something about an impending phone call always makes Cora uneasy.

She agreed to go out with Harvey and Yifei, in part because the sound of her phone ringing had unraveled her so much she would have agreed to sell her own organs if Yifei had asked, and partly because she'd been thinking of ways to celebrate her negative COVID test. It feels like one of those things that should make her happy, but thinking of the test at all reminds her of the heat of a man's saliva in the seam of her lips.

But Cora knows that trying different restaurants counts

as a hobby for a lot of people, so maybe Cora can become a foodie, if she can force herself to just eat and not think about where each ingredient came from. She can write Yelp reviews for restaurants, start a food blog, be the kind of person people want to go out with because she knows all the best places.

Harvey bites into what turns out to be a soup dumpling and dribbles hot broth across the table.

"Control yourself," Yifei mumbles, unpacking the other boxes.

"I'll lick it off the table later," Harvey says, reaching out for napkins, which Cora passes to him.

"That sounds COVID-safe," Yifei says. "I'm sure these public tables are sterile."

The sun is low in the sky—they were supposed to meet earlier, but Harvey was late as always, and now the setting sun puts Cora on edge. Something about darkness feels so expansive these days. Like the world only opens its eyes after dusk.

Harvey is talking about a movie neither she nor Yifei have seen, and Cora thinks the only reason Yifei isn't interrupting is that it stops Harvey from eating all the dumplings.

Yifei probably thinks Cora doesn't notice the way she watches her. Ever since she went to Yifei's apartment, Yifei has been texting her to check in, everything from *Hey what's up?* to the more direct *See any ghosts today?* Cora knows that she's transparent glass for anyone who actually looks at her, but most people don't want to. They think her reticence is impenetrable, that her pale skin is poured concrete, her body a fortress. But Cora knows—and now, so does Yifei—that all of her words are full of secrets.

Cora texted Yifei back with emojis instead of words, scared of what she might reveal if she tried to explain. She definitely did not tell her about the dusty footprints in the crypt.

Yifei is nice, at least nice enough to worry about Cora.

But Father Thomas is nice, Auntie Lois is mostly nice, lots of people are nice—surface-level niceness is meaningless. Nice people have the power to send Cora away if they think her mind has fractured. They'll tie her down and tell themselves they're doing the right thing. So Cora pointedly ignores Yifei putting dumplings on her plate. Besides, if Cora wants to be a normal person, she needs friends besides Yifei and Harvey. They're probably the least normal friends she could possibly have.

Two white men come out of the store with boxes in their hands and take the table next to them. Cora pops a dumpling in her mouth and scoots slightly closer to Yifei, who's just as likely to have COVID as those men, but if she has to get it from someone, she'd rather it be Yifei than strangers.

"Anyway, you need to watch it," Harvey says, quickly followed by, "Who the hell ate all the soup dumplings?"

"You can't be trusted with them," Yifei says.

The men beside them are oddly silent as they unbox their food, picking up dumplings with forks. One of them stabs a soup dumpling and all the broth leaks out. He swears, grabbing a napkin.

"Is food supposed to ooze?" he says.

"It's soup, dumbass," says the other.

The first one grumbles something Cora can't hear.

"I heard they put rats in these," the first man says.

Cora stops chewing. She shares a look with Yifei, who mumbles *jackass* in Chinese before taking a sip of Sprite.

"Don't you mean bats?" the other one says, and they both laugh, the loudest sound they've made since sitting down.

A thought skewers Cora's mind like a lobotomy—her therapist once said they were called intrusive thoughts, the most terrible, cruel things that you know you would never do but can't help but think. Except her therapist has no way of knowing what Cora will or will not do, what's an intrusive thought and what's a wish.

This time, Cora sees herself holding Harvey's bat in one hand, jamming her fist into the white man's mouth, down his throat, punching into his stomach. She sees the bat living inside him, scratching at his stomach lining, trying to claw its way back up, scraping his insides raw. His body is the vent in Zihan Huang's apartment, nothing but a cold metal cage, and he will hear the sounds of dying deep inside him, he will remember it always, feel the fear that Zihan felt.

Who's the bat eater now?

The thought bursts, and Cora realizes she's made eye contact with the man. She turns away too quickly, too obviously.

Harvey and Yifei have stopped eating, chopsticks hanging limp in their hands. Yifei stands up suddenly, slamming the lids back on the boxes.

"Yifei?" Cora says.

"Let's eat somewhere else," she says loudly. "It suddenly smells like shit out here."

The white men don't make eye contact, but they angle themselves away from Yifei as she jams her bag over her shoulder and somehow balances all the boxes, while Harvey and Cora scramble to gather their own things. She barely makes it two feet before the store window explodes.

There's a crunch and a twinkling sound, then shards are raining down on Cora and Harvey, who are closest to the window. Cora shields her face the second she feels something sharp on the back of her neck, and then Harvey pushes her down on the bench, braces his body over hers. Someone screams, footsteps crunch over glass, and Cora can't see anything but the wood seat of the bench under her cheek.

Then Harvey is gone and Cora flinches at a hand on her

wrist. It's only Yifei, hands suddenly empty. Where did she put the dumplings?

"Are you okay?" she says. "Cora?"

Cora looks down at her bare arms. Something stings on her neck and she puts a hand to it, pulls away a piece of glass, and a thin line of blood runs down her finger. She turns to Harvey, who's standing and facing the shattered window.

The staff are gathered around the shards, staring at a brick on the ground in the center of the store. There's a few spots of blood, but whoever it hit must be mostly in one piece because there's no one lying there dead, just a lot of staff talking and yelling. Cora turns to the street, sees a few delivery bikes pulled over to see what happened, a crowd of people flowing in all directions.

Cora stares at the brick, feels a bit like one has shattered her brain as well because she was *doing everything right.* She was out trying to be social, to not hide away in her apartment, to eat food she didn't prepare herself, make small talk about movies, things normal twenty-four-year-olds do. But still, no matter how hard she tries to just have a simple life, everything around her always breaks. And Cora doesn't think it's a coincidence that this happened in Chinatown, at a Chinese take-out place. Even when she is no one at all, just an echo of a dead person, she's still Chinese and no one will let her forget it. That's all anyone cares about, all anyone wants to see.

"Cora?"

Cora blinks hard, turns back to Yifei. "Yeah, I'm fine," she says. "Harvey?"

Harvey turns around. There's a thin stripe of blood down the side of his face. "Yeah, I'm good," he says, face oddly pale, but he's not gushing blood or anything, seems more surprised than anything else. "Jesus, I thought a bomb went off or something."

Yifei shouts something at the staff in Cantonese and one of them shouts back, shaking his head.

"They don't want us to call the cops," she says.

"This place is fucking crazy," one of the white men says. Then they leave their table, abandoning their food that, in all fairness, is probably covered in glass shards.

"Let's leave in case someone calls them anyway," Yifei says, picking up the only take-out box that didn't burst when it hit the ground. "I don't want to talk to cops."

That's how they end up on a park bench brushing glass from each other's hair while sharing the remaining five dumplings between them. They don't say much after that, aside from Harvey commenting on how good the dumplings are, how sad he is that they can't go back for more.

The sun sets and the lights come on in the park and Cora feels prickly, sure there's glass lodged somewhere she can't see, like inside her ear canal. It will slide deeper and deeper while she lies on her side in bed, carve paths in her brain, as if her mind isn't already an egg over easy. She barely eats the dumplings, afraid that glass has somehow lodged itself in them through the thin gaps in the Styrofoam.

When they get to Canal Street, Yifei passes Cora her blue cardigan.

"Wear this," she says. "Give it back to me later."

Cora takes the cardigan, stares down at it. "Why?" she says. It's late August and still too hot for Cora's liking.

"You're wearing all black," Yifei says.

Cora frowns. Does Yifei care that much about her style? Cora has always known she's not as fashionable as Delilah, but she's a crime scene cleaner, not a supermodel.

"It's bad luck this month," Yifei says when Cora doesn't answer.

This month. "Oh," Cora says. So she puts the cardigan on

even though it's too hot, rides the train for a few stops before Harvey and Yifei switch to a different train, gets out at the station a few blocks from her apartment.

The sun has fully set now, the streetlights weak circles of brightness like small islands, the darkness a deep river filling the sidewalk. The street is quiet, but the kind of quiet that feels wide-awake, apprehensive. Even though Cora doesn't live near any tourist traps, normally there are still people out at this hour. But the night is silent, undisturbed.

Cora hugs the cardigan closed, arms tight around her stomach. Her apartment is only a few blocks away and her street isn't particularly seedy, but she suddenly wishes she'd gone home with Yifei because the distance between streetlights feels wider and wider with every step.

It's trash day tomorrow and piles of it block the sidewalk. Cora steps off the curb, and as a cold breeze blows up from the sewer grate and caresses her ankles, she feels it—an opening, like the world has yawned wide, wet throat exposed.

A whisper of air blows down the street, too cool to be a summer breeze. Cora jumps back onto the sidewalk, teetering around the sodden trash bags. The air continues, an endless sigh that trails off into a whisper, a word that Cora can't quite hear.

She's freezing cold now, suddenly grateful for Yifei's cardigan. The whisper repeats itself, rustling the trash bags behind her, one of them tumbling over and spilling onto the street with a clink of cans and crinkle of plastic.

Cora starts walking faster. She feels like the sidewalk is vanishing in chunks behind her, a great chasm biting at her heels, the seams of the world ripping open. There is something following her.

She walks even faster, stumbling over the uneven concrete.

She turns the corner to her street, and like a door has closed, the whispering vanishes.

"Cora."

She stops walking.

Cora knows that voice. She remembers it, even though she was certain that after so many months, she would forget.

"Cora," it says again, clear as day.

Cora closes her eyes, clenches her fists.

Yifei says that hungry ghosts are real, and every part of Cora wants to believe her. It's a dangerous thought—the idea that it's not Cora's own mind that is bending, but the barriers between worlds. She doesn't want this secret that no one will believe. She has a *history*, after all. She's the perfect person to haunt because no one will trust the things she says ever again. Whatever she finds, it will be for her and her alone. No one will help her. No one will save her.

"Cora."

Her heartbeat is so loud, her heels at the edge of a great precipice, wind rushing all around her. She doesn't want to look back. For so long, she couldn't bear to.

But clearly, it's not a choice anymore. Closing your eyes doesn't stop monsters from devouring you.

"Okay," Cora says, opening her eyes to the sky but not turning around. "Okay, I'm here. I'm listening. What do you want?"

No one answers. Cora starts to turn, but a hand on her shoulder stops her, honed fingernails pricking her skin.

"Cora," the voice says, the words so close that Cora feels the air whisper past her ear, rustle her hair. "Don't turn around."

A shiver rips through Cora's blood. She feels that there is an entire universe just behind her, but she's not allowed to look.

"Why?" Cora whispers.

The hand slides across her collarbone to her throat. The

skin is rough, sandpapery, scratches against Cora's neck as the fingers settle over her racing pulse.

"Why?" Cora says again, feeling the word vibrate against the freezing cold palm.

"Don't turn around," the voice says again.

But, like always, Cora needs to know.

She turns around.

The street is empty. A trash bag plops over onto its side. Somewhere at the end of the street, a dog howls. Cora presses her hand to her throat, feels her freezing skin, the bruising ghost of the touch. A heaviness drags down her shoulders, makes her feel a thousand years old. If she hadn't turned around, would Delilah have kept talking to her? Cora yanks her cardigan closed again, fingers biting into the fabric, and storms back to her apartment.

She rushes up the stairs, jams her keys into the lock on her door, undoes the dead bolts, slips inside, does up the bolts behind her, one, two, three. She clings to the sound of Delilah's voice, replaying it in her mind even though she can already feel the memory rebuilding itself, growing quieter, less truthful by the moment. Cora's memory will eat holes in it soon, her mind full of hungry moths. Then it will be gone, like every other part of Delilah.

Delilah was always supposed to be here, but that was just another one of her lies.

Cora remembers being ten years old, trailing after Delilah and her friends on a Friday night while they played Truth or Dare on the roof of a college library. Delilah stuck Cora in the corner behind the planters with a book she'd already read and passed around a bag of chips for everyone else.

Truth: What are you most afraid of?

Cora set down the book and walked to the edge. She cannot remember the name of the city anymore, but she remembers the skyscrapers in the distance, three of them like syringes, a foamy bath of treetops below.

Truth: Where are you most afraid of going?

Cora's mom had just become the fourth wife of a cult leader. Cora's dad had just remarried in China. Cora didn't know Delilah that well yet, but Delilah's mama wouldn't let Cora go anywhere alone because she was too young. Everyone in Cora's family had examined her like an old sweater off the clearance rack and politely said "No, thank you," hung her back up for someone else to take.

Dare: jump.

Cora leaned forward. A breeze rushed up from between the trees, birds shivering into the gray sky, and Cora wanted to join them, to fly until she found somewhere brighter, warmer. She would later learn that this was just another intrusive thought, but in that moment, it felt realer than anything in her so-called life.

A hand closed around her wrist.

Cora turned around and there was Delilah, completely unbothered, like she had already read the story of Cora's life. "Get down," Delilah said.

Cora shook her head. "I wasn't—"

"If you want to sit with us, just sit with us," Delilah said, tugging her down from the ledge.

"You don't want me to," Cora said, because all that ever mattered was what Delilah wanted.

Truth: Who are you most afraid of?

Delilah shrugged, and some small part of Cora was glad that she didn't deny it, that she hadn't lied to her. "You're my sister."

"That's just a word," Cora said.

Delilah scrunched her face up. "All words are just words," she said. "We're sisters, so us being together is inevitable. It doesn't matter how we feel about it. Just like it doesn't matter how we feel about the sun setting. It happens anyway."

It didn't feel that way at the time, but it was one of the kindest things Delilah ever said. She gave Cora something better than an abstract idea of love: a promise. That whenever Cora drew too close to the ledge, Delilah would be there.

Cora should have known better than to believe her.

She sighs and presses her forehead against the door of her apartment, dropping her bag to the floor. Delilah left her in life and in death, and she is never coming back.

Cora turns around and heads for the bathroom, but her hands go numb, keys slipping from her fingers, crashing to the ground.

There is a woman in her living room.

Her throat is needle-thin, no more than a whispered silver thread. Her eyes are deep chasms of black, skin a translucent tarp pulled taut over her cheekbones, the knife edge of her jaw, her withered black lips.

She sinks her teeth into Cora's coffee table and it fractures easily, a cloud of sawdust gasped into the air, tiny pieces floating past the cool city lights through the window where the curtains are just barely parted. The woman casts a shadow on the pale wall, but it is not an echo of the shape that Cora sees. It is a stain of darkness devouring the paint, opening up a window into night. A soft and rancid breeze sighs through it, like it is the maw of some massive creature.

Cora claps a hand over her mouth. She cannot scream, because the neighbors will come and they will not see what Cora sees; they will send her away.

The woman stiffens, head bobbing on her needle neck like a withered dandelion, and turns to face Cora.

The Hunger that Comes After

The living think they know hunger when their stomachs spasm, when their mouths go dry, when they grow weak.

But they do not even begin to understand it until they cross over into the land of death.

Food will not sate the dead, but they don't realize it at first. They fill their mouths with rice, yet the hunger grows deeper, opens wider within them.

Then they fill their mouths with bread, and the ache grows sharp, as if everything they eat is glass.

Finally, they fill their mouths with blood, and at last the pain in their stomachs grows quiet.

Auntie Z

TEN

The creature has no eyes, but Cora knows it sees her—Cora has a prey sense for when she's being watched. She has always been a white rabbit ready to dart away, knows all too well the prickle of eyes on skin, the cold rush of blood, the clench of her heart.

Sawdust spills from the woman's lips mixed with a viscous saliva, drooling in a beige slop to Cora's floor. She wears a thin white dress that pools around her, melting into the ground. Her head sways slowly back and forth like a pendulum on the thin wire of her neck, which truly shouldn't be able to hold her head up—Cora is reminded of her sister's purple allium flowers, round bulbs that grew too big for their stems and had to be bound in a cage of wires to stand upright.

A train rushes past the window in a blur of red and white lights, and the creature vanishes.

Cora doesn't feel herself sinking until she hits the floor, pulse hammering in her head. The train goes on and on, brakes screeching, casting flashing lights across her face. Cora raises a trembling hand to her chest, pressing hard against her beating heart, feeling it *knock knock knock* against her rib cage, like something awful is trapped inside her, begging to be set free.

The train passes and cool dark falls over the apartment, a sudden gasp of silence. Cora doesn't dare to breathe, her heartbeat the loudest sound in the world.

She moves forward on all fours, spreading her weight as if afraid the floor will fracture like a frozen pond beneath her, drawing closer to her broken coffee table. She picks up the sharp pieces, turns them over in her hands, runs her soft fingertips over their jagged points. They are real—at least, as real as anything else Cora has ever seen. Her fingers trace the teeth marks of the broken wound at the edge of the table.

She eyes the light switch at the other end of the room and feels that, for some reason, she will be safe once it's on. She feels like a child cowering under her covers, but then she thinks of the yawning darkness on her wall and she rises on unsteady feet, realizes she hasn't even taken her shoes off. Her shadow rolls across the wall, her weak reflection whispered over the window as she crosses the room, sure that the darkness is looming larger behind her, reaching out for her.

With a click, she flicks on the light switch.

The sharp brightness casts judgment down on Cora's footprints in the sawdust, the broken shards of table, the subway slop tracked in from Cora's shoes. She slips off her sneakers and lines them up in the hallway, turns toward her room.

The woman stands at the end of the hall.

Too tall for Cora's ceilings, hunched over, head lolling to the side, wire neck curved in a limp U, and stiff black hair hanging down. She is pressed into the archway of Cora's bedroom as if trapped in the shadows.

Cora throws herself at the light switch to her left, but her socked feet slip and her hand swipes down the wall. She hauls herself into the kitchen and presses herself back against the cabinets, out of sight of the woman.

A footstep echoes down the hallway.

It's wet, like the woman is walking through mud. Another step comes, and Cora bites her lip and scoots back until she's pressed against the fridge. She reaches up toward the counter and feels around for her knife block, but it's too far away and Cora can't stand, doesn't think her legs will hold her, so she folds into herself and hopes she'll disappear like the creature did in the light of the train. She presses her eyes closed, claps a hand over her mouth, *Wake up wake up wake up, please, God, wake up!* When nothing changes, she tries to cast her consciousness out somewhere far away, to go numb the way she sometimes does when the world is too loud, but she stays locked in the prison of her own trembling bones.

The shadow appears first, rolling across the open doorway, a buzzing black, like Cora's floaters converging into a sparkling darkness. It devours all of the hallway that Cora can see from her corner, her apartment gone, nothing but an empty chasm beyond her kitchen.

Then a skeletal hand grabs the edge of the wall, nails ripping into the paint, and the woman fills the doorway.

Cora lets out a breath that sounds like dying, crushing herself into the corner.

The creature only grows larger as she comes closer, a cape of night trailing behind her. She smells of deep earth and decay, a scent Cora knows all too well.

The creature kneels down to her level, bones creaking, and Cora's fingertips feel numb; she knows she's breathing too fast, but her hands are tight fists that she can't unclench. She remembers the glossy feeling of Yifei's scar beneath her fingertips and knows she is going to die before this creature even touches her because her heart is going to burst. She wants to look away from the puckered craters of the creature's eyes but her gaze feels locked.

The creature reaches forward, hand unfurling palm-side up, fingers nothing but bones blurred with a glassy webbing of skin so thin it's hardly there. But it does not come closer to Cora. It waits.

A jade bracelet swings slowly back and forth on its wrist, rattling against the bones. A gold plate glimmers on the bottom, but Cora cannot read it.

A question burns at Cora's lips, but she can't find her voice. Her fists come unclenched slowly, a breath hissing through her teeth, the air sharp and cold. She reaches forward because she needs to know, the unknowing is worse than the knowing.

Her fingers close around the cold jade, turning the bracelet until the gold plate is on the top, light glinting off the Chinese character for *hope.*

Cora snaps her hand back. The bracelet swings and spins around the bony wrist, and the creature does not move.

"Delilah?" Cora whispers.

The creature clenches and unclenches her fingers, sliding her hand closer to Cora.

She thinks of all her missing food, how Yifei had called the ghosts *hungry.*

Slowly, not peeling her gaze from the creature, Cora slides to the side, pulling the fridge open. The creature angles herself away from the light and Cora slips her hand inside, feeling around until her hand closes on an orange. She nudges the fridge shut and slowly sets the orange in the creature's hand.

The creature's fingers clamp shut around the orange, nails stabbing into the skin, juice dribbling to the floor. She raises the fruit to her mouth and unlatches her jaw until it looks like a silent scream, cramming the entire orange in her mouth.

She devours it, peel and all, a burst of juice raining down on the floor. She swallows in two bites, the fat shape moving down her needle throat, stretching it. It moves slowly, tediously, and the creature makes a keening sound as if in pain until the shape disappears beneath its dress.

Cora's throat tightens and she gasps down a drowning breath, tears scorching her skin. She buries her face in her hands and sobs, curling up against her fridge.

She did this to Delilah.

She didn't burn joss paper, she didn't pray for her. She never even went to her grave after the funeral.

It felt easier that way, to try to spackle over all the holes Delilah had left behind as quickly as possible. Cora was supposed to be the one who suffered. Cora was good at suffering, it was nothing new to her. Nothing she did was supposed to hurt Delilah anymore. Because even if Cora thought she hated her sister sometimes, even if she hated her even more for dying, she didn't want her to suffer.

The creature does not move, does not speak. And Cora can't stand the hollow look in her face that says more than words ever could. Cora grabs the fridge handle and wrenches the door all the way open. The light spills across the kitchen and Delilah vanishes, nothing but a pool of orange juice at Cora's feet.

ELEVEN

Cora sleeps with the lights on. But even then, she worries that Delilah will appear in the darkness behind her eyes, so she stares at the ceiling and tries not to sleep. When sleep comes for her anyway, pulling her under before she can stop it, she dreams of a darkness that begins in her living room wall and spreads wider and wider until it devours the entire world.

Cora has started to notice all the shadows in her apartment. Even with the shades up and lights on, the five legs of her rolling desk chair cast a pale, spidery shadow underneath the seat. Then there's the tiny inch of darkness underneath her oven door, and the space behind the refrigerator. Even Cora herself has a shadow that she can't escape. She finds herself rearranging lamps, or shining her phone's flashlight periodically on the pockets of darkness, petrified that Delilah will crawl out of every thin sliver of shadow.

A horrible part of Cora realizes that Delilah is no longer beautiful, that she has swung to the polar opposite of how she was in life, and for a single traitorous moment, Cora thinks that Delilah deserves it. To be looked at with fear instead of jealousy. Because Delilah had never known anything but adoration, and a grim part of Cora is satisfied that for once, Delilah has to occupy a body that is gross and jagged like hers.

The thought is so unfair that Cora immediately strips down for her second shower, scrubbing herself as if to purge the cruelty from her mind. Her therapist would dismiss it as another intrusive thought, but Cora thinks it's just pettiness.

She sleeps too late the next morning because she forgot to charge her phone and her alarm never went off. There are two missed calls from Harvey and three from Yifei, followed by a slew of texts about how Yifei is going to come over after work if Cora doesn't answer.

Cora gets dressed with the windows open, sunshine blaring inside, caring more about ghosts than nosy neighbors, and stumbles out the door while plugging the job address into her phone with one hand and looping her masks around her ears with the other hand. The sunshine has wiped the morning clean, and it is almost too easy to pretend everything was a dream. The sun is so sharp that Cora can't fathom the shadows of last night.

She remembers, in a flash, Delilah bent in half in the shape of her doorway. Cora's hand tightens around her phone and she wonders if it's too late for joss paper now.

I can just leave the lights on forever, Cora thinks, and the thought feels safe, a buoy to cling to. But she wonders if Delilah is truly gone when the lights are off, or if she's still there, starving and silent and invisible.

Cora draws to a stop in the hallway, takes a moment to fold that terrible thought up into smaller and smaller squares, tuck it away deep inside of her. She turns back to her phone, and when the app loads walking directions instead of the subway, Cora realizes that the address is only a few blocks away.

Her footsteps slow. She thumbs the elevator button and cross-checks the address from both Harvey's and Yifei's texts to confirm.

Cora knows the building.

It's a hotel in the Bowery where Auntie Lois stayed once, back when she tried harder to keep an eye on Cora. Cora doesn't think the neighborhood is that much swankier than where she lives, but Auntie Lois acted like anything inside Chinatown was a war zone, like every stranger wanted to steal her knockoff purse and she was safer the minute she set foot anywhere without *China* in the name. She chose the hotel because of the security guards at every entrance and on every floor, the constant CCTV. How had someone managed a messy death in this hotel?

Cora finds the truck parked a block away from the site. She jams her key into it, bundles a hazmat suit under her arm, and shoves past the caution tape, through the spinning doors, the gilded lobby with koi fountains and sculptures of vaguely phallic shapes. She dresses in the elevator, yanking her hair back and pulling on her face shield just as she reaches the seventh floor.

Harvey and Yifei—Cora can't tell which is which under their hazmat suits—are dragging a hose from the bathroom, searching through the brush bag, gallons of Blood Buster already unpacked.

Cora steps inside, an apology on her lips, but the words fall away when she turns to the wall Harvey and Yifei are facing.

The bed is black with soaked-up blood, a starburst of it splashed against the backboard where someone must have been sleeping. Above it, glossy brown-red blood is smeared across the wall. Cora can see the whispers of brushstrokes—the murderer packed a paintbrush?—the sharp lines of thin bones, jagged wings, cavernous ears. The blood drips down, like the creature is melting into the bed. A hideous, dripping bat.

"Batman was here," says the voice of Harvey, the hazmat suit on the left, holding up a bucket of Blood Buster.

"You're not funny," Yifei says. "Cora, are you okay?"

"Did they catch the person who did this?" Cora says.

Harvey shakes his head. "Paul said they only found her because she didn't check out in time."

"She?" Cora echoes, wishing Harvey hadn't said that. Because it's easier to imagine her now. Cora can see her silhouette painted into the bed with blood.

"Travel nurse," Harvey says. "Ai Wu."

"We already cleaned the hall," Yifei says, an unusual stiffness to her words. "There were bloody shoe prints. He didn't even clean himself up, yet none of these ten thousand cops saw a damn thing."

Cora stands there, feeling useless in her heavy hazmat suit. People covered in blood cannot just disappear.

"And there's still been jack shit about it in the news," Harvey says. "Don't you think people should know that bloody Batman is ravaging Chinatown?"

"The police think it's the same person?" Cora says.

"It's a serial killer calling card," Harvey says, jerking his hand to the dripping bat mural. "Paul said there were some live ones here too, crammed in her guts."

"And the cops haven't mentioned the bats in any public reports," Yifei says. "No one on the outside should know about them. It's not like it's easy to get bats around here—you can't just pick them up at Petco."

Cora swallows. "Maybe the police have reasons to…to…"

"To keep this quiet?" Yifei says, her tone implying she doesn't believe it.

Cora wants to argue, not because she's particularly loyal to the police, but because she wants this to not be her problem. The police never found Delilah's killer, after all, so there's only so much faith she can give them. She wants to believe in a world where the police always catch the bad guys, where they get thrown in jail for the rest of their lives, where the survivors can mourn and move on and learn to be happy again. But only children can believe in that world.

"They've had their time to figure this out," Yifei says, dunking a sponge into the bucket of Blood Buster. "I'm done waiting."

Cora doesn't know what she means, and she doesn't ask. They scrub the rest of the room in silence until the blood is only a whisper of gray that can be painted over easily, until the bedding is bagged for the trash and the room smells of dizzy sharp chemicals.

But when they pass through the throng of reporters, this time Yifei does not walk away. She grabs the reporter with golden-retriever hair, whispers something in his ear, and storms back to the truck.

"What did you do?" Harvey says. "My uncle—"

"We're talking to the press tonight," Yifei says, hurling her face shield into the trunk, unzipping her hazmat suit with too much force, the zipper snagging.

"We?" Cora says.

"Yes," Yifei says, balling up her suit and tossing it in with the cleaning supplies.

Harvey groans, drops his shoulders. "But my uncle—"

"Your uncle doesn't pay me enough to keep quiet about something like this," Yifei says. "People need to know, Harvey. I didn't come to America by myself when I was fifteen just to end up gutted in my own bed with a bat shoved down my throat. I am not going to be one of those bodies that we have to scrape off the ceiling, okay? Because you know damn well that when that happens, all anyone sees you as is a mess, a biohazard, something no one wants to touch. Or worse, I'll turn into gore porn for weirdos who spend all night on Reddit reading about how another pretty Asian girl got chopped up, and then nothing I did before in my life will matter at all, just the death that I didn't choose. I am not going to let anyone take away what makes me a human. Because that's what this guy is doing, Harvey. You blast people to bits or hack them apart because you don't see them as human—you take away the shape of their body and then no one else can see them as human either. I know blood and guts is fun for you, but this could just as easily have been me or Cora. Would you joke around when you mopped us off the floor? Or drop your two-dollar Sonic key chain in what used to be our brains? No, I'm not going to sit back and shut up for twenty bucks an hour, which, by the way, is not enough to live in fucking Manhattan. I want every person in this whole city to keep their lights on and look for this asshole, to lock their doors and buy those handguns that you Americans love so much, because I'm tired of scrubbing Asian women off the walls. I'm so fucking tired."

Harvey blinks at Yifei. He looks like he's been slapped. After a moment, he swallows, fishes ChapStick from his pocket, and rolls it across his lips. Cora pulls at the sleeves of her hazmat suit, wishes she could ball herself up like Yifei's clothes and toss herself into the oblivion of the trunk.

This is the difference between Yifei and Cora—Yifei turns her pain into a plan, while Cora scrubs her pain away with Blood Buster. Cora is aware all at once that she should be the one fighting. She's the one whose sister died because of people like the one Harvey calls Batman. All that anger should be hers. But instead, she's hiding behind two masks and a baggy hazmat suit because the thought that she could do anything meaningful never even occurred to her. Cora cannot fathom her actions mattering beyond her own mind. She feels herself slump smaller, as if her hazmat suit is eating her alive.

"Okay," Harvey says at last. "What time are we meeting this guy?"

TWELVE

"You're twitchy," Yifei says to Cora, waving the bartender over.

Cora has not been to a bar since the Before Times. It's only been a month since bars were cleared to reopen, and Cora still feels a bit like she's standing on a land mine. Even though they're technically outdoors, the temporary plywood plexiglass structure feels like a tiny room and she can taste the spit of all the other customers in the air. The bartender wears a mask and makes a show of sterilizing the glasses in a blue light box, but Cora still hates the grime of the barstool seat against her bare legs, the greasy table under her elbows. She sanitizes her hands again, even though she isn't putting any food directly from her hands into her mouth, but she thinks maybe the scent of alcohol will purify the air if she uses enough of it.

"We could probably pour some vodka over your hands, if that's easier," Harvey says.

Cora doesn't laugh. She didn't want to come here. She thought they'd meet in some secret alleyway, or someone's apartment. But Yifei had suggested the bar and Harvey hadn't seemed the least bit bothered, so Cora couldn't just say that the air was full of COVID, because two out of three people thought it was fine and Cora is always too careful. Instead, she and Yifei took the train all the way to Hell's Kitchen and Cora had to walk through the crush of Times Square, the blaring lights and tour buses trapped in the crosswalk where Cora lost a shoe and had to backtrack and pray she didn't get crushed.

She's already untethered and the reporter isn't even here yet. Part of it probably has to do with the guy who followed her and Yifei halfway here. A few blocks from the bar, a white man started asking where they were going, if they wanted to change their plans and come with him instead, and when Yifei told him in no uncertain terms exactly how interested they were, he called them Chinks and wouldn't stop following them until Harvey met them outside the bar and loudly asked who their friend was. With every car that passed, Cora thought the man might push them both in front of it, and even now at the bar, her hands are still shaking.

So she takes another shot, waiting for the first three to kick in.

Yifei shoves a bowl of peanuts at her, but Cora would sooner die than stick her fingers in a communal peanut bowl, so she ignores it.

"You want something else?" Yifei says, watching Cora edge away from the nuts. Cora shakes her head, but Yifei turns to the bartender anyway. "Hey, can I get some fries and water?" she says.

The bartender passes her the water a few moments later, and she slides it in front of Cora. Taking the hint, Cora drinks half the glass.

The reporter comes in as Cora spills water down her neck

and has to grab some cheap napkins to wipe it up. He has a notepad tucked under his arm and looks younger without the mask, like a teenager who stole his dad's work clothes. Yifei said his name was Devin McSomething.

"Thank you so much for meeting with me," he says, mostly to Yifei, then turns to the bartender. "Can I get a vodka soda and another drink for all of them?"

Yifei glances pointedly at Cora's collection of used shot glasses, and Cora feels her judgment, but at least Yifei doesn't embarrass her by saying anything out loud.

The reporter opens up his notebook, flips to a blank page. "Can I get your names?"

Yifei stiffens, smoothing it over by tipping the rest of her drink into her mouth just in time for the bartender to hand her another. Cora's next drink comes along with the fries Yifei ordered for her, so she sets the water aside.

"No," Yifei says, taking a sip of her new drink.

"No?" The reporter's face looks a bit red. Cora thinks most of it is because of Yifei, who looks more like she's dressed for a date than to spill secrets to a reporter.

"No, because we're talking about a serial killer here," Yifei says. "You think we want our names in the paper saying we outed him?"

"Serial killer?" the reporter echoes, eyes wide. A smile creeps across his face, and something about it turns Cora's next sip sour.

Harvey has ordered a burger and is letting Yifei do the talking, so Cora follows his lead and picks at her fries after cleaning her hands once more. She should have asked for a fork, but it's too late now—her hand is already covered in hot grease.

"He calls him Batman," Yifei says, jerking a finger at Harvey, who makes a sound of acknowledgment around his burger. "His calling card is bats."

"Bats," the reporter says, nodding quickly and scribbling the word *BATS* in all caps across his notebook.

Yifei goes on to describe the crime scenes in morbid detail, from Yuxi He's brains in the bathtub and bat in her drain to this morning's bat mural, and Cora can see the exact moment the reporter regrets talking to them. It's somewhere between the words "skull fragments" and "ropes of intestines." His pen starts to slow down until he's just staring at Yifei, not even writing. As it happens, Cora begins to feel the shots kicking in. Her stomach is warm, her head hard to hold up.

Yifei stops to take a drink, and the reporter clears his throat. "So," he says. "You believe there's a serial killer in Chinatown because you've found…bats?"

"Yes," Yifei says, staring the reporter down, like this is the most obvious thing in the world.

He hums. "Even though all three women were killed in different ways?"

Yifei frowns. "Are you a detective?"

"Well, there's such a thing as journalistic integrity," the reporter says. "I have to ask questions. I can't put out stories that I think aren't true."

Yifei scoffs. "Unbelievable," she says. "You accost us outside every crime scene and you don't even believe what we say?"

"Hey," Harvey says, wiping his mouth and dropping the used napkins too close to Cora, "I think she's right. I work there too. I've worked with serial killers before. Well, not *with* them, but like, cleaned up after them, you know?"

"You're an expert?" the reporter says, picking up his pen again.

Yifei barely hides her scoff behind her glass.

"Absolutely," Harvey says. "I know a serial killer when I see one. I can tell you, in all the years I've been doing this,

I've never seen so many fucking bats. That has to mean something, right?"

"Well," the reporter says, taking a tentative sip that feels more like an intentional delay than a move to quench any kind of thirst, "there are bats indigenous to New York."

Cora reaches for another fry, wipes her hands, angles herself around Harvey to find the bathroom so she can finally wash the grease off her—

Delilah is standing by the entrance.

Just like in Cora's apartment, the doorway is too short for her willowy neck, and she curves into its arch. She glows pale blue from the echoes of the neon sign above the counter.

Cora jumps to her feet before she realizes it, grabbing onto the counter when the world sloshes back and forth. The neon sign flickers and Delilah blinks in and out of existence with it.

"Cora?" Yifei says. "Are you okay?"

At the end of the hall, Delilah reaches out a skeletal hand, palm facing up. The neon light flashes to red, casting Delilah in warm light. The shadow behind her begins to eat away at the wall, the door to the bathrooms a spinning vortex.

Delilah is like this because of me, Cora thinks. But she turns back to the reporter, to Yifei's tense expression, and remembers that *no, that's not exactly true*. It's because of someone else too.

Her skin itches as if covered in spiders. She hugs her arms to stifle the feeling.

"The bats were torn up," Cora says. The words are gummed together, slow but clear.

"Sorry?" the reporter says.

Cora swallows, turns toward the reporter, and the alcohol makes it easier to ignore the creeping threat of shadows behind her. "The bats in the vent had wings torn up so badly they never could have flown to the roof," she says. "It doesn't matter if there are bats in New York. Someone maimed these ones and put them in the vents."

"And you don't think the victim put them there?" the reporter asks.

Cora lets out a sharp laugh. "Why, because it's normal for Chinese people to keep bats for pets?"

The reporter grimaces. "I meant—"

"Because Chinese people like to shove bats down our own throats before blowing our brains out, or paint bat murals on our walls after slitting our own throats with hunting knives? When this whole city—this whole country—calls us bat eaters?"

Devin McSomething says nothing, inching his notepad closer to his body. Cora knows that she's scared him, said something normal people don't say—she knows that look in his eyes. But the words come out unstopped and she doesn't care, not five shots deep into the night, not with a ragged echo of her sister looming in the doorway, not when she's standing in a bar in the middle of a goddamn pandemic just to beg a white man to listen to her.

"Did you know that the human head can explode?" Cora says, louder than she should. "If you hit it with enough force all at once, it bursts. My sister's face hit the express train through Broadway and burst like a fucking melon. Her mom begged them to put her head back together for the funeral, but eventually they had to tell her that there wasn't anything left, that her whole head was just gone, pieces so small they'd never find them. At least, that's what they told us. At night, I wonder if my sister's head is still down there somewhere in the tracks, if no one bothered to get it back because we're just fucking bat eaters, because we're dirty and eat the wrong kinds of animals. All I could tell the cops about the man who pushed her was that he was white. He had a mask and hat on, all I saw was his hand and his eyes, and that's enough to tell that someone's white but not much else. And you know what the cops told me? They said that's not enough to go on. *We can't just look for white men. You should have looked harder,* they said. But white men are going after Asian girls, and that's all *they* have to go on, us being Asian. No one wants to look harder at *us*. To imagine that we're real people. Every day I clean up their brains and blood and I know that a white man coming for me isn't an *if*, it's a *when*. And the worst part is I know no one will find out who did it, no one will write about it in the newspapers, because who cares if another Chinese girl is dead—they'll hear me screaming and just put in their headphones and keep walking. Even now, you want to walk away from us because it's gross, because blood and guts make you uncomfortable. But it doesn't matter if we're uncomfortable—we don't get to look away. We're dying and no one can hear us."

"Cora."

Yifei's hand is on Cora's arm. She pushes a glass of water at her and Cora drinks it all at once.

"We're leaving," Cora hears Yifei say. The world is a nauseous blur and Cora tries to tell Harvey and Yifei not to take her away from the light, but her ankles feel loose and her head is heavy. All Cora can look at is the pavement, and she thinks she sees a blur of black hair, but it might be her own, might be Yifei's, might be Delilah's.

"I'm sorry," she whispers, but she doesn't know who she's talking to.

"You didn't do anything wrong," Yifei says. "I don't know why I bothered with that asshole."

Harvey and Yifei keep talking, but their words blur together until Yifei tugs Cora's arm up higher around her shoulder and says, "I don't want her puking on the subway."

Then they are somehow in the back of a car, and Cora's head is in Yifei's lap and the city lights are a carousel outside the window. They don't arrive at Cora's apartment but Yifei's, where the elevator is thankfully working.

Paisley and Ryan are half-naked in the kitchen when Yifei shoves the door open. They roll their eyes at Yifei, who waves like she doesn't notice and dumps Cora on the couch, grabbing three bottles of water from the fridge while Ryan buttons his pants.

"You want fish?" Yifei says to Paisley in accented English, whipping out a bag of sardines from the fridge and waving it in Ryan's face. "I cook for you."

"Ugh, no," Paisley says, shaking her head. "Who the hell eats fish at midnight?"

She and Ryan hurry into their room and shut the door, and the smile drops off Yifei's face. She shoves the fish back in the fridge.

Cora looks up as Harvey sits on the arm of the couch, staring down at Cora oddly as he sips his water. He smacks his lips, screws the cap on.

"I'm sorry," he says.

Cora doesn't know what to say. She lets the couch eat her.

Yifei snaps off the lights and Cora bolts upright.

"Turn it on!" she says.

Yifei's eyes go wide, but she obeys. "Why?" she asks.

And now, with Cora's mouth loose from alcohol, she tells them both. About Delilah. About the hungry ghost. She is sure that by the end of it they'll call to have her put away, but as tears burn her face she can't seem to care, because at least then someone will watch her sleep, keep the lights on.

But when she finishes, no one reaches for their phone to call someone else to deal with her. No one tries to make her take a sleeping pill, or worse, discreetly crush one under a spoon and stir it into her water and slip it to her as if she doesn't know what they're doing.

Yifei just groans and goes to a cabinet, pulls out a bottle of vodka, and pours herself another shot. "I told you to burn the fucking joss paper," she says.

"Seriously," Harvey says, holding his hand out for the bottle. "I thought quiet types were supposed to be smart. You fucked around with a hungry ghost?"

"You believe me?" Cora says, throat dry, clutching the edge of the couch.

"Duh," Yifei says. "Cora, I already told you I'd seen a hungry ghost before. Obviously I'm not the only one who can see them, or I'd be fucking crazy."

Cora's gaze drifts to Harvey.

"I saw a ghost once," he says, shrugging. Then, quieter, "Down in the basement." Yifei hands him the bottle and a mug, which he fills too high and drinks too fast.

"So," he says, slamming the glass down on the coffee table, "I guess we're ghostbusters now."

"Minus the leaf blower," Yifei says.

Harvey frowns. "It's a proton pack."

Yifei waves her hand to shut him up. "Whatever. I doubt that Hollywood shit matters to Chinese ghosts."

"Oh, so you're an expert?" Harvey says.

Yifei shakes her head, but she's staring out past the window, thinking. "Cora," she says, and Cora doesn't like the way she says her name, not at all. Because she knows that whatever comes next is something Yifei is scared to say. "Everything you said to the reporter… Was that true?"

Cora leans back, stares up at the ceiling. "Yes," she says.

"Okay," Yifei says, the word so gentle, as if preparing Cora for what's next. "Then I think I might have an idea why you've got a hungry ghost on your hands."

"Um, because she was pushed in front of a fucking train?" Harvey says, crossing his arms. Yifei shoots him a cold look, but Cora only grimaces.

"That's probably part of it," Yifei says. "But, Cora, you know how in ancient China, decapitation was considered the worst kind of execution?"

Cora knows no such thing, but she nods anyway, sure that Yifei wouldn't lie at a time like this.

"It's bad for the spirit not to leave a body intact," Yifei says, as if she can sense Cora's lie. "Maybe the cops are right and her head wasn't…salvageable, in which case, it's a dead end. But if they just didn't want to shut the trains down to look… Well, maybe we should see for ourselves."

Cora stays very still, letting Yifei's words wash over her. The idea of her sister's head rotting in a crevice of the subway is one of those thoughts she's done her best to push to the periphery of her mind.

"Would it even still be there?" Harvey says. "Wouldn't rats have…" He glances at Cora, wincing. "Sorry, I mean, I meant—"

"Rats don't eat bones," Yifei says, rolling her eyes. "I think maybe, if we could bury your sister whole, that might solve the problem."

"The problem," Cora echoes. The problem of her sister's existence.

"Young people don't usually come back as hungry ghosts," Yifei says.

"Young people don't usually eat train sandwiches," Harvey says.

Yifei scowls. "Are you just going to whine and say stupid shit?" she says. "This isn't a joke, Harvey."

"Liu, you're talking about breaking into the subway after hours to look for body parts," Harvey says. "I'll fuck around with horror movie shit when I'm getting paid to do it legally, but this is something else."

"Horror movie shit?" Yifei says, crossing her arms. "Is that what our job is to you?"

Harvey pulls back, face gray, knows he's said too much.

"Corpses aren't Halloween decorations, dumbass," Yifei says. "You clean up entrails but never thought about where they came from? *Who* they came from?"

"Don't act like *you* hang out with corpses all the time," Harvey says quietly, looking away. "It's easy to act brave now. I'm just being honest with myself."

Yifei stills. Her next words are low and cold. "You think I haven't seen dead bodies?" Yifei says. There is a dangerous edge to her words, daring Harvey to keep pushing, keep talking.

Harvey casts a nervous glance to Cora where she's slumped on the couch, a glance that Yifei follows, her expression smoothing over. "You wouldn't do it for Cora?" Yifei says.

Harvey hesitates, mouth crinkling as he watches her. Cora's sure she looks miserable, drunk and sweaty and draped over the couch like a discarded toy, listening to her coworkers talk about rats eating her sister's face.

"Do you want to do that, Cora?" Harvey says, his voice softer.

Cora blinks, reaches a hand out for a bottle of water that Yifei hands her, takes a drink, tries to wipe her mouth with the back of her sleeve and ends up punching herself in the face because her limbs are still uncoordinated.

No, Cora doesn't particularly want to look for her sister's head. But the problem is—has always been—that there are many things Cora does not want and very few things that she does want. Cora doesn't want to see her sister's ghost either, but there are no good options left.

She looks to Yifei, whose expression is stern, and Harvey, who looks like he'd rather throw himself out the window than be here. Then she looks outside, where the light beyond the thin curtains shifts, long hair blowing past the window, backlit by city lights.

Yifei thinks this will help Delilah, so Cora needs to try.

"Yes," Cora says.

Harvey groans. "She's drunk," he says. "Ask her again in the morning."

"Don't come if you're gonna be a baby about it," Yifei says, crossing her arms.

"I can't let you two get eaten by hungry ghosts alone!" Harvey says. "Besides, there are three ghostbusters, not two. I have to come."

Harvey and Yifei keep arguing, but Cora sinks deeper into the couch, lets them think she's still drunk. The whisper of hair beyond the window converges into the silhouette of a hand, but Cora closes her eyes, and in the darkness of her dreams, it cannot touch her.

THIRTEEN

There are police cars outside Cora's apartment.

Her hand tightens on her bag as she draws closer. She managed to fall asleep on Yifei's couch last night, too drunk to argue for an Uber, but her skin felt tight and caked with grease, her eyes crusted, hair tangled. Not to mention the low simmer of nausea that was normally only an abstract thought had transformed into a tangible threat low in her stomach.

She adjusts the nosebands of her masks and approaches the caution tape. An officer is already telling her to step back but she tells him twice that she lives here. He asks for her apartment number, confirms with another cop that she's not on *that* floor, then lifts the caution tape and another officer escorts her upstairs.

"What happened?" she asks him.

"Under investigation," he says.

But as they pass the third floor, Cora smells blood. She knows its sharpness too well, how its salt can cut through layers of cloth and plastic under her hazmat suit.

Lots of things can cause people to bleed, Cora tells herself. People accidentally cut themselves with kitchen knives, or faint and hit their heads on coffee tables, or get random nosebleeds that just don't stop. A lot of blood doesn't necessarily mean a murder, Cora knows this. Maybe the police are having a slow day and are just being thorough.

Cora has to believe that, because she cannot think about a murder in her own building. It's one thing to commute to a crime scene, to see the broken locks on the front door held in place by tiny screws, or the shattered garden-level windows. It's another thing entirely to see how weak the doors of your own building truly are, to know that the walls you want to think are impenetrable are no obstacle for someone who truly wants to break in. That's why Cora installed the extra dead bolts, screwed them in with extra-long screws, but there's not much she can do about the weakness of the wood. Her apartment will never be a fortress unless she knocks down the walls and rebuilds them with cement.

The cop leaves her in the hallway outside her apartment. Cora takes out her keys, eager to escape the smell of blood, the way it spins her mind, but hesitates just before unlocking the door.

Her doormat is off-center.

Cora is always very careful to align it perfectly after she wipes off her feet—she cut it herself to the exact width of the door. But now it is two inches to the left, the right corner tugged slightly forward.

Cora adjusts it with her foot, wipes her shoes, lifts her key to the lock—

Her hand stills. She lowers her keys.

There is a footprint on her door, just above the lock. Like someone tried to kick her door in.

They wouldn't have had much luck—Cora had her door reinforced with steel, double-bolted. But someone *tried.*

Cora turns around, contemplates going back to Yifei's place. But her skin itches with grime, and the shadows shift toward the end of the hall, and whoever came for her clearly hadn't succeeded, or her door would be broken. She doubts Yifei's home is any more secure than hers, so is it really safer? Don't they say lightning never strikes twice? Maybe it's the same for burglars.

She unlocks her door, punches on all the lights before anything else, then double-checks the dead bolts, still firm and intact. No one made it inside her apartment. She has the only key.

It's still safe in here, she tells herself. *The shoe print is just proof of how safe it is.* Even if Cora had been home when someone tried to break in, the dead bolt would have been strong enough to buy her time to call the cops.

But the scent of blood is still coating the back of her throat. That could have been her, spilled open in the hallway. Did someone come for her and slink down to the third floor to settle for someone else when they realized they'd attract too much attention breaking down her reinforced door? Cora doesn't know why anyone would want to kill her, but then again, Yuxi He and Zihan Huang probably didn't know either.

Maybe it was just a burglary gone wrong? Something about Cora's doormat could be too flashy, indicative of wealth? She should get rid of it just to be safe, even though the idea of wiping her shoes off inside her apartment makes her clench her teeth.

Cora knows she should probably feel lucky, but she doesn't. She feels like her turn is coming soon. And Cora doesn't honestly know what's worse—the ghost of her sister warped into her doorways or the thought of someone breaking in and shoving a bat down her throat.

Cora showers with the curtain open, water spraying all over the floor, because the curtain casts too many shadows that the overhead light can't reach. She watches herself in the mirror across the room, skin vivid pink, until the room fills with steam and she is nothing at all.

The next job is different. It's another Chinatown job, but unlike their usual scenes, the cops are still there when Cora arrives at the apartment complex, their lights spinning red and blue all down the street. They whisper, stand with their arms crossed, keep the reporters back.

"A cop got shot," Harvey says, lifting the caution tape for Cora. Yifei is late, but Harvey says she texted him, so Cora tells herself there's no reason to worry. "Paul said his name was Wang."

"*His* name?" Cora repeats. Harvey's voice is always shrill enough to hear through his mask, but Cora needs to be sure.

"Yep," Harvey says. "No bats either. It's our lucky day. Just a run-of-the-mill shoot-and-run."

They head up to the second floor, where more cops let them through the tangle of caution tape. Two paramedics are coming out with a stretcher, and Cora catches a glimpse of a purpled hand hanging limp off the side.

"They're just taking the body out now?" Cora says, edging closer to the wall to let them pass. The bodies are usually gone hours before they get the call.

Harvey shrugs. "They're running late, I guess?"

The excuse feels tenuous, but Cora says nothing. They enter the room, and Cora knows at once that it's the freshest scene she's ever been to.

Usually, by the time the paramedics and police and photographers have been through, the blood on the walls has hardened into a rusty brown and the carpet has finished drinking up the bodily fluids. But this room looks like the raw walls inside a beating heart, pulsing with blood that's still rolling down the crown molding, pools of glossy brains slick across the pillow.

The room is alive, and suddenly Cora wants to be anywhere but here.

She can still see the silhouette of the corpse beneath the sheet, his blackened nails, the blood staining his knuckles. She can imagine that same hand when the man was still alive, flesh warm and pink. Normally, these crime scenes feel like a distant echo of a scream, but this one is wailing in Cora's ears.

Harvey reaches for the light switch, but it won't work. A heaviness settles in Cora's bones, a numb sort of acceptance when she realizes that they'll be working with nothing but dim ribbons of sunlight through the shutters. They can't exactly throw open the shades and let the neighbors across the street see the mess, after all.

Harvey puts his hands on his hips, examines the bloodstained sheets.

"Headshot," he says after a moment. "Machine gun, judging by the splatter. Seems like overkill if you ask me. Dude was asleep."

"He was killed off duty," Cora says, not quite a question, though the end of the sentence rises up like dust, floats away. She's cleaned up after dead cops before, but they're usually shot while pursuing someone. Not asleep in their beds.

Harvey hums. "It's fresh. You think soap and water will be enough?"

He sets down his bag, fishes out a spray bottle, douses the wall above the headboard. Cora pulls out a biohazard bag and starts to strip the bed. She jams the pillow into the bag, is reaching for the next one when a hand closes around her ankle.

She makes a sound, but it is so small and pathetic that the noise is swallowed by the hazmat suit and Harvey doesn't hear a thing. Cora's gaze drops down to the skeletal hand jutting out from under the bed, jade bracelet swinging back and forth.

"Harvey," Cora whispers, but he's scrubbing the ceiling and can't hear her.

The hand clenches, nails stabbing holes into the plastic of her suit.

Then it releases her, turns palm facing up, jerking two fingers as if gesturing for Cora to come closer. The hand disappears beneath the bed skirt.

Cora lets out a shaky breath, her whole body bathed in sweat, baking inside her plastic suit. Harvey is still grumbling at the wall, scrubbing away at the red haze. Cora's knees feel weak, yet she slowly crouches beside the bed. Maybe it's the hazmat suit that makes her feel braver. It is not armor, it will not protect her from anything but bodily fluids and gases, yet something about every inch of her skin being hidden feels safe. So Cora keeps leaning down until her head is on the ground, gloved hand curled around the bed skirt. The shadows murmur beneath the bed; Cora's own shadow a dark eclipse across the floor.

She lifts the bed skirt.

No one is there. Nothing but a tiny rectangle, its sharp corner departing from the shadows. Cora reaches forward and pulls it out into the light, turns it over in her palm.

A thumb drive.

"Cora?"

Cora closes her fist, looks up. Harvey is standing with his hands on his hips, facing the wall above the bed, where the bloodstain has only grown into a wash of soapy red.

"No shortcuts today," he says.

Then Yifei stomps into the room, not even wearing her mask or hood. Her face is pink, eyes searing. Cora wonders how she can stand the smell without her mask, but she looks too furious to notice. She has something balled in her hand, which isn't even gloved.

"Took you long enough," Harvey said.

"Shut up," Yifei says, uncrumpling the paper in her hands and shoving it in his face. Harvey reaches for it with a gloved hand before remembering his hands are covered in blood.

"Uh, I—"

Yifei scoffs and turns the paper back toward herself. Cora can tell from the color and size that it's part of a newspaper.

"'Residents praise increased security in Lower East Side,'" she reads. "'Crime in Chinatown has gone down significantly since Mayor Webb increased police budget by 5 percent this quarter and sent additional units to patrol the streets.'"

She lets out a strangled sound and balls up the paper once more, casting it down to the puddle. The fresh blood eats it up immediately, drowning the pages in red.

Cora doesn't know if any of that is true, but it certainly doesn't feel like it. As a crime scene cleaner, she knows better than Mayor Webb when there's been an uptick in violent crime. Cora doesn't particularly trust the mayor's word at this point either. His platform has always been More Police Everywhere All the Time, and in times of fear, a lot of people think that's enough to keep them safe. But a few months ago, the city had protested for days after the police shot a Black man trying to fix his flat bike tire on the sidewalk. The NYPD drove a police car into a crowd of protestors and all the mayor had to say was that the protestors shouldn't have surrounded the police car in the first place.

Cora had watched from her window as protestors with

their hands up got pepper sprayed; she heard their chants and screams all night, growing louder when curfew came, a terrible crescendo of agony until it finally went quiet. The silence was harder to sleep through than the screams.

Besides, Mayor Webb is hardly credible even with his supporters. Last month, he got caught cheating on his wife with a Korean international student at NYU and gave a painful explanation about how she'd "charmed" him and how his focus was back on his family and not "outside temptations." The girl got so many death threats she had to quit school and move out of the city and probably change her name too.

"That Devin guy we talked with?" Yifei says. "He wrote this."

"What?" Cora and Harvey say at the same time, though Harvey's word swallows Cora's.

"I know," Yifei says. "That's why I was late. I went to his office to chew him out. He got all pale and teary and said, *I tried, I swear I tried, my boss wouldn't let me print what you wrote, blah blah blah, I could get arrested.* Cry me a fucking river."

"Arrested?" Cora says. "Not fired?"

"I..." Yifei trails off, frowning. "Yeah, he definitely said *arrested.*"

"Jesus, is writing about hate crimes illegal now?" Harvey says.

"No," Yifei says. "I don't know why the fuck he said that. It doesn't matter. He's spineless, all of them are. They only printed bullshit copaganda during the Black Lives Matter protests—of course they're not gonna help us either. Sorry I dragged you guys into it."

Harvey shrugs. "I got a burger out of it."

"It's fine," Cora says. "You tried."

Yifei grimaces. Her gaze shifts to the blood spatter on the wall. "Let me guess. Machine gun?"

"What are you doing?" someone shouts from the hallway.

The three of them turn, Yifei taking a step back. A man in a black uniform and camera is standing in the doorway, looking at them like they're the ones who murdered a cop.

"Um…cleaning?" Harvey says.

"You can't do that!" the man says, his voice echoing up and down the empty stairwell, rage resonating through every floor. "You're interfering with a crime scene!"

"It's not a crime scene anymore, it's just a mess," Yifei says. "We're professionals and we're paid to be here, so who the hell are you?"

"A police photographer!" the man says, shaking his camera in her face. "You know, the guy who's supposed to be photographing the crime scene *before* it gets cleaned up!"

Cora's next breath catches in her throat. The crime scene hadn't been photographed yet? Cora doesn't know a lot about crime scene protocol, but she's fairly certain no one is supposed to start washing the walls before the scene is photographed.

Yifei turns to Harvey, her expression pained. "Who told your uncle about this job?" she says in Chinese.

Harvey throws his hands up. "I don't know!" he says. "I didn't ask! Usually the families, or the landlords if they don't have any."

"And where the hell is the body?" the photographer says, knuckles white on his camera, like he's about to snap it in half.

"Hey, that wasn't us," Yifei says. "We don't get paid enough to handle corpses."

The man looks like he's about to start screaming, but Harvey steps forward first. "Look, man, we're just cleaners," he says. "Someone calls us and we come. Take it up with the customer."

The man scoffs. "I'll take it up with the police, who will arrest you for *tampering with a crime scene!*"

Cora's knees shake, and she doesn't know why this is a more terrifying prospect to her than a ghost grabbing her ankle. Wasn't she supposed to outgrow the childish reflex of crying when men scold her? Some part of her feels like she's still a little girl in pigtails and overalls that her third grade teacher can put in time-out.

"Okay, fuck this," Yifei says. "Let's go. Harvey, tell your uncle I'm not going to jail for this job."

She shoves past the man with the camera while Harvey and Cora scramble to pick up their things and hurry after her.

"You can't just leave!" the photographer says. Cora tries to slink past him, to roll across the wall like a shadow so he can't yell at her anymore, but he reaches for her arm and she goes still, a prey animal waiting for teeth to close around her neck. That's all Cora ever does—sits around and waits to die.

Harvey grabs the man's arm before it touches her. Knocks it away, wedges himself between them. Harvey is not an intimidating person, but the hazmat suit makes him look bulkier than he is, and the smell of blood on his hands makes the photographer's expression curl. He flinches away, grimacing at the bloodstain Harvey left on the sleeve of his jacket.

"We're leaving," Harvey says, his voice low. "You got what you wanted."

Cora peels herself from the wall, gravitates toward Yifei, who drags Cora behind her and glares at the photographer.

The man turns his searing gaze to his own colorless reflection in the tinted plastic of Harvey's face shield.

"Fucking Chinks," he says under his breath, shoving past Harvey and into the apartment. Yifei flips him off to his back, then they hurry out before anyone can question them.

Once they're back in the truck, Harvey calls his uncle to

ask who called him about the job, and soon his uncle starts yelling so loud Cora can hear it from the back seat. Even though it's hard for her to understand Mandarin on a good day, Harvey's uncle enunciates when he's angry.

"Yes, dumbass, I'm sure it was a real call!" Harvey's uncle says. *"I know the landlord."*

"Did he know that police have to clear the scene first?" Harvey says.

"Of course I told him, you think I've never done this before?" Harvey's uncle says. *"How did you even get in if the police didn't clear the scene?"*

Cora remembers the police at the front door who hadn't even blinked when she ducked under the caution tape. Maybe they didn't know what she was doing?

"I don't know," Harvey says, his voice small. "But this guy threatened to call the cops on us."

Cora doesn't understand what Harvey's uncle says next, but she assumes it's a swear. *"Stay away,"* he says. *"I'll make some calls."* Then he hangs up.

Harvey lowers his phone, turns back and grimaces at Cora and Yifei. "No answers," he says, as if they hadn't heard the whole thing. "This was a waste of time, but hopefully we'll still get paid."

But Cora thinks that maybe it wasn't a waste of time. Because in her pocket she can still feel the USB that Delilah gave her pressed tight against her thigh. She lays a hand over her leg, trying to make the gesture look casual, then presses down, making sure that it's real.

In the Before Times, it would have been impossible to search the subway tunnels for body parts, because the trains ran twenty-four hours a day. But only fools and poor people take the subway these days, so the trains stop running at 1 a.m.

Cora's usually in bed by eleven, trying and failing to sleep. But Yifei handed her a paper cup of black coffee an hour ago as they sat on a bench outside East Broadway, and now Cora feels just as tired but also nauseous and has to pee. Her stomach eats itself for fuel whenever she gets the coffee-to-food ratio wrong.

Harvey arrives at one thirty, crushing a can of Red Bull with both hands before tossing it at a trash can and missing, scrambling to pick it up. The street is quiet, the moon a hazy eye overhead, watching them.

Cora has never done anything like this before, not even close.

There's an odd thrill to descending the frozen escalator, and part of it is probably exhaustion, but a bigger part of it is fear, knowing that she's doing something wrong as they ignore the signs about the shutdown and hop over the turnstiles. She wonders if this is how her high school classmates felt when they snuck out to drink on rooftops and smoke in parks and make out at house parties when their parents thought they were fast asleep. Cora spent those years reading under the covers with a flashlight, being a Good Kid, and in some ways she looks back on her life and thinks it's much paler for it.

The platforms are damp and smell faintly of Clorox from the after-hours cleaning, and the knife-sharp scent helps Cora center herself, calm her heartbeat. There is no ladder down to the tracks at the platform they've chosen, but it's a short drop. Yifei shines her flashlight onto the gravel, hands it to Cora, and hops down.

It's like she's jumped into the dark sea, the night swallowing her whole as she drops out of the circle of light.

Cora hears Yifei's feet hit the gravel and stumble a bit before Cora's flashlight finds her again and she raises a hand to shield her eyes. Harvey tosses his backpack down first, then drops a bit less gracefully than Yifei, falling onto his hands and knees. Then the two of them are looking up at Cora, who's standing with only a flashlight in her hand, looking into the mouth of darkness. On both sides, the tunnels seem to go on forever, and Cora is struck with the sudden thought that if she falls into the dark, she'll never be able to climb back up.

"Come on, it's not that far," Yifei says. Both of their flashlights are pointed at Cora, and she feels alone and exposed on the platform.

"Here, sit down first," Harvey says, handing his flashlight to Yifei and stepping forward. His head is just below the top of the platform. "Just put your hands on my shoulders."

"Cora's still not going to fuck you," Yifei says.

Harvey rolls his eyes. "That's not what I'm doing." He turns to Cora. "I'll catch you."

Cora sits down, dangles her feet over the edge, sets her flashlight on the ledge beside her. She knows logically that it's only gravel below her, but the roiling sea of dark dances in the periphery of her vision, a trap. She takes a breath, reaches for Harvey's shoulders, has to stretch out farther than she wants. But once she touches his T-shirt, feels his bones under her palms, she lets out a breath. He pulls her toward him, catches her waist, and sets her down on the solid ground, then plucks her flashlight from the platform and hands it to her. The ground still feels unsteady, an ocean beneath the gravel.

"Which way?" Yifei says.

Cora points to the left, the direction the train had been heading. That is not something she could ever forget.

Harvey and Yifei shine their lights on the edges of the tracks, skirting the third rail, checking all the crevices. But now that she's down here, Cora can only clutch her flashlight to her chest, a small circle of light on the gravel in front of her.

She knows logically that the train isn't running at this

hour, but being here in the dark, she swears she can hear its low rumble in the distance, that at any moment it's going to shatter through the wall of night and the last thing she'll see will be its brilliant headlights.

More than anything, Cora does not want to find her sister's head.

She imagines it with skin intact, one half of Delilah's face puckered where it hit the train, nose crunched inside itself, teeth a jagged mess of cracked enamel and bloody gums and exposed nerves, eyeball hanging loose where it spilled out after the eye socket burst. But she knows that Delilah's head—if it's even here—will only be a skull by now, and in a way, that's worse. Knowing that rodents peeled her flesh away from her face, ripped it apart with their tiny hands and ground their teeth down eating it. Cora keeps her flashlight as close to her as possible and pretends to search, hoping that Harvey or Yifei will be the ones to find it.

Slowly, they move farther down the track. The deeper they walk into the tunnel, away from the emergency lights of the platform, the thicker the darkness becomes, an impenetrable wall ahead and behind.

Cora drags her feet across the gravel, but one stone in particular makes her pause. She kneels down and plucks it from the ground, turning it over in her hands. It's small, grayed, sharp enough to draw blood. Anyone else might have dismissed it as a strange stone or piece of glass.

But Cora has a lot of experience with skull fragments.

This could be part of Delilah, she thinks. *It probably is. How many people's skulls have exploded at this train station? But it could also belong to an animal.*

"I think we're close," Cora says, dropping the stone, watching it mix in with the gravel. They're a short distance from the platform, close to the first turn in the tunnel.

"All I've found are cigarette butts," Harvey says. "And a few condoms."

"And rats," Yifei says, shivering and moving farther down the track. Cora has seen none of these things, her flashlight clutched too close to her body to see much of anything.

"I can't see shit," Harvey says, followed by the sound of a zipper. There's a click of his flashlight turning off, then blue light glows across the tracks in its place. It's one of the UV lights they use at crime scenes to make sure they've cleaned up all the blood spatter. Blood shows up as black under the lights, even through layers of paint. Cora tends to leave that task to Harvey, since the UV light also illuminates semen, and Cora doesn't want to go down the rabbit hole of imagining how much semen she's accidentally touched.

But Harvey hands her a UV light and she isn't sure how to say *No, I came all this way but don't want this anymore*, so she takes it and stuffs the other light in her bag.

She wonders, briefly, why Delilah hasn't shown her face at all down here in the ample darkness.

Then she realizes that the darkness is so inky and thick that maybe Delilah is here, just behind her, but the only thing Cora can see is where she shines the light, the places Delilah can't manifest.

Cora shuffles forward along with Yifei and Harvey, the train tracks glowing silver under the blue of the UV light, each piece of gravel a ghostly gray. She realizes she's falling behind and doesn't want to be left alone, so she hurries forward.

That's when the ground beneath her feet turns dark, a sudden wave of tar-black splashed across the gravel. She follows the trail to the left, toward Harvey, who's already drawn to a stop, UV light cast over the wall of the tunnel where it curves sharply to the right.

A ragged black splatter glows under his light, coming from

a crater in the wall about ten feet high. An echo of black blood oozes from it, pooling in the gravel below.

This is not fresh blood, Cora reminds herself. *This is just the ghost of blood.*

It makes sense, all things considered. The train probably lost speed as it turned the corner. It could have ripped Delilah's head clean off her shoulders, carried it along until the train slowed down at the first turn and the slick blood made her head slip loose and lodge in the wall.

But there is nothing in the hole, nothing on the ground below it. Maybe Delilah's head burst against the wall, maybe some of it was left and rats carried it away, made it their den, crawling in and out of the eye sockets.

Cora remembers Delilah telling her once that she never wanted to grow old.

It's like slowly rotting to death, Delilah had said, patting anti-aging cream under her eyes with her ring finger while looking in the mirror, at herself, even though she was talking to Cora. *I want to be remembered like I am now.*

At the time, Cora didn't understand what Delilah meant by that. Because all Cora could see when she looked at her sister was a seashell polished by the ocean, full of echoes and air on the inside. Delilah needed her beautiful shell because inside of her, there was nothing.

But Delilah didn't get to leave a pretty corpse.

"Shit," Harvey whispers.

"Shit," Yifei echoes. She turns to Cora. "I think this is..."

"Yeah," Cora says because she doesn't want them to say it out loud. "Yeah, I think so."

"Do you want to keep going?" Yifei says, one hand on Cora's shoulder.

"No," Cora says. There is no head here. If rats carried it

away, Cora will never find it. It's more likely that Delilah's skull is in a thousand fragments, mixed in with the gravel.

Yifei nods and hooks her arm around Cora's and they start walking back to the first platform.

"Told you this would be a bust," Harvey says.

"Harvey, shut up," Yifei says. For a while, they walk in silence back toward the entrance.

The sound starts quietly at first, hard to distinguish over the echoes of their footsteps in the empty tunnel. It is a whisper somewhere so far away that Cora thinks it's just her own simmering thoughts.

But when it grows louder—crisp and repetitive—and Harvey and Yifei both look up, Cora realizes that it's not the murmurs of her anxious mind.

It's footsteps on gravel.

It comes from far behind them, in the darkness of the tunnel around the corner, where it curves off to the right.

"Shit," Harvey says. "We've been caught."

"By who?" Yifei whispers. "You think the transit police patrol the tunnels without flashlights? It's probably a homeless person."

"Hell of a place to set up camp," Harvey says.

Then he turns his light toward the footsteps.

It illuminates the next thirty feet or so of the tunnel, gray gravel and smooth tracks. But after that point, the darkness swallows the light.

The footsteps grow louder, closer, and Cora's skin prickles, her heartbeat beginning to pick up. It is the unknowing of the darkness that unnerves her. The secrets that it keeps.

"Yo, what the hell do you want?" Harvey shouts into the tunnel.

Yifei punches his shoulder. "The fuck is wrong with you?" she says.

But the footsteps keep coming, and Cora starts backing up.

"We should go," she whispers. But no one hears Cora, no one ever hears Cora, because her thoughts are only half out loud and half in her mind, anxious sounds that haven't quite coagulated into words.

The footsteps stop.

Harvey and Yifei look at each other, neither sure what to do next. The silence stretches out around them, and Cora can hear the scurrying of rats, the low buzzing of their flashlights, her own thunderous heartbeat.

Then the footsteps start again, closer.

This time, they're running.

"Nope, no no no, no way," Harvey says, spinning around and running in the other direction. Yifei seems to agree, because she turns and runs after him. Cora hesitates only a moment longer, joints still locked tight, before she hears Yifei call for her.

She turns and runs.

Gravel pounds under her feet. It's hard to run and keep a flashlight pointing straight ahead in her shaking hand, and Cora runs too stiff and slow, afraid she'll step on the third rail, or that the darkness will slam into her like a brick wall. Harvey and Yifei are flickering stars ahead of her, flashlights jumping as their arms pump.

Whatever this is, it cannot be Delilah.

It's ghost month, after all, and there are lots of hungry ghosts besides her sister. Auntie Zeng always told Cora not to stay out late at night in August. Delilah might have latched on to Cora because they were family, but other ghosts didn't need a formal invitation. Cora vaguely remembers her aunt saying something about not touching anyone's shoulder and putting out their "spiritual torches" and winces at the memory of her hands gripping Harvey. How many rules has she broken in one night?

Cora sprints, gravel slipping out under her feet. Up ahead, Yifei's and Harvey's lights have stopped swinging. Cora catches a glimpse of Yifei hurling her flashlight onto a platform and hauling herself up. Cora's flashlight slips from her hands and spins across the tracks, but she keeps running forward unseeing, the footsteps close behind her.

Yifei's flashlight is spinning in circles where she dropped it on the platform. It bumps into a pillar and blinks out, and suddenly Cora is running through an infinity of cool darkness. She can no longer hear her footsteps on the ground or feel the sharpness of the gravel beneath her feet.

In that moment, she wishes that Delilah—however she is—were here.

Cora knows how pathetic that makes her. She's twenty-four, not fourteen, and she should know how to navigate without her sister. But she has always felt like she's out at sea with only a star map and no stars at all overhead, voyaging somewhere far and nameless, and Delilah always knew where to go. All Cora can do is tread water until her arms grow numb, and float on her back and let the current rock her like a piece of garbage. It is a slow and quiet drowning, to not know your destination.

Something grabs the back of her shirt and Cora can't scream, all her words extinguished in her chest. This is when she dies. The weak link, the boring character in a horror movie who nobody liked anyway, the one with no defining traits, a name no one can remember. Here, in this same filthy train station where her sister died. Even when she dies, she'll just be copying Delilah again.

The hand tugs and Cora's shirt pulls taut against her chest, collar choking her back, and this is the part where she'll fall to the ground and never get up again, where her body will shatter and she won't be human anymore.

I don't want to die here, Cora thinks, and the loudness of the thought shocks her, because it's been a long time since she's wanted anything this badly. But the thought sinks its teeth in, and the thought that comes after is an electric current zapping through her veins: *I will not die like my sister in this disgusting train station.*

With her next step, she grinds the ball of her foot into the gravel and pushes forward, yanking herself away from the hand, T-shirt snapping back as it's torn from the hands of a ghost.

Harvey's light blinks back on and Cora reaches for it, reaches for the hand that breaks through the darkness.

Her fingers grip the edge of the platform, but her palms are sweaty and slip straight off. Harvey and Yifei are shouting something but their words and their echoes blur and Cora can't make out either one of them. Harvey grabs one of her hands and Yifei grabs the other and they pull her up, but not before Cora feels a hand close around her ankle; it catches in her shoelace as she pulls away, snagging her pant leg. The shoe loosens on her ankle, dragging down, but Harvey and Yifei lift her up and she swings her legs up onto the platform.

The air goes still and silent. Harvey moves his light to the left, looking down the tunnel, then to the right, but no one is there.

At least, no one they can see.

Cora's flashlight sits twenty feet away, casting a circle of light at the far wall, where a rat scurries past.

"Yeah, no thanks," Harvey says, taking Cora's arm and pulling her to her feet. "Not how I want to die. Let's get out of here."

"For once, I agree," Yifei says. "I think this is a dead end anyway. Sorry, Cora. I really thought this might work."

Cora shakes her head. "It's fine," she says, staring across the ocean of black, the other world just below the lip of the platform, the flickering light from her abandoned flashlight growing paler as the battery dies.

"Ghostbusters never get the ghost on the first try," Harvey says as they hop over the turnstiles, and Cora thinks he's trying to make a joke, but she can't even bring herself to pretend to laugh. They emerge into the night and Cora can't stop shivering even though it can't be less than eighty degrees. Yifei pulls out her phone and starts typing something while Cora bends down to retie her shoe.

"I have one other idea," Yifei says at last.

Cora ties her laces too tight, imagining hands reaching up from the sewer grates to rip her sneakers off. She looks up as Harvey balances on a bike rack.

"Please tell me this one doesn't involve rats and used condoms," Harvey says.

"*That's* your objection to what just happened?" Yifei says. "The condoms?"

"What's your idea?" Cora says, because she's shivering harder now; she can still feel a hand on her ankle.

Yifei turns to her, gaze softening. She puts an arm over Cora's shoulder and pulls her closer, and the closeness feels wrong during a pandemic, but Yifei is so warm. "On the fifteenth day of ghost month, people in China hold a feast for the dead," Yifei says. "We can hold one for your sister, and maybe that will make up for not burning joss paper."

"So, we order a bunch of ghost pizzas?" Harvey says, wobbling on the bike rack.

"No, we'll cook actual food," Yifei says, glaring. "The proper way. That's in three days. Well, two now, since it's after midnight."

Two days. It's objectively not that long, but Cora has barely slept at all since this whole situation began, will definitely not be sleeping tonight either. Yifei might have gotten a glimpse of the ghost in the tunnel, but Yifei wasn't the one Delilah was following around. Of course it was easy for her to wait, to plan a dinner party.

"There's nothing else we can try first?" Cora says.

"Yeah," Harvey says, "I mean, didn't you feel that thing back there? I don't know if spicy chicken is gonna be enough to fix this."

"This isn't the first time I've done this," Yifei says, dropping her arm from Cora's shoulders, zipping her jacket up. Cora remembers the bite mark below her ribs. "This will work, and next year—" she turns to Cora "—burn the fucking joss paper."

Cora looks down at her too-tight shoes, nods. She doesn't need Yifei to tell her this is all her fault.

"Hey, I've never burned joss paper before and no ghosts are tailing me," Harvey says.

"Probably because you'd annoy them to double-death," Yifei says. "Look, I'll make a grocery list. Come with me to H Mart on Wednesday and we'll cook at my place, then all of this will be a creepy story to tell people ten years from now."

Cora cannot imagine who she would ever tell this to besides Harvey and Yifei—nobody else would believe her. She especially can't imagine herself ten years from now. Even thinking about the next year of her life is like staring off the edge of a canyon. Maybe it's a sign that she will end like Delilah—one moment she'll be everything all at once, the next she'll be in pieces too small to be human, not even worth saving.

FOURTEEN

When Cora finally goes home that night to her stark bright apartment, she slips the USB into her computer. She has just showered and her heartbeat feels slow, every part of her half-asleep already, but there is something she has to do first.

The drive felt heavy in her bag all day and night, and for a while Cora thought she might just toss it in a drawer and never think about it again. She wonders if she'll regret plugging a device into her computer that was delivered to her by a hungry ghost. Harvey has told her at length about horror movies where people see things they're not supposed to and soon it's all they can see—the girl at the bottom of a well staring up at the circle of bright sky, fingernails splintering on rocks, grainy black-and-white images, curses that sparkle into your eyes from the television static.

But this is a message from Delilah.

And even if Cora can't stand to look at her, she thinks Delilah at least deserves to be heard. Besides, it's not going to be some cursed tape that blinds her or sentences her to death or anything like that. Delilah would never hurt her.

Cora opens the Finder and the device pops up with the name BACKUP. Cora hesitates, cursor hovering over the icon. She feels like she's eighteen again, packing for NYU because Delilah said so. Part of her had always liked not having to decide. The world often felt like an endless hallway of doors, and Cora never knew which ones to open. Part of her trusted Delilah, and part of her just liked being *pulled*, innocent and blameless when it all inevitably fell apart. Even now, after her death, Delilah is pulling her.

Nothing good can come from looking at the hidden USB of a cop shot to death in his bed. Cora *knows*, in the way she always knows terrible things before they happen, that the USB will not contain family vacation photos, or college term papers, or old tax returns. Those kinds of things aren't worth hiding. Cora tries to imagine the worst thing it could possibly be—a trick her therapist taught her once, to defang her worst fears—but she cannot conjure a single image except a looming sense of rot, a nameless darkness, a box of white spiders.

In the end, not knowing is worse.

Cora double-clicks on the thumb drive.

A box pops up, prompting Cora to enter a password.

She lets out a stiff breath, sinking back into her desk chair, ashamed at the relief that once again, it's not her choice anymore. She will not look at BACKUP tonight because she can't.

"Sorry, Delilah," she says, ripping out the thumb drive, shoving it to the back of her nightstand drawer. "I'm going to need more than that."

But even with the USB out of sight, she feels it there, like a sleeping animal caged beside her head. In her dreams, the drawer rattles, whispers secrets that she can't decipher.

★ ★ ★

Cora's fridge is hanging open the next morning, nothing but weak light and cool air left inside, empty plastic drawers cast across the floor. All of her cabinets are thrown open, a faint dusting of instant oatmeal on her counters but no sign of the packaging. She focuses only on quietly closing each door, wiping down the drawers with Clorox wipes, cleaning away the oatmeal powder and the handprints left in it.

As she's closing the fridge, in the brief moment when it is only a sliver open and the automatic light shuts off, Cora swears she sees grayed fingers inside, reaching for her.

She slams the fridge shut, and before she can think more about it, grabs her reusable shopping bags from the hook on the wall, toes on her sneakers, and puts on both masks as she locks the door behind her. She needs to go grocery shopping now anyway, and since she hasn't showered yet, it's the perfect time—she always does a full wipe down after grocery trips, Lysol on plastic surfaces, cardboard boxes quarantined, outdoor clothes straight in the hamper. Besides, ghosts don't appear in brightly lit grocery stores, do they? What's Delilah going to do, hide under a pile of bananas? Cora is certain she'll be safe there, at least until the fear of COVID in such a crowded space starts to tip the scales and worry her more than the fear of ghosts. She can probably only stand to be there for an hour at most.

Cora hugs her bags to her chest like a polypropylene shield—the plastic coating is easy to wipe down on both sides, so it smells like chemicals and the scent feels sharp and new and safe. An unmasked couple passes Cora and she presses the bags closer to her face, as if the chemicals will scorch germs from the air.

The angle of the late-morning sun is kind to her at this hour—the shadows are short and thin and self-contained, no threat of bleeding darkness opening up beneath her feet. The only shadows she has to pass through are the narrow strips cast by the streetlights on the sidewalk. She holds her breath as she passes over them, feeling like each one is a step across a chasm. One by one, she rushes across them, faster and faster until she lets out a breath at the end of the street, toes to the curb as she waits for the light at the crosswalk.

The light changes and Cora's about to step down when she sees something fall across the subway entrance—a shimmering curtain of black, jagged at the ends as if raked through with scissors, hanging in tatters.

Hair.

Someone bumps into Cora and she stumbles into the street, forces herself to cross rather than stand open-mouthed in the middle of an intersection, draws to a stop once she reaches the safety of the sidewalk once more.

Bony fingers curl around the lip of the subway entrance, and Delilah's skeletal face appears upside down in the shadows of the staircase, hair hanging wild around her.

The bags in Cora's hands crinkle as she hugs them tighter. She supposes she could always walk to and from the grocery store. It adds another twenty minutes each way, which she'll probably regret when her bags are full, but technically she doesn't have to take the subway.

Then she remembers the USB. She tucked it into her backpack that morning, afraid it would be eaten like her coffee table if she left it out, and now her bag feels impossibly heavy.

Delilah's ghost might be driven by some inhuman hunger, but part of her humanity was left—she wanted to tell Cora something.

Cora knows she shouldn't try to talk to the dead. She doesn't need Auntie Zeng to tell her that to know it's a bad idea. Besides, nothing Delilah had ever said to Cora was that important, unless it was bad news. It would be very much like Delilah to send Cora on a wild-goose chase just to tell her to stop wearing Delilah's dresses to church because they don't match her skin tone. Besides, Delilah was going to leave her for a pipe dream of being a model. Cora doesn't owe her a second of her time.

But, as always, just like a moon pulled into orbit, Cora finds herself drawing closer to the subway, readying her MetroCard, closing her eyes as she descends into darkness and the curtain of stiff hair brushes her face.

She taps her card, follows the thin shadow that rolls across the walls even though no one is there. Cora steps onto the platform as an inbound train rushes into the station, boards it with no destination in mind, and as the world rushes away through the dirty windows and the train surges into the dark tunnels, she waits for a sign.

There are more people on the subway than a few months ago, but most people are still staying aboveground, in their Ubers or taxis or bicycles, afraid to be trapped down below with so many poor people breathing the same stale air. But there are things far more fearsome than COVID—Cora knows that now.

When the doors to the next station slide open, Delilah is waiting for her.

In the stark shadow of a pillar, she looms tall and thin and gray. The darkness isn't enough to cage all of her, and her thin throat leans off to the side, head invisible in the light. She is only narrow shoulders and a neck that tapers off into a hungry whisper.

Cora glances around, but no one else seems to notice. Delilah is apparently her curse alone.

The doors beep and Cora rushes to get off the train, doors slamming into her once before they open again and she stumbles onto the platform, where Delilah has vanished. Cora looks around for her, but the light is too bright and she suddenly feels very alone, at a station she's never been to before.

She ascends the stairs and emerges into the sunlight, peels her masks off, wanting to call out for Delilah like a child.

But she doesn't have to.

The mouth of the exit sits right in front of a police station.

Cora finds herself sitting in a plastic folding chair while she waits her turn for a secretary, unsure what she's even supposed to say. It was so like Delilah to drag her somewhere new and then vanish, leaving her drowning in dark waters.

Maybe Delilah wants her to tell the police what the reporter wouldn't print. Maybe she's supposed to press for more details about Delilah's death.

Cora remembers the hand around her ankle from under the bed, the first time Delilah had touched her. Delilah hadn't seemed to want anything beyond food until Cora set foot in Officer Wang's apartment, when Delilah gave her the USB.

Cora peers through the window on the door behind the secretary, squinting at people rushing back and forth carrying manila folders. Could Officer Wang's office be in here somewhere? Maybe the password to his USB is in this building.

Cora presses back against the wall as the man next to her yells at the secretary. He has a nosebleed and gets louder every time the secretary offers medical attention.

"I want to file a police report, not get a fucking Band-Aid," he says.

"I need some ID," she says.

"What part of 'I was just mugged' do you not understand?"

Cora crosses her arms and sinks lower into her chair. When

the man with the nosebleed finally leaves, the secretary sighs, shuffles some paperwork, and looks down at Cora.

"You need a translator?" she says after a moment.

Cora sits up, realizes her reticence has been read as not speaking English.

"No," she says. "I need…" She trails off, glancing through the door at the nameplates she can't make out. She'll have to take a chance. "I'm here about Officer Wang," she says at last.

The secretary freezes. "Oh," she says.

"I'm his wife," Cora says, probably too quickly. The lie is so easy it scares her. Cora is always telling quiet lies, making her aunts think she's fine. No one ever wants to know the full truth of the carousel of Cora's mind; she learned that lesson the hard way. But this lie is bold, even for her.

She knows that Officer Wang was killed in bed and that he was in bed alone, so she's fairly certain he doesn't have a real wife, no one to contradict her. She knows the secretary thinks she looks Asian enough to not speak English, and people always assume all Asians are either married or siblings anyway. "I'm here to clean out his office," she says, her voice smaller this time.

The secretary's expression softens. "Sorry, but it's already been cleaned out," she says.

It's been less than twenty-four hours and his things are already gone? Cora thinks. "By who?" she says, trying to sound teary so the woman won't ask too many questions.

"You have to understand, a lot of his paperwork was confidential," the secretary says. "We can't leave that kind of stuff sitting around."

Cora nods, lips pressed together. There must be something here, or else Delilah wouldn't have sent her. "Wasn't there anything I could take? Picture frames? I think he had an extra set of house keys in his desk."

The secretary regards her for a long moment, and at first Cora thinks she's pushed too far. She clutches her bags tight against her chest, ready to run.

But the secretary sighs and stands up. "Let me check," she says. "Stay here." She turns and opens the door that Cora peered through, closes it, her shadow moving across the frosted glass.

And another shadow appears.

Across the glass of the door on the opposite side of the desk, a shadow looms too tall for the doorway, just a silhouette of a bony torso and a long wire of a neck. Delilah extends a thin finger and points at the secretary's desk.

Cora glances around, but no one is paying attention to her. Slowly, she rises to her feet, peers over the counter.

A paper shredder.

She looks back to the door, but Delilah is gone. She's left Cora alone to do the hardest part. It doesn't matter if Cora is scared, Delilah can't get her hands dirty.

Cora huffs, setting her bags down, and looks back at the shredder.

The secretary said they needed to get rid of all the confidential information in Officer Wang's office. That probably meant they went right into a shredder, and this one bulges with paper scraps, lid barely holding on. And Delilah wants her to just...take it?

Cora wants to scream. It's one thing when Yifei snatches trinkets from the dead who won't miss them, but Cora is not prepared to do jail time. She will cry the moment an officer starts questioning her. Then she'll say too much and they'll lock her away in a soft cell.

Delilah pounds a fist against the door. Cora jolts, turning back to her. Nails scrape down the glass, the sound so horrid that Cora wants to tear her own ears off. But Delilah wants this badly, enough to claw her way back from hell for it.

And Cora always does what Delilah wants.

She swallows, stands up, and rounds the desk, calm and unhurried because Cora is very good at pretending everything is fine.

She pops the lid off the shredder, shimmies the bag out, ties it off, and pops the lid back on. She lets out a breath once she's back on the safe side of the desk, jams the bag into her backpack, zips it up, and heads for the door.

"Hey!"

Cora freezes. The secretary is hurrying toward her, and Cora can't run, can only turn around and feel tears already start to blur her vision at how badly she's messed up. But the secretary places a picture frame in her hands.

The photo is old and faded, and Cora realizes it must be Officer Wang as a kid. He's on the shoulders of a man in a striped blue shirt who's being hugged by a woman with permed hair in a pink dress, a coastline behind them.

Cora only met Officer Wang as a purple hand in a hallway and a burst of blood across the wall. She doesn't like knowing more about the crime scenes, doesn't like seeing who the people used to be. Tears well in her eyes and Cora knows she's doing a good job of pretending to be a grieving widow, but the secretary doesn't understand that you don't have to know someone to mourn them, that Cora has seen this man be unmade, and now she knows what his smile used to look like, the smile that was blasted off his face with a machine gun.

"This was all we could find," the secretary says, her voice quiet.

"Thank you," Cora says, tucking it against her chest. And she turns away because she doesn't want to lie right now—

she's angry at Delilah for making her play this game, angrier at herself for listening. She clutches the picture to her chest as she leaves the police station, steps out into the sunlight that will bleach her sister away.

FIFTEEN

"I have an idea," Harvey says.

For a moment, Cora isn't sure why she's dreaming about Harvey Chen. She would know his shrill voice anywhere, and it's certainly sharp enough to wake her from a deep sleep, but he shouldn't be in Cora's apartment.

"Cora? Hello?"

She blinks, realizes she's answered her phone in a half-asleep daze. She remembers a ringtone slicing through her dreams, the instinctive muscle memory of trying to stop the sound. Cora pulls the phone from her face, looks at the time.

It's 1:26 a.m. It's Tuesday—now Wednesday morning. They snuck into the train station two nights ago and haven't had much of a chance to debrief since then. Yesterday, after Cora went to the police station, they got called in for two back-to-back jobs—one Korean girl hacked apart with push saws while still alive, one Chinese girl drowned in her bathtub fully clothed. Cora left the bag of shredded paper by her apartment door, intending to bring it over to Yifei's because whatever secrets are in that bag, Cora doesn't want to find them alone.

"What?" Cora says, rubbing her eyes. She wakes up too fast because the lights are always on in her apartment these days. Every night now, she floats in shallow waters of sleep, still aware of the feeling of sheets on her skin and face pressed into her pillow, never fully submerged or unaware, and she wakes feeling like she's been treading water rather than resting.

But Harvey must think she means *what is your idea* and not *what the hell is going on.*

"Have you ever seen *Mr. Vampire*?" Harvey says.

"Uh, I don't know," Cora says. "Was that on Disney Channel?"

"No, it's an old Hong Kong movie," Harvey says. "About those Chinese hopping corpses, you know? Jiangshi?"

"I… Yeah, I've heard of them," Cora says, rubbing her eyes and sitting up. She remembers a TV show with ancient Chinese scholars with gray skin, limbs stiff from rigor mortis, hopping around and drinking other people's blood to sustain themselves. Like a cross between American zombies and vampires.

"Well, I was rewatching *Mr. Vampire IV*, and I started thinking, they're not so different from hungry ghosts. They're resurrected dead who hide in the dark and wreak havoc on the living, right?"

"I guess," Cora says.

"Well, there's a lot of information out there about how to get rid of jiangshi," Harvey says. "Folktales and stuff. I think we should give some of it a try."

Cora hugs a pillow to her chest, rests her chin on it. "Have you talked to Yifei about this?" she says, because Cora isn't the right person to run this kind of idea by.

"She doesn't answer her phone after eight," he says. "Well,

at least she doesn't answer *me* after eight. But, Cora... I don't know if we should tell her about this."

"Why?" Cora says, frowning.

Cora hears Harvey crack open a soda can, the hiss of bubbles rising in a glass. "Look, Yifei never told me exactly what happened with her family," Harvey says, "but whatever it was, it was bad. She said something about an inheritance once that made it sound like her whole family was dead."

Since Yifei never talked about her family, Cora assumed they were either dead or had disowned her, and her suspicions leaned toward disowning when she found out Yifei was a klepto. But it wasn't any of Cora's business.

"What does that have to do with anything?" Cora says.

Harvey lowers his voice, as if Yifei can somehow hear them through the phone. "I don't think she's being objective about this," Harvey says. "I think it's personal for her. Just because something worked for her family doesn't mean it will work for yours, but she doesn't want to hear that."

"You don't think Yifei's plan will work?" Cora says.

"Fuck if I know," Harvey says. "But I hate waiting around until the fifteenth just to throw a ghost party. Do you really think something like that is just going to eat a couple dumplings and say, *Thanks, I'll go home now*?"

"Something," Cora echoes. "You mean my sister."

Harvey goes quiet. A sudden silence expands across the line and Cora realizes Harvey was typing, that his fingers have stopped moving. "Cora," he says, "a hungry ghost isn't your sister anymore. You know that, right?"

But Cora doesn't know that, doesn't agree. Because maybe a hungry ghost has changed, but it is still her sister's soul somewhere deep inside of it, suffering. If it weren't her sister, it wouldn't be here with her. Cora and Delilah were always drawn to each other. It was inevitable, that's what Delilah said. At least, until the end.

Harvey sighs, starts typing again. "Cora, I can't even turn off the lights now," he says, softer this time. "Not since what happened at the train station. And I know I'm being a little bitch about it, but I don't think it would hurt to try something else. If it doesn't work, Yifei doesn't need to know."

Cora doesn't think she could lie to Yifei even if she wanted to—she's certain Yifei would smell it on her. But Harvey is right about one thing—sitting around doing nothing while Yifei draws up grocery lists feels like it's not enough. Delilah is rotting in the shadows, and Cora is too cowardly to look her in the eyes, but that doesn't mean she's not there.

"What do you want to do?" Cora says.

"Depends on what I can find in my kitchen," Harvey says. "I'll see what I can grab. Want to meet me at Foley Square in half an hour to try some stuff out?"

"Outside?" Cora says.

"I don't want jiangshi in my house, do you?" Harvey says.

It's a bad idea—going out alone this late at night with a serial killer running around, entertaining Harvey's ideas. But Cora thinks of running alone in the dark subway tunnel, and she's starting to think that maybe it doesn't matter which direction she runs as long as she goes *somewhere*.

"I can be there in ten," Cora says.

Cora arrives first and sits on a bench, hugging her legs to her chest. The park is mostly stone, an interlocking pattern of cement hexagons beneath her feet, caged in by concrete buildings with a few sparse trees in between. Cora sits in a circle of benches around dying foliage and watches cars pass by the Supreme Courthouse, trash blowing past her feet. The park is filled with a rotation of modern art, so at night the grass crawls with jagged shapes, abstract shadows. One of the new statues is something that looks like a splatter-painted octopus coatrack with long tendrils ten times its size. On the other side are birdcages shaped like crinoline, roped loosely to the nearby trees.

Cora is almost never outside at this hour, has never seen New York so quiet. They say it's the city that never sleeps, but six months into this pandemic, Cora still sees pockets of darkness, places where the city closes its eyes just for a single, defenseless moment.

Harvey texts her that he's running late, like always. Cora hugs her bag to her chest and turns her chin up to the moon, and that's when she feels it.

At the far end of the park, an upright silhouette presses close to an oak tree, and the glare of the streetlight falls at exactly the right angle to shroud it in impenetrable light. The wind nudges the tree branches and the shadows shift along with them but this one doesn't move, as if painted into the light. Even though Cora can't make out the edges of the silhouette, or see any eyes, she knows the way she knows her own name that she's being watched.

It can't be Delilah, because this figure hides in the brightest light of the park. Cora's mind flashes through memories of crime scenes, gallons of blood spilling through floorboards and raining down on the apartment below, women being unmade, piece by piece. She pictures Harvey and Yifei being called to the park to clean up her blood, wondering why she isn't answering her phone.

Cora slips her hand into the front pocket of her bag, where she packed a letter opener before leaving. It's a pathetic weapon, really. She doesn't eat much meat so she doesn't have any steak knives, and she didn't trust herself not to slice her own fingers off with a full-sized Chinese cleaver floating around in her backpack. She really should ask Yifei for a Swiss Army knife or can of pepper spray or something.

"Hey."

Cora turns toward Harvey's voice. He's wearing one backpack on his back and another on his chest, a broom in one hand and a tote bag in the other. He hands Cora the broom. She stands up, glancing across the park, but the light shifts as she stands and the figure is gone.

"Peachwood," he says, nodding to the broom as he unzips his bag. "At least, I think it is. Jiangshi hate peaches."

"Why?" Cora says, running her hands across the smooth wood.

"Who knows?" Harvey says. He sets down his bags, pulls out a sack of rice, a satchel that jingles, and a handheld mirror, then lines them up on the bench.

"Am I supposed to sweep the jiangshi away?" Cora says.

"What?" Harvey says. "No, forget the broom end. Think of it like one of those staffs in kung fu movies," Harvey says.

"I don't watch kung fu movies."

"Okay, then let's just…start with this," Harvey says, handing Cora the mirror, reflective side facing her, so she's forced to look at the dark circles under her eyes. "Jiangshi hate their reflections," he says.

"Okay," Cora says.

Harvey shakes the satchel, dropping some coins into his hand. "There are some stories about pouring out coins so jiangshi have to stop and count all of them. Some people say the same thing about rice, so I figured we can try both. There are lots of other stories about what we can do, but this is all I had at home. We can go buy some jujubes if you want? Supposedly nailing seven of them into a jiangshi's spine will kill them."

"I…" Cora shakes her head. "That sounds a lot harder than the rice."

"Right," Harvey says, something changing in his expression, like clouds rolling over the sun. He sits down, unzips his second backpack, and pulls out two steamed buns wrapped in plastic, handing one to Cora.

"And this is for?"

"Eating," Harvey says, unwrapping the one in his hands.

"To…stop the jiangshi?"

"To stop my stomach from rumbling," Harvey says. "Midnight snack."

Cora examines the bun. It's wrapped in unbroken plastic, so Harvey hasn't touched it with his bare hands. Cora's hands are dirty from the broom, but if she can eat it while touching only the plastic, it should be fine. Carefully, she rips the seam, edges the bun out from the bottom, takes a bite, and considers for half a second after tasting the custard whether Harvey should have refrigerated this, but it's late enough that her thoughts are muted, and she shoves that particular one back down.

"Cora," Harvey says, the word too careful.

Cora stops chewing.

"It seemed a lot cooler when I was on a sugar high researching this in my room," he says quietly to the squished half of bun in his lap. "Now that I'm explaining it to you, it all sounds kind of…dumb."

Cora shifts her legs, plastic crinkling in her lap. "It's not that it's dumb," she says. "It's just that…" She stares at the bun, the oozing custard. *It's that you're asking me to believe in folktales when I don't believe in anything at all*, she thinks.

"It seems too easy?" Harvey says, and Cora nods, because that sounds kinder.

"This is more or less what I expected when you woke me up talking about vampire movies," she says.

Harvey looks at her, expression pained. "Then why did you come?"

Cora crinkles the plastic in her lap. "It seemed like you thought it would work," she says.

"But *you* didn't think so?"

"It doesn't matter what I think," Cora says. Half the things she thinks aren't even real. Thoughts are nothing at all, they come from nowhere and disappear into nothing and you can't wade in their river as they pass by—that's what her therapist said. But Cora knows that her therapist means *Cora's* thoughts, not everyone's thoughts.

"How can that not matter?" Harvey says. But Cora doesn't know how to answer that in a way Harvey will understand, so she takes another bite of the bun.

Harvey sighs. "I just want to make sure you know it's not a joke to me, Cora. Even if all this—" he gestures to the sack of rice falling over on the ground "—looks stupid. I didn't mean it that way."

"I know," Cora says quietly. Because she knows Harvey Chen may be a hot-air balloon on a loose tether most days, but he knows when to come back down to earth. Cora wants to believe in him, wants him to whip some magic spell out of his backpack that would solve all their problems. But as she looks at the trinkets and sack of rice slumped over on the ground, she agrees that it all seems like child's play.

Harvey is slumped over, knees on his elbows, squishing his bun but not eating it. Cora knows he wanted this to work as much as she does, maybe even more because Harvey lets himself believe in things.

"Well, we came all the way here," Cora says. "We might as well give it a try, right?"

"You actually want to?" Harvey says, looking up.

"Yes," Cora says, though probably not for the reasons Harvey thinks.

Harvey straightens up and shoves the rest of his bun in his mouth, pocketing the wrapper. "Let's try the rice," he says, grunting as he lifts up the bag and starts liberally pouring it around the path. "Worst-case scenario, we've got some happy pigeons."

Cora grabs a few handfuls and sprinkles them around the bushes. Harvey tosses the coins in after them, but there are noticeably fewer of those because "Who carries change anymore?" Harvey says.

"All right, ghosts, come and get it!" Harvey says to the empty night. Of course no one answers. "Happy pigeons it is," he says, shrugging and picking up the broom and mirror, passing them to Cora. "Okay, last thing, we should practice with the broom. Pretend that I'm a jiangshi."

Cora grimaces, holding up the mirror half-heartedly, feeling childish. Harvey rolls his eyes, then sticks his arms out in front of him. His tongue lolls out of his mouth and he lets out a grunt that Cora assumes is supposed to sound like a zombie. Cora waves the mirror at him again, but he breaks character and swats it away.

"That won't work—my reflection isn't ugly," he says.

Cora smirks and jabs him in the stomach with the end of the broom.

"Ow! Okay, fuck, don't actually gut me," he says.

"Do you want me to joke around or not?" Cora says. "Make up your mind."

"I just don't want the cream bun to come back up," he says.

"Okay, so I'll avoid your stomach," Cora says, jamming the end of the broom into his cheek.

"Ow, Jesus, I'd like to keep my teeth too!" he says, laughing and smacking the broom away.

"A real ghost wouldn't complain this much."

"Okay, okay, let me get into character," he says, taking a deep breath. Then his jaw falls slack and his arms stick out as he walks stiffly toward Cora, slipping on the rice and letting out a strangled sound.

Cora can't help but laugh, can't help but wonder if, under different circumstances, Harvey could be her friend and not her designated corpse-finder. Cora gave up on real friends a long time ago. All she ever had was Delilah, the one person she thought could never leave. She knows that she and Harvey are only hanging out by circumstance, because both of them are too strange for anyone else.

She braces the handle of the broom against Harvey's chest as he approaches, holding him back.

"You're leaving my hands free," Harvey says, limp wrists knocking at Cora's cheeks. "I could rip your head off."

Cora twists the broom handle clockwise, knocking Harvey's stiff arms into his face, forcing him back into the trunk of a birch tree.

But the sound of Harvey's back colliding with the trunk is wrong.

There's no hard *thump* against rigid wood, no trembling branches overhead. Harvey falls against the tree with only a whisper of a sound, like it's pillow-soft, yielding against Harvey's spine. Its bark hangs like loose skin, translucent, cut through with moonlight. Its branches come to sharp, taloned points. Cora's gaze traces up the willowy line of its trunk, up the needle-thin white branch that leads to its face, the hollowness in the eyes made bare by the streetlight.

The mirror slips from Cora's hands, shattering on the ground.

"That's bad luck," Harvey says. Then he reads Cora's expression. "What?" he says. When she doesn't answer, he follows her gaze, turns around, and comes face-to-face with what's left of Delilah Zeng.

SIXTEEN

Harvey takes a quick step back, bumping into Cora, who clutches the broom to her chest as if it could do anything to protect her. Delilah crouches down, her head staying level with Harvey's face even as her palms press flat into the ground, spine arched like a cat ready to strike.

Cora knows that Delilah would never hurt *her*, but Delilah has no idea who Harvey is.

A hungry ghost isn't your sister anymore, Harvey said. Cora knows she should put herself between Harvey and Delilah, or at least say something to get Delilah's attention on her instead of Harvey, but her mouth feels gummed shut and she can feel the grains of rice beneath her sneakers but can't get her feet to move. *Fear is a sin*, she hears Auntie Lois say, and it certainly feels like one as Cora stands here, waiting for Delilah to take a bite out of Harvey, who only came here to help her. Cora is not the kind of person who can save someone's life—she has known this since Delilah died three feet away from her.

Even when all she has to do is take a single step, say a single word, all Cora can do is watch other people die.

Cora has another one of her thoughts, the kind that steamroll all the others away: Delilah taking a bite out of Harvey's throat, his esophagus like a wet noodle as she slurps it down, and Harvey can't make a sound, can only fall forward and turn and look at Cora, his empty throat like a second mouth screaming for him, and through it Cora can see all his wet insides, but the worst part is his wide-open eyes, asking Cora to do something, anything, but like always she does nothing at all.

But the thought disperses like mist and Delilah tears her gaze from Harvey, turns her face to the ground, a gray tongue slithering out of her mouth. With a scraping sound, she drags it across the pavement, lapping up the spilled grains of rice.

Harvey's back is pressed against Cora, the broom crushed between them, and she can feel his thundering heartbeat through his jacket.

"Holy shit," he whispers. "Cora, the rice worked. It really worked."

The broom trembles in Cora's hands. Delilah's tongue makes an awful sound, like a knife scratched against the lip of a glass bottle. She must truly be starving to lick uncooked rice off New York City pavement, and seeing Delilah this debased is somehow even worse than seeing her in this twisted, unnatural body.

Then, across the park, in the dark oceans between the safety of the streetlamps, the trees begin to multiply.

Willowy white figures stand in a silent forest across the green of the park, their mouths moving but wordless, gnawing on air. Their gray heads bob back and forth on their needle-thin necks, a field of dandelions in a breeze.

They begin to cross the park, coming closer, and Harvey tries to back up into Cora but there are more behind her, there's nowhere for her to go. Just like Delilah, the ghosts crouch down on all fours and begin to lick up the rice. The park fills with the ripping and scraping sounds of their tongues, like a machine that will rend itself apart. Cora and Harvey stand frozen in the center.

"Jesus," Harvey whispers, "how many of those things are tailing you?"

"Just one," Cora says. "Just Delilah."

Harvey finally breaks from his trance, glancing over his shoulder, brown eyes meeting Cora's. It's so much like Cora imagined Harvey would look with his throat ripped out—that raw fear, begging for Cora to do *something*, to be someone else. "Then where the hell did these ones come from?" he says.

Cora swallows, afraid the broom will snap in half in her hands as one of the ghosts laps at the grains under her shoe. She realizes Harvey is gripping her wrist, doesn't know when that happened, but his hands are trembling.

"You fed them," Cora whispers. "You told them to come."

"Shit," Harvey says. "They were supposed to count it, not eat it."

One of the ghosts finishes licking up the rice from beneath a bench. It scrapes its palms across the ground as if feeling for more, and when it finds none, turns to Harvey.

Harvey lets go of Cora, takes a step away, and for a moment she thinks he's going to run away without her and she can't even blame him, but instead he kicks over the rest of his bag of rice. It pours out across the pavement and the hungry ghost descends on it, forgetting about Harvey.

"Let's get out of here," he says, grabbing Cora's arm, not waiting for her answer.

They run back to Cora's place because it's closer, and Cora doesn't realize until she's unlocking her door that no one has ever come to her apartment before.

Harvey takes his shoes off by the door without being asked,

spends a moment staring at the sterile white walls, probably smelling the bleach and Lysol.

"Shiny," he says at last, setting down his backpacks beside the shoe rack. "Where's your bathroom? I almost pissed myself back there and would like to avoid it if anything else pops up."

Cora points, relieved that this means Harvey has to wash his hands before he touches anything else in her home. She imagines his footprints in vivid, radioactive orange, tracking the outside world in. She puts on her house slippers, pops her phone in the blue light sterilizer and slams the lid, washes her hands at the kitchen sink. It's easier to think about all these things than the sound of her sister licking rice off the ground. She hears the toilet flush and the water run and counts the seconds—Harvey washes for twenty seconds, which isn't enough but it's close enough that Cora can live with it. Cora's clock says it's 3:12 in the morning, and Cora feels wide-awake.

Harvey pokes his head out of the bathroom door, smiling at Cora seated stiff as a mannequin on her couch.

"Your place smells nice," Harvey says, stepping closer. "Better than mine, but I guess that's not saying much. You want some pineapple cakes?"

He starts rifling through his bag before she can answer, and Cora wonders what it must be like to be Harvey, to switch in and out of realities so easily, to think about pineapple cakes after escaping a flock of hungry ghosts. Cora is perpetually trapped in her one broken world.

Harvey sits down beside her, slaps a package of pineapple cakes on the table. He gives her a sideways glance, then pops one in his mouth.

"You're stressed," he says. "Eat a pineapple cake."

"That's not how stress works," Cora says.

"I beg to fucking differ," Harvey says, pushing the package

toward her. "If anyone deserves a pineapple cake at three a.m., it's you, Cora."

Cora grimaces. It's not really about deserving. "I want to sleep," she says, which isn't a lie, even though she's not tired. She wants to be unconscious.

"Okay," Harvey says, stuffing another pineapple cake in his mouth and standing up. "Where are we going?"

"I..." Cora glances obviously at the couch without meaning to. Harvey knows how much she makes, can see that she lives alone. Surely he doesn't think she can afford a two-bedroom apartment in Manhattan all by herself?

Harvey finishes chewing and wipes his mouth on the back of his sleeve. "I'll sleep on the floor, don't worry," he says. "But there's no way in hell I'm sleeping alone in your sterile asylum living room, sorry."

"Asylum?" Cora echoes weakly.

"Yeah, it's like a padded room in here," Harvey says. "You don't have any decorations. It's like no one lives here. Like some sort of minimalist Ikea showroom."

Cora lets out a tense breath. Some asylums have decorations, but of course Harvey Chen doesn't know that.

She grabs a couple cushions and a throw blanket from her couch and shows Harvey to her room, dropping them on the ground. She doesn't feel too bad because she knows her carpet is freshly vacuumed and bathed in Lysol spray. She offers Harvey one of her large T-shirts and then changes into her pajamas in the bathroom, coming back to find Harvey eating more pineapple cakes on the floor.

"I'm not tired," Harvey says, "but I can shut up if you need to sleep."

"Can you?" Cora says, not trying to sound mean but realizing belatedly that she failed. Harvey snorts, pulling up his blanket.

"I'm not tired either," Cora says, sliding under her covers. In the stark brightness of her room, it's an odd parody of intimacy. Cora has never fallen asleep beside anyone but Delilah. Briefly, she imagines a world where she and Harvey fall asleep in the same bed, say good-night, shut off the lights, grow used to the sound of each other's breathing. It's not a fantasy anchored in Harvey, specifically, just *someone.* Cora wonders how that would feel, instead of this stiff awkwardness, this hyperawareness of her breathing. Cora would dare to say that Harvey probably thinks of her as a friend, but right now it feels like they're strangers forced to share a cab or shoved together into an uncomfortably long elevator ride.

"I used to count silverfish to fall sleep," Harvey says quietly. Cora turns her head toward him, sensing that there's more he might say if she lets him, like the night they buried the bats. But he laughs stiffly and shakes his head as if erasing the thought. "I don't suppose you have any bugs we can count?"

"If you see any, please kill them immediately," Cora says.

"Hey, bugs have rights too."

"Not in my apartment they don't." She thinks she sounds too angry, knows it when Harvey goes quiet, the smile fading from his face.

"Is that one of your things?" he says.

"My *things,*" Cora says, even though she knows exactly what Harvey means.

"Yeah, like with your hands?" Harvey says, mimicking rubbing hand sanitizer into his palms.

Cora doesn't know how to answer. She's not stupid—she knows she doesn't do a perfect job of hiding things like that from Harvey or Yifei, but the fact that Harvey is saying it out loud makes her feel like he's peeled all her skin off and is staring at the map of her veins. She's sure he would stop asking if she lied about it, but what would be the point? He already knows. He knows and for some reason he wants to know more. He's not making excuses to leave.

"Just white spiders," she says at last. "That's the only... *thing.* I don't like other bugs, but in the same way most people don't like them."

"Okay," Harvey says. Then, softly, "I'll kill any if I see them."

Cora pictures Harvey squashing spiders like bats with a cast-iron skillet, putting holes in her walls.

"Thank you," she says, for more than just the spiders, but she doesn't say the rest out loud, hopes that Harvey knows.

Harvey goes quiet after that, and Cora thinks maybe he's trying to sleep or at least trying to be quiet so *she* can sleep, but Cora is still thinking about little Harvey counting silverfish in the basement, about what else he saw down there.

"Harvey," she says. "You said you saw a ghost in the basement."

Cora isn't looking at Harvey, but she hears his breathing stop. "You remember that? You were trashed."

"I was mostly coming down by then," Cora says. "How did you make it go away?"

Harvey doesn't answer at first, so Cora rolls over to face him, finds him corpse-stiff under the throw blanket. He blinks, and that is the only sign that he's alive at all.

"I didn't," he says at last. "She's probably still there now."

Cora clutches her blanket in her fist, huddles it close to her. "It didn't hurt you?"

"There are lots of different kinds of ghosts," Harvey says, his voice wary, like every word is forbidden. "She didn't move. Didn't say anything. She was just...*there.*"

"There," Cora repeats, as if testing the word. That's how Cora feels—like she's just passively existing while the world turns around her. If Cora ever becomes a ghost, she'd be like that one.

"Yeah," Harvey says. "Just kind of lying there, you know? At the bottom of the stairs. Part of her head was crushed in, kind of like a smashed milk carton."

Cora tenses up, tugging the blanket tighter around her. She wants Harvey to stop talking now, but as always, he goes on.

"She never said anything. She just breathed, but it sounded all wrong, like her windpipe was squeezed and she was breathing hard through a thin straw, all high-pitched and wet. But whenever my dad opened the door, she was gone."

Cora's blankets are taut around her, tight enough to cut off circulation. She imagines young Harvey in the basement with the vivid image of a corpse at his feet, crying out for a dad who wouldn't—couldn't—believe him because there was nothing to see.

"Maybe someone died in your basement," Cora says.

"Yeah," Harvey says softly, "someone did."

Then he rolls over, his back to Cora as she processes his words. *Harvey knows exactly who died*, she thinks, but Harvey whispers something that sounds like "good night," and Cora won't ask any more questions. You can only scrape so much out of a person in one day. She pictures the ghost in Harvey's basement like a mangled piece of furniture, never asking for anything, never touching a soul, yet haunting Harvey all these years later just the same. In a strange way, she feels sad for the ghost. Maybe she never wanted to haunt anyone—it wasn't her fault that death cracked her skull open, made her terrifying and ugly, took away everything that made her human.

Cora suddenly feels very tired. Something about Harvey's story makes her feel heavy, seasick. She falls asleep imagining a staircase with a terrible monster at the bottom, but the staircase winds farther and farther down into the darkness and still she can't see it. Only when she reaches the bottom stair and hears the door far above her click shut does she truly understand.

★ ★ ★

Cora doesn't know the time when she wakes because her room is always sun bright, but she feels like she's only just closed her eyes. Outside her window, the sky is still dark, not even a whisper of sunrise, so it can't have been more than an hour or so.

She tenses when she realizes what woke her—there is a hand on her leg.

"Harvey," she mumbles, shifting her leg so his hand will slide away. But the hand only clamps down harder into her thigh, nails biting in.

Cora's eyes open. "Harvey?" she whispers.

But she can hear Harvey breathing, knows that he's down on the floor, not beside her. He can't reach her from there.

She stills her breathing as the hand crawls upward, scoring a path of small cuts with its fingers, trailing up past her hips, her navel, resting just below her breastbone. A second hand joins it, holding tight to her hip. The blankets shift as if draped over a nauseous sea.

Cora lies still as death, some pathetic prey instinct, as if her stillness means that whatever this is won't notice her. And she doesn't understand, because her apartment is so glaringly bright that she thought it would scorch away all ghosts. She was supposed to be safe here.

But, from across the room, she spots a place she's missed.

Just to the left of her bookshelf is a thin shadow where the lamplight can't reach, a pale ribbon of darkness.

Gray fingers are wiggling through it, like a child with fingers beneath the seam of a door. With a crunching sound, a grayed hand forces its way through, scraping at her bookshelf.

More fingers are squirming wetly in the narrow strip of darkness cast by her picture frames, beneath her doorknob, the legs of her desk chair. It is like being inside a tomb while maggots crawl around. Cora should have realized that she can't eliminate darkness completely. It's everywhere.

It's even beneath her blanket.

It was bad enough worrying about one hungry ghost in her apartment, but apparently the ghosts Harvey summoned had finished their rice and wanted more.

The blanket swells and a heavy weight crushes against Cora, a sharp rib cage pressed against the softness of her stomach, long hair falling across her arms, itching like straw.

Something unlatches in her throat and she chokes out Harvey's name, but he doesn't answer.

A hand traces its way up to the base of her throat. The one on her hip bites down, and a third rests on her bare stomach.

All Cora needs to do is pull the blanket off and the light will sear the ghost away, but with its weight on top of her she feels breathless, limbs dead.

The hands tug her shirt up, and a warm wetness presses against her rib cage. Something sharp prickles at her skin, and Cora realizes all at once that it's *teeth*.

She shoves the blanket off and falls out of bed, tripping into Harvey, who jerks awake with a shout. The falling blanket floats down toward them and Cora kicks it away, ripping off Harvey's blanket for good measure.

"What the hell?" Harvey says, rolling to his feet half-awake, squinting in the bright light. He spins around, gaze settling on the writhing fingers by the bookshelf, his next words dying in his throat.

Cora grabs her phone and fumbles for the flashlight, casting it on the shadows by the bookcase. The fingers twitch and jerk as if slammed in a car door, then slide back into the wall. The scratches they clawed on the side of her bookshelf remain, a mocking reminder.

"Jesus," Harvey says, reaching for his phone and flashing

light onto the fingers jammed through the keyhole. "Fuck." He sits down, rubbing his arms, which have broken out in goose bumps. "That's some *Silent Hill* shit. Cora, I think we fucked up."

"We?" Cora says.

"Okay, fair," Harvey says, rubbing his eyes. "As much as I'm not looking forward to it, we should probably talk to Yifei."

Cora nods, knowing Harvey is probably going to end up bearing the brunt of the blame anyway. Her phone says it's 4:02 a.m.

"She's not going to answer her phone for a few more hours," Cora says.

Harvey sighs, looking out the window at the dark sky. "Got any coffee?"

SEVENTEEN

Yifei calls them back at eight.

Harvey's phone rings, and then Yifei is yelling so loudly that Cora can hear it from across the room where she holds a cold cup of coffee.

"You better be fucking dying!" Yifei says. *"You know when you call more than once, it pushes the call through even if I have Do Not Disturb on? You called four times!"*

"I know, I know, I'm sorry," Harvey says, sitting on the floor where his phone is plugged into Cora's wall socket. "We had a bit of a jiangshi situation."

"I beg your pardon?" Yifei says. *"And who is 'we'?"*

"Me and Cora," Harvey says, and Cora winces, already knowing what's going to happen before Yifei starts yelling even louder.

"You were with Cora last night at four a.m.?" she says. *"Harvey, I swear to god if you two are fucking—"*

"Give me the phone," Cora says, crossing the room, because listening to this is too painful. She would rather face Yifei's wrath.

Harvey all but throws the phone at her, going back to his coffee and pointedly looking away as he drains his fourth cup.

"Hi," Cora says, turning the volume down so Harvey won't have to hear the insults she's sure Yifei is going to start shouting.

"Cora, I know everyone gets lonely during a pandemic," she says, "but Harvey—"

"It's not like that," Cora says as Harvey clutches his mug with both hands, trying to look like he's not listening. "He came over and we tried some ways to get rid of jiangshi on Delilah."

The only sound on the other end for an unbearably long time is Yifei's breathing. "Cora, you know that hungry ghosts and jiangshi are not the same thing?" she says at last, like it's taking every ounce of her willpower not to yell, a courtesy she's sure wouldn't be extended to Harvey.

"Yes," Cora says quietly. "We thought it might help anyway."

"We?" Yifei says. "You mean Harvey?"

Cora's silence is enough of an answer.

"Cora, give the phone to Harvey."

Wordlessly, Cora passes the phone back to him. She's glad that she can't hear what comes next, though the grimace on Harvey's face tells her enough. He makes a few pathetic sounds of affirmation, then puts the phone on speaker.

"Go ahead," Harvey says.

"Okay," Yifei says. "Since I apparently wasn't clear enough about this last time, *we are going to take care of this problem today.* We are going to feed these hungry ghosts actual food, not whatever disrespectful shit you two threw at them last night, and they are going to go away because this isn't a goddamn kung fu movie and this is how it works in real life. You two will meet me at H Mart at one o'clock today. You will pay for everything I buy, then you will help me cook this ghost feast so we can wash our hands of this forever. Got it?"

"Yes," Harvey and Cora say quietly.

"Great," Yifei says, then hangs up.

Cora isn't sure she can make it until nightfall. Her mind spins thinking of all the sources of darkness where fingers could emerge—her mailbox, between her shower curtains, under her oven. Then she thinks of all the darkness in her body—beneath her eyelids, her hair, her ear canal. Was Delilah inside the darkness of her eyes this whole time, causing the floaters? She stands up to grab some Dramamine just so she doesn't spiral.

Harvey sits cross-legged on her couch, fully dissociating into whatever mobile game he's playing on his phone. Cora chews the Dramamine tablet, swishes water around in her mouth to scrape the chalkiness from her molars, lies down on the couch and waits for it to carry her away even though she knows it won't take effect for at least an hour.

"You want something stronger?" Harvey says. "We can stop by a liquor store."

"Is that your solution to everything?" Cora says, dropping a hand over her eyes, then thinking better of it when she remembers that she's only creating more pockets of darkness. It was a mean thing to say, but she's barely slept at all and can't find it in her to be patient with the guy who summoned fifty ghosts to her apartment.

Harvey's thumbs stop moving over his phone. He looks up at Cora, expression flat. "It's the best one I've got, and it doesn't seem like you've got a better one," he says. His tone isn't unkind, but the truth of it stings. She shouldn't be criticizing Harvey when she doesn't have any better ideas. She went along with his horror movie jiangshi plan when she could have just hung up on him. She's the reason Delilah is here at all.

In a normal world, one where Cora had slept for at least five hours and hadn't looked for her sister's head two days ago, Cora would have just gone quiet and turned away to hide her expression. But she's exhausted, and tears fill her eyes and streak down her face. She claps a hand over her eyes to hide it but is sure Harvey can see her crumpled expression because she hears his phone hit the floor.

"Oh, uh, Jesus," he says. "I'm sorry, I didn't mean—"

"No, you didn't do anything," Cora says.

"Um, are you sure?" Harvey says.

Cora's nose starts running, so she stands up and goes to the kitchen for a paper towel rather than answer Harvey. He stands in the doorway while she blows her nose, wipes her face, and gets herself a glass of water to calm down because crying in front of Harvey Chen was not how she wanted this day to start.

Her phone rings and Cora nearly chokes on her water, half of it spilling down her throat. Harvey is staring at her like he's on the other side of the glass in a sad zoo exhibit and Auntie Zeng is calling Cora for the hundredth time in the last few days, probably angry that Cora still hasn't called her back.

Cora almost declines the call out of habit, but hesitates just before hitting the button. All her life, she half-heartedly entertained Auntie Zeng's beliefs, kneeled before every shrine and swept every grave like a puppet in some elaborate play because at least Auntie Zeng was *there*, and that was worth something. Cora always thought she was just too American, that Auntie Zeng's gods didn't want her, and that was why she felt nothing when she knelt before them. But now everything Auntie Zeng warned her about is coming true, and maybe her aunt knows how to undo Cora's mistakes.

Cora turns to Harvey, who's still standing in the doorway like a scolded child.

"Want to meet my aunt?" Cora says.

One hour later, Cora and Harvey sit on the couch while Auntie Zeng rips Cora's clothes off the drying rack. She brought over some dumplings, which Cora doesn't really have the stomach for after the dumpling shop incident, but Harvey seems to have no trouble eating.

"Thank you, Auntie!" he says, very nearly splashing soy sauce on his shirt—Cora's shirt that she let him borrow. The first thing Auntie Zeng did when she arrived was roll her eyes at Cora and Harvey for wearing black and white—bad luck, just like Yifei said. Cora pulled on one of Delilah's orange shirts and lent Harvey a green summer camp T-shirt two sizes too big for her.

All Cora told Auntie Zeng was that she was worried about hungry ghosts. That was all she needed to say—Cora never tells Auntie Zeng when something worries her until it's too late. And when she does, Auntie Zeng offers no empty platitudes, no kind reassurances. She finds the root of Cora's problem and rips it from the ground.

In ten minutes, Auntie Zeng was on her way to Cora's apartment with a bag of frozen dumplings and Chinese talismans that now hang in Cora's windows. The shadows seem to soften and pale as soon as Auntie Zeng arrives, like her presence alone is starbright. Cora thought about telling her everything. But at the end of the day, Auntie Zeng reports to Cora's dad. She's the one who decides if Cora is Fine.

Auntie Zeng drops the pile of Cora's stiff clothes from the drying rack on the arm of the couch. "Did you leave these out on your fire escape all night?" she says in such a way that tells Cora she already knows the answer and is disappointed in Cora for it.

"I forgot they were there," Cora says quietly.

Auntie Zeng raises an eyebrow. "It's an invitation to ghosts," Auntie Zeng says. "They'll borrow your clothes for the night."

In the past, Cora might have listened only because it would make Auntie Zeng happy. But now, she commits the fact to memory and begins folding her clothes. She will have to find another way to dry them, because drying them inside will cause mold to grow on her wallpaper, black fungus that chokes her in her sleep. Cora doesn't know what's scarier—the ghosts or the mold.

By the time Cora finishes folding, Auntie Zeng has dragged a chair over from the kitchen and is standing precariously on it, hanging a red knot decoration above Cora's doorway. She hops down and carries the chair back before reappearing with a fresh packet of joss paper, slapping it down on the coffee table. Harvey slides the dumplings to the side while Auntie Zeng digs around inside the chasm of her reusable shopping bag and pulls out a tube of incense.

"I don't have—" Cora starts to say, but then Auntie Zeng pulls out an incense burner shaped like a lotus, jams a stick into the end, and lights it.

She sits cross-legged in front of Cora and Harvey, across the coffee table, and looks at them both so sternly that Harvey stops chewing.

"No swimming," she says. "No hiking, no picking up coins in the street, no turning around for strange sounds or voices." Cora grimaces, deciding not to mention that she already did one of those things.

"Will you write me a list?" Cora says. She doesn't think

she could forget anything this important, but she likes having something solid to look back to because sometimes her mind lies to her—that's what everyone says.

"Why, you can't remember four things?" Auntie Zeng says, tearing open a package of joss paper. "You don't need to write this down, just listen. Really listen to me."

"I always listen to you," Cora says, taken aback. She'd done every damn thing her aunt had ever asked of her.

"No," her aunt says, beginning to unfold the honeycomb of pink paper into a 3D shape. "You hear me, Cora, but you don't listen to me. There's a difference."

Cora opens her mouth to protest but the sharpness in her aunt's gaze silences her.

"I know you've grown up in two worlds," her aunt says, manicured fingers working quickly across the joss paper, a miniature house taking shape. "I would never force you to believe in what I believe, as long as you were respectful. But now you've seen something, and it sounds like you're ready to start listening."

Cora keeps her gaze fixed on the joss paper, which now stands as a miniature mansion. "I haven't seen—"

"Don't lie to me," her aunt says, pulling out a matchbox. "Get me a plate."

Then she strikes the match and Cora has to run to fetch a plate because she's certain that Auntie Zeng will set fire to the joss paper right on top of her very flammable coffee table if she doesn't. She manages to slide the plate under the joss paper house a moment before Auntie Zeng drops the match.

The fire tears through the house all at once. The paper walls fall in toward each other, eaten through with searing black holes, curling up on itself the way insects do when they die. The fire echoes in the blackness of Auntie Zeng's eyes, flames expanding, lashing out wide, forcing Cora and Harvey to lean back against the couch. Smoke begins to fill the room and it gets harder to breathe.

And then, in the bright tongues of fire, Cora sees something she's not supposed to see.

The searing white at the hottest point of the fire converges into a light so bright that it strips away the colors at the edges of Cora's vision. Just as the darkness of Delilah's shadow led into an infinite chasm of night, the bright white is another door into a place Cora doesn't want to go. It is the unknown beyond of the doorway in the crypt; it is the secrets of the sun, the reason they tell children not to stare at it directly; it is the star explosion that will one day destroy everything and everyone. The roaring of flames devouring paper begins to sound like screams, a thousand different voices, parched throats scraped raw.

Cora moves closer, sliding to her knees in front of the coffee table, and the heat of the flames scalds her face but she doesn't care, stares deeper into the ribbons of infinite white.

I am staring into hell, Cora realizes all at once, the flames lashing higher as if in agreement, the smoke blurring away the rest of the room. The flames are whispers of hands, orange silk scarves clawing at the remains of the house, dragging it down with them. They reach for Cora's face, but the paper is nothing but withered black on the plate and the flames are growing smaller and smaller, the door closing. The flames die out in a tiny flicker of yellow light, like a last word cut off, spiraling into silent smoke.

"Cora?" Harvey says somewhere behind her. Cora is still staring at the smoldering ashes on the plate, tiny flickers of red buried in the black. "Are you okay?"

Is she? Cora feels a bit like she's just showered, peeled all her skin off. Bath by white-hot flame, nothing but raw, bloody muscles and blue veins left of her. She's more okay than she's felt in weeks, the haze of exhaustion stripped away. Is this how her Auntie Lois feels when she talks to God?

She looks up at her aunt. Through the haze of smoke, she looks like a dream that a breeze will blow away. "Why does it seem so real now?" Cora says.

"It's always been real," her aunt says.

Cora begins to register the sting of smoke in her eyes, but the sensation is welcome, it sharpens her vision. "I've never…" She trails off. Never thought it was possible? Never wanted to trust in something beyond herself? In many ways, it doesn't make sense. Cora would make the perfect member of any religion, the kind of person who doesn't want to decide, who wants a textbook to tell her what to do. But Cora has always kept that kind of unwavering trust reserved for only one person. Delilah has always been Cora's God. For one brief, sharp moment, Cora thinks of her mother singing from treetops above kale farms and wonders which of them is crazier, what part of them shattered and made them want to hand their souls to someone else.

Even now, with Delilah dragged down to some sort of hell, or purgatory, Cora is still following her.

Cora lets out a short, sharp laugh. Her eyes water involuntarily from all the smoke, and the tears drip down her face, chasing the sting away. "Auntie Lois will hate this," she says. "She's tried so hard to make me a Christian."

"You can't make someone believe," Auntie Zeng says, frowning. "But you still can be a Christian, if you want to."

"How?" Cora says.

Auntie Zeng's eyes water. She rises to her feet, opens a window, lets plumes of smoke into the sky. "It's not about my gods or your Auntie Lois's God being the right one. There are thousands of gods that open thousands of doors to anyone who knocks. It's about deciding which doors you want to open."

But Cora doesn't feel like she's decided anything. She feels like someone has grabbed her chin and taped her eyelids open and forced her to stare at something she never wanted to see. She never asked for these ghosts. Delilah is dragging her across planes. Even in death, she has Cora on a string, pulling taut around her throat.

This time, it's too much.

Cora might have followed her sister to China, but all of these ghosts under her blankets, rooting through her fridge, peering through her keyholes—this is too much, even for Cora. She needs to send her sister back to wherever she came from.

"Is there anything else?" Cora says, her voice oddly calm even though her throat feels scraped through with glass.

Her aunt nods. "Where is the jade bracelet I gave you?"

Cora rises to her feet, roots through her desk drawer, brings it back to the living room. The character for *love* glimmers on the gold plate.

"Put it on," Auntie Zeng says. "Whatever you do, don't take it off."

Cora nods, commits that to memory as well. The jade is cool on her skin. Once upon a time, she liked wearing it because it matched Delilah's bracelet. She and Delilah were never the kind of sisters who wore cute matching clothes or jewelry, even as kids, and she secretly loved that Auntie Zeng had tricked Delilah into it. But now the matching set is broken; Cora's bracelet is the only one because Delilah's is buried with her. Cora spins the bangle with her right hand, the smooth stone soothing over the skin of her inner wrist, cold and unyielding.

EIGHTEEN

By nightfall, Yifei is making biangbiang noodles in her kitchen and Cora and Harvey have been exiled to the living room, where they're taping together Cora's stolen paper strips. Cora doesn't know the name of everything Yifei is cooking, but the last dish was so spicy that the air is actually hurting Cora's eyes and making her nose run, so she's grateful that the food is for the ghosts and not them.

When Cora first upended the bag of paper shreds onto Yifei's carpet, she didn't think they had a chance in hell of putting them together. The bag had compressed some of the air out, so Cora hadn't realized the sheer quantity of thin, white, nearly identical paper strips she'd been carrying.

"Holy hell, Cora," Harvey said. "You're so badass."

"I'm impressed," Yifei said. "I didn't know you had it in you, Cora."

Except Cora doesn't, not really. She just does what Delilah says. And of course, Delilah isn't going to appear to help her do the tedious, boring part of putting the papers back together.

Cora approaches the task the same way she approaches a blood-soaked apartment—one problem at a time. She sets aside all the strips with photographs, since those will be the easiest to match up. Harvey passes them to her, doing his best to line up the rest of the strips text-side up, taping them down on one end so they don't keep blowing away every time someone breathes too hard.

The room smells like rice, then garlic, then Sichuan peppers, then fish as Yifei cooks, having long ago decided that Cora and Harvey were more of a nuisance than a help, only good for pushing grocery carts and fetching items from the shelves at H Mart. Harvey takes frequent breaks to eat honey butter chips and look over Yifei's shoulder, but Cora stays cross-legged on the carpet as the explosion of paper slowly resolves itself to clean piles.

Her hands are covered in paper cuts even though she can't remember getting any. The blood stains the edges of the paper, but the color reminds her what pieces she's already examined, so she lets it be.

Slowly, she starts to assemble the photographs.

It's impossible to realign the papers perfectly, so the mug shots she pieces together look just slightly off, eyes just barely misaligned, lips too high on one side, jawline jagged, as if they're almost human but not quite. She tapes five of them together and passes them to Harvey, who uses the text below the photos to find the rest of the paper, finishing the sentences letter by letter.

"Got one," Harvey says, passing Cora the Frankenstein paper, limp and sticky in her hands from the tape hanging off the edges.

It's the first page of a case file on someone named Jimmy Watts. Twenty-nine, life insurance salesman from Jersey, unmarried, unmemorable face. Someone—probably Officer

Wang—has scrawled notes in the margins, which Harvey hasn't aligned perfectly, but Cora can make out the words *linked to case 15?*

"So he's a boring office dude," Harvey says from over Cora's shoulder, scanning the paper. Then he points halfway down the page. "'Member of The Allegiance,'" he reads. "That's fucking vague. Allegiance to what?"

"It's a neo-Nazi group," Yifei says.

Cora looks up. Yifei has stopped stirring, is staring into a steaming pot like she can see beyond it. "They crashed a Black Lives Matter protest around here a few years back," she says. "Curb-stomped a few people."

"You *saw* that?" Harvey says, recoiling.

Cora clenches her jaw, can almost hear the sound of teeth shattering on concrete, can feel the ghost of an ache in her molars.

Yifei drops a handful of star anise in the pot and doesn't answer.

"So, not a boring office dude," Harvey says, flopping back against the couch. "Great."

Cora's hands move faster now, caring less about perfectly aligning the faces as long as she's certain she has the right strips. The world around her falls away and she sees nothing but the slices of skin, puzzling them together. More and more jagged mug shots start to form and Harvey tells her he can't keep up but she doesn't stop until she's torn through her pile, until she's pieced together ten faces and there's nothing left. She helps Harvey with the rest, and they move faster as there are fewer and fewer strips to choose from. When the last strip of paper is gone, they stare down at ten profiles.

Half of the profiles are men from neo-Nazi groups afraid that white people are a dying race. Some just seem like regular white people working cubicle jobs, though. Wang typed up a few overly descriptive notes about their colorful browsing histories, a few screenshots of *hentai* or videos with titles like "submissive Asian bitch gets railed by monster cock" that Harvey finds hilarious. The rest of the notes in the margins are mostly useless without context. They say things like *Possible connections?* and *Same person?!*

Maybe it's the fact that they're puzzled together, but none of the photos look particularly memorable. They all have the same cropped brown to medium blond hair, stern jawline, eyes staring straight ahead.

"Here," Yifei says.

Cora looks up, and before she can stop it, Yifei is stuffing a dumpling into her mouth with chopsticks. Cora covers her mouth so she doesn't spill over the papers.

"Where's mine?" Harvey says, opening his mouth expectantly.

"Fuck off, these are for Cora's sister," Yifei says. "We're just making sure they don't taste like shit. Are they okay, Cora?"

Cora nods, giving Yifei a thumbs-up, grateful that Yifei at least passed it to her with chopsticks and not her bare hands. No one ever washes their hands enough when handling raw meat.

"Officer Wang was studying boring people," Harvey says, squinting down at the lopsided text. "This one sold car insurance. Oh, the horror! Lock him up."

"Insurance salesmen are basically crooks," Yifei says.

Cora ignores them, trying to discern some of Officer Wang's notes, but his handwriting is either awful, or— "Harvey, this one's wrong," Cora says, pulling up the strip, scanning the floor, swapping it with another one.

As she tapes the new strip down, Officer Wang's handwriting lines up perfectly, three words that make Cora's hands freeze.

Huang Zihan's neighbor?

"'Huang Zihan,'" Harvey reads, leaning over Cora's shoulder. "The girl who got axed?"

"With bats in her vent," Cora says, hugging her knees. "Officer Wang was on that case?"

"Apparently not for long," Yifei says. "That was what, a week ago? Two weeks?"

"And this was as far as he got," Cora says.

Harvey straightens, picking up another case file. "Then he must have been getting close."

"And you know this because you're an expert crime analyst?" Yifei says, slamming a lid down on a pot.

Harvey clambers up onto the couch, shaking his head. "Don't you get it?" he says. "What happens to people who go after serial killers when they get too close?" He mimics a gun with one hand, pressing the two-finger barrel against his temple. "Brains all over the wall, evidence in the paper shredder. Corpses can't talk." He points down at the case files on the carpet. "I'd bet you anything that one of these guys is Batman."

"Stop calling him that," Yifei says. "Batman is a good guy."

Cora sits very still on the floor. She looks down at the case files, the jagged black-and-white photographs of men. She wants to believe Harvey, but there's only one problem:

Delilah wanted her to see this.

It's not like Delilah to go out of her way to help others. Delilah lived inside her own snow globe world, beautiful and glittery and plastic. Everything she did was for her own benefit. It wasn't that Delilah wanted to hurt other people, she just never thought about them at all.

A spot of darkness catches Cora's gaze, and she's about to ignore it as another one of her floaters, but then there's a flash of light, a single clear thread swinging in front of the window, a tiny spider dangling from it. It's white, the size of Cora's thumb, landing softly on the windowsill and scurrying toward the curtain. It rushes into the shadow behind the fabric and does not emerge, as if the darkness has swallowed it whole.

And Cora realizes, all at once, that the only reason Delilah would send her after a serial killer is if he's the one who pushed her.

The kind of person who would shove a Chinese girl in front of a moving train is the same kind of person who would hack a Chinese girl to death in her own bed. Delilah was pulling Cora again, but this time not toward NYU, or an art history degree—toward her killer.

The ten jagged faces scattered across the floor suddenly look sinister in their asymmetry, hideous broken mouths, skewed eyes, gnarled teeth. One of these ordinary, unmemorable men killed her sister.

Cora sinks her fingers into the carpet, hangs her head, breathes through the sudden wave of nausea, hears nothing but a faraway train, the loudest sound in the world. But she can also feel something new, joss paper burning in her chest, a kind of hurt that she wants to lean into, to feel more brilliantly. It is different from the kind of hurt that makes her want to scratch off her own skin. This pain is a fever that makes her feel more alive in its awfulness, the kind of ache that reminds you that you *are*, that there is something left inside you.

Over the distant whir of the train, Cora hears the words of Auntie Lois's priest.

And the Lord said, "I will be merciful to their unrighteousness, and their sins and their iniquities will I remember no more."

But Cora remembers.

She remembers his pale hands, the crunch of a skull shattering, the taste of her sister's blood. This sharp fire feels much better than God's forgiveness ever could.

Auntie Zeng said there are thousands of doors that will open to anyone who knocks. This is the door that Cora chooses—the one that opens up in the starbright fires of hell.

The rice cooker beeps out a cheerful song and Yifei pops it open with a cloud of steam, fluffing it with the rice paddle. Cora remembers, in a cold wave, that all of this food is meant to send Delilah away.

"We need to find these people," Cora says. "Their addresses are here. If we can get proof that one of them is the killer, then the police—"

"The police had this information," Yifei says. "They shredded it."

Cora huffs, fingers twitching. "The press, then. That reporter wanted proof, right? Maybe we can give it to him."

"You think we should tail a serial killer?" Harvey says.

Cora looks between Harvey and Yifei, already knowing that they won't do it from the look in their eyes. They've seen the entrails of people who get too close to this man.

She wants to scream. This has to be what Delilah wanted her to do, right? Why else would she show her this?

"Let's just start with research," Yifei says, perhaps sensing Cora's mood darkening. "Maybe if we can narrow it down a bit, we can find a reporter who will take it off our hands."

"Take it off our hands?" Cora says. "Delilah gave this to me to handle."

"Delilah is going to rest again," Yifei says, her eyes narrowing. She gestures to the stove. "That's what we're doing here, Cora."

"But what if she can help us find the killer?" Cora says. Her words taste jagged, and she knows she's talking in the way her aunts don't like, that her eyes are probably fever bright.

This is why Cora is always quiet—when something actually matters, it matters too much, and everyone can taste it in her words. It scares them, how much it matters to her.

Yifei presses her lips together, closes the rice cooker.

"Cora," she says, setting down the rice paddle with uncharacteristic gentleness, "keeping a hungry ghost around is never a good idea." Her hands trace the spot on her ribs, the scar Cora touched. "Death changes you."

"Delilah wouldn't hurt me," Cora says, and Yifei flinches back. Cora bites down before she can speak anymore.

Yifei opens her mouth as if considering, then shakes her head. "She's suffering, Cora," she says.

The words punch the air out of Cora's lungs. She'd forgotten that part. She looks to the window, but even in the deep shadows, Delilah isn't there. "Right," she says. "Sorry, you're right."

"She's given us a lot to work with," Harvey says. "That's probably all she can do anyway."

Cora nods, too fast and too hard, but it's hard to lie to your friends and yourself at the same time.

"Why don't you get started on her altar?" Yifei says.

Cora nods, moves robotically to her backpack, starts digging around it with numb hands.

Yifei thought they should make an altar for Delilah before the feast, and Cora realized an hour before she left that she didn't actually know what goes on an altar, so she jammed a few handfuls of things from Delilah's boxes into her bag. Yifei has already cleared off a foldable card table for her, a few tea candles scattered across the top. Cora squats in front of it and unloads her bag.

The first thing she takes out is a framed picture of Delilah, one of the few pictures Cora managed to pluck from the walls before Delilah's mama came through and took the rest.

Most people don't hang framed pictures of themselves on their walls, but of course Delilah did. It was one of the shots from a boudoir session Delilah did during her brief attempt to get into modeling, where Delilah is posing in a sheepskin rug and lacy white bra. It looks like something Cora isn't supposed to see, but Delilah hung it up across from her bed and said, *Where else am I supposed to hang a picture of me in my underwear except in our room?* And Cora couldn't really argue with that. But as beautiful as the woman in the photo is, Cora doesn't think it really looks like her sister. Delilah never showed up in photographs the way Cora saw her, the way her presence was sometimes a whisper and sometimes a tsunami.

"Damn," Harvey says over Cora's shoulder. "Your sister was hot."

"Harvey," Yifei says.

"Sorry, sorry," he says. "She looks kind of like you."

Cora grimaces and reaches back into her bag. It's the other way around—Cora looks like Delilah, but stretched out in afternoon shadows, the delicate nuances of her soft features sharpened, her night-black hair dulled to a lightless brown.

"Stop hitting on Cora," Yifei says. "She already told you no."

Cora sets Delilah's hairbrush down on the table, along with one of her pink lipsticks, a green perfume bottle that leaked a bit in Cora's purse and made everything smell like a magazine, one of Delilah's lavender essential oils, and a handful of rocks that might have been some of Delilah's special stones or might have been something she just grabbed on the beach, Cora's not sure which.

"Is that enough?" Cora says.

Yifei looks up from her cooking. Her expression is strange as she crosses the room and sets a hand on Cora's shoulder.

"That's great, Cora," she says, squeezing gently. Harvey

copies the gesture, and Cora realizes that they think she's being quiet because she's sad.

The feeling in Cora is not quite sadness.

She remembers, back in her worst days, watching a video about black salve, a substance so caustic that it eats through flesh overnight, leaving holes Swiss-cheesed through your body. Cora never bought it, of course, but the thought haunted her for weeks, for all the spots she could never clean deep enough, the spots she wanted to hole-punch out of herself.

Delilah was never there when it was that bad. Emotions were a mess she couldn't dirty her hands with. Instead, she was a lighthouse for Cora to look to in the distance, a reward at the end of it all. *When you're normal, you get your sister back.*

Cora's stomach feels a bit like it's full of black salve now, like a circle has been punched out of her middle and air is blowing through.

"She would have liked this," Cora says. "People staring at a picture of her in her underwear. Too bad now all her flesh is gone."

Harvey lets out a sharp laugh, while Yifei only grimaces and tightens her grip on Cora's shoulder. "Cora..."

"I think that's what she hates more than anything," Cora says. "Not being pretty anymore."

Harvey and Yifei say nothing, and Cora knows she has broken a rule: don't speak ill of the dead. But their sympathy makes her skin crawl. She doesn't want it.

"She wouldn't have eaten any of this," Cora says, nodding to Yifei's food. "She just sort of picked at everything on her plate, broke it apart into smaller and smaller pieces. She always watched me eat, though. The way people look at squirrels breaking nuts apart. She never said anything, but I never wanted to eat when she watched me like that because her thoughts were so damn loud. Whatever she hated, I had to hate too. I started eating at weird hours just so she wouldn't be there. I ate in the bathroom sometimes. The day she died, I ate a grilled cheese sandwich at our kitchen table, and it tasted like nothing but it was the first time I'd ever done that. I think being a hungry ghost isn't that different for her, because I'm sure she was always hungry when she was alive."

Yifei and Harvey are no longer touching her. Cora realizes, belatedly, that she's not sure if she's actually conveyed the essence of Delilah, or if she's just made herself sound insane. Delilah was a study in contradictions, and that was why Cora never talked about her when she was alive. It seems impossible to explain her now when they'll never actually meet her, see how she is, was.

"Forget it," Cora says rather than waiting for Harvey and Yifei to think of how to respond. It's not the kind of story people like, the kind where you know what to say afterward.

Yifei stands up, rifles through a drawer, comes back with a matchbox and lights the tea candles. Their flames are reflected in the glass of Delilah's boudoir photo, brightening the reflection of Cora's own face overlaid across Delilah, and for a single moment, their faces are the same.

"What else is left?" Cora says.

"Just setting the table," Yifei says, so Cora busies herself setting out plates. Harvey and Yifei watch her a moment before moving to help her.

"You're sure we can't eat any of this?" Harvey asks once they're done.

The feast is spread out in front of them, so big that they had to drag over the coffee table to fit everything. Cora set an empty place setting for Delilah at the head of the table. The sun is going down, and they've turned off all the lights except for a few candles on the table. The wall is a dark canvas, free for Delilah to enter.

"If this works, there shouldn't be anything left," Yifei says. "We have bigger problems than your stomach at the moment, Harvey."

He huffs, sits back in his chair. "So how do we do it?" he says.

Yifei turns to Cora. "You said you fed Delilah before, right?"

Cora nods stiffly. She feels a bit like she's at Delilah's second funeral. This is supposed to be a good thing, but Cora would rather be anywhere but here.

"How did you do it?" Yifei asks when Cora doesn't do anything.

Cora shrugs, thinking of the orange. "I just sort of...gave it to her?"

"Can you try it again?"

Cora purses her lips, stabs a slice of apple with her chopsticks, and holds it out to Delilah's empty seat. Seconds roll by, their shadows trembling across the walls as the flames flicker, but still, Delilah isn't there.

"Normally she just kind of appears," Cora says, feeling stupid as she lowers the apple slice.

"Maybe she hates Yifei's cooking," Harvey says.

"She ate my coffee table," Cora says. "I don't think the food is the problem."

Then the door slams open and the lights burst on.

Cora squints, shielding her eyes.

"Oh, you're here," Paisley says, Ryan looming in the doorway behind her. "You're eating in the dark?"

"Uh," Yifei says, eyes darting between Cora and Harvey, "Chinese dinner," she says, and that seems to be enough of an explanation for Paisley, who shrugs and steps into the apartment. "I thought they were staying over at his place," Yifei says in Chinese, grimacing.

"That smells amazing," Ryan says, eyes wide as he leans over the table. "Can I grab a plate?"

"She made so much," Paisley says. "You don't mind if we eat too?"

"Uh, no no," Yifei says, eyes wide, probably unsure how to say, *We're trying to summon the dead with this food*, in broken English.

But Paisley either thinks she means *No, I don't mind* or doesn't care what she meant because Ryan sits down in Delilah's seat and Paisley grabs her own plate and sits across from him.

"It's, uh, very spicy," Yifei tries again, probably thinking that will deter them. Paisley hesitates, but Ryan shrugs, standing up when he realizes there are only chopsticks and no forks.

"I eat Chipotle salsa all the time," he says, grabbing a fork from the silverware drawer while Paisley takes a scoop of white rice.

"Is this...bad?" Cora manages to say in Chinese, not sure how to say, *Did they just ruin everything?*

"I don't know," Yifei says, with a smile that looks more like a grimace. "This has never happened before."

"You made it sound like you knew for a fact that I couldn't eat anything," Harvey says in Chinese, crossing his arms.

Yifei says something Cora doesn't understand, but she assumes it's an insult from the way Harvey pouts and sinks deeper into his chair.

"Why aren't they eating?" Ryan says, sitting back down with his fork. "They're just staring at us."

Paisley shrugs. "Chinese prayer or something?"

A sound like a bolt of lightning shocks through the ceiling, and the power cuts out, dropping darkness over them.

Ryan's fork clatters to the floor. Cora tenses, eyes adjusting to the dim candlelight once more.

"Shit," Paisley says, looking to the ceiling. She turns to Yifei. "Has this been happening a lot? Is this why you had candles?"

Yifei shrugs, and Paisley sighs. "We should've stayed at your place," she says to Ryan.

"My place doesn't have food," he says, popping up from under the table with his fork and stabbing it into a dumpling without so much as wiping it off.

The windows clatter open, a hot breeze rushing inside and bathing them in a wet heat.

"No, no, all the cold air will get out," Paisley says, rushing across the room.

Cora watches her, and that's how she notices that the room is growing...lighter.

The shadows are peeling themselves from the walls like a sheet of dead skin, dropping to the floor, the carpet a black abyss yawning wider.

"Yifei," Cora whispers, nodding to the ground. Yifei follows her gaze, eyes wide, but she stays rooted to her seat.

The darkness slinks across the room, and Cora grips the bottom of her chair, remembering the first time a shadow ate a hole in her wall. It moves slowly, silently across the floor, pooling under Delilah's chair, and then it begins to rise.

Ryan keeps eating dumplings while the shadows stretch to the ceiling, growing legs, and arms, and finally, a needle-thin neck.

"Holy shit," Harvey says. "It fucking worked."

Ryan pauses before he can take his next bite, staring at Harvey. "I thought you didn't speak English," he says.

Then Delilah's jaw drops open with a *crack*, and she leans forward and closes her mouth around Ryan's head.

★ ★ ★

Ryan's neck cracks, a startled sound lost in the cavern of Delilah's throat. Delilah's lips seal all the way around his head, then tear it off with a sound like ripping Velcro. His body slams into the table, a bowl of hot soup overturning, blood spraying from the stump of his neck as the bulbous shape of his skull forces its way down Delilah's throat.

Cora and Harvey jump to their feet so they won't get scalded but can't seem to move any farther than that as Delilah crams the rest of Ryan's body into her mouth.

It won't fit, Cora thinks. Ryan's body resists, limbs twitching as Delilah's bony hands grab at it, angling, twisting, forcing it down. Cora thinks that surely Delilah's thin throat will break and her head will roll to the floor, but piece by piece, Ryan is crushed into her trash-compactor jaw, rammed down into her stomach.

Other ghosts begin crawling out of Delilah's shadow, shredding through couch cushions, licking hot oil splashes from the floor by the oven, tearing off the hinges of the fridge. But Delilah is the only one standing, the only one who was invited to the feast.

Delilah turns to Paisley, who is standing frozen and slack-jawed by the window. She backs away, slamming against the glass, and for a moment Cora thinks she might jump out.

But Delilah is too fast.

She clambers across the couch like a spider, jaw clamping around Paisley's head, screams swallowed in the chamber of Delilah's throat. Paisley's body snaps in half at the rib cage, legs flopping down to the carpet, ribbons of organs twitching as the upper half of her body pulses down Delilah's throat. Delilah grabs a leg in each hand and holds the rest of Paisley up in the air, feeds her into her mouth with a wet slurp.

Then Delilah turns back toward them.

Her jaw drips with blood and guts and things Cora is all too familiar with, the cape of darkness behind her humming like the tunnel of a subway.

Cora should run. She knows she should. Yifei is right—death has changed Delilah. She's a feral ghost who could kill them all easily.

But she's also suffering, and Cora can't leave her like this.

"Fuck this, I'm out," Harvey says, backing away.

"Wait," Cora says, the word firm, impenetrable. She reaches slowly toward the table, fingers closing around her chopsticks. "We came this far. Let's finish it."

"Finish it?" Yifei echoes, still frozen in her seat, deathly pale.

Cora slowly sits down, picks up a dumpling, and deposits it on Delilah's bloody plate.

"It's for you," she says.

For a moment, Delilah doesn't move.

Cora just saw her rush across the room, knows she can move quickly if she wants to, knows that in a single blink she could wrench Cora's head from her neck.

But Delilah wouldn't do that. Cora knows, the way she knows things even when they go against all logic.

Slowly, Delilah steps forward, each footstep heavy, wet.

"Sit the fuck down, Harvey," Yifei whispers.

Harvey falls into the closest chair, jaw still hanging open.

Delilah sits down and surveys the feast. Her long neck bobs to the side, then curves around and brings her face inches from Yifei's. Yifei sucks in a breath, rigid in her chair.

Delilah pivots and looks at Harvey, then Cora.

Cora steels her expression, glares back at Delilah. *I will not be afraid of my sister*, she thinks. And maybe it's a lie, but Delilah always liked beautiful lies.

"Eat," Cora says. "We've been waiting for you."

Delilah's neck pulls back, a fishing line reeled in, examining her plate. She shoves the dumpling into her mouth, the round form rolling down her throat.

Then she plants both hands on the edge of the table, lifts it up, and slides the entire feast into her mouth.

All of the bowls and plates rush toward her gaping mouth, disappearing into its dark chasm. She crunches down on porcelain and candles and meat knives and napkins. Harvey raises his hands and slides his chair back as if afraid she'll inhale his fingers too. All around them the other ghosts murmur, the kitchen cabinets shuddering open and shut, spices falling and bursting on the ground where the other ghosts lick them up.

The jagged mass rolls down Delilah's throat, and she rises to her feet. She turns to Cora, and Cora wonders if, finally, Delilah will speak.

Then, with a low buzz, the lights burst back on.

The kitchen is soaked with blood. Stray shards of plates are strewn across the floor, the back window is splattered with more blood and tufts of blond hair, and the ghosts are gone.

The three look at each other across the mess, faces speckled red, pants soaked with soup.

"She ate all my plates," Yifei whispers.

"She ate your roommate!" Harvey says. "Isn't that the bigger problem?" Then he folds forward onto the table, groaning. "I'm gonna pass out."

"Then get on the floor, I'm not catching you," Yifei says, but her voice is oddly quiet. She stares at the empty table with wide eyes, hands folded in her lap.

Cora slowly becomes aware of the sticky sensation of someone else's blood on her face, gumming her hair together, rolling down her neck under her shirt. But her whole body feels like an echo, her mind like TV static. She replays the sound of Ryan's neck snapping, of Paisley's muffled screams from inside the cavern of Delilah's throat. Cora's hands twitch. She licks her lips by accident and tastes Paisley's blood, spits on the floor and gets dizzy when she sees the pattern of the kitchen tiles, the reflective pool of blood.

The shadows on the wall feel quieter, a soft, flat gray. These past few weeks, shadows have been making Cora's skin itch like her bones want to escape, her prey sense choking her heartbeat in her throat. But now, in the silent aftermath, Cora doesn't sense Delilah anymore.

"I think it worked," Cora whispers.

Cora knows it's supposed to be a good thing, that Delilah isn't suffering anymore. But now Cora is the only one left suffering, and somehow that doesn't feel like a victory.

"Okay, so that's one problem solved," Harvey says, peeling his face from the table, "and two more—arguably bigger—problems created."

He looks between Cora and Yifei like they'll have the answers, but when neither of them speak, he covers his face with his hands. "I just wanted dinner!" he says. "What the fuck are we supposed to do now? Who's going to believe this isn't our fault?"

"No one," Yifei whispers, still pale and unmoving, staring into the vortex of the kitchen table. She blinks hard, clenches her fists as if pulling herself back to reality. "No one, that's why we can't tell anyone."

Cora tears her gaze from the floor, turns to Yifei. "You want to hide this?" she says, needing Yifei to say it out loud.

She nods. "Harvey, you have the keys to your uncle's place, right?"

"Yeah," Harvey says. "But—"

"So we're gonna need a few gallons of Blood Buster and some biohazard bags."

"Liu, I can't go to jail," Harvey says. "My uncle's not even here legally—"

"There are no bodies," Yifei says. "No one can even prove they're dead. We have no motive. All that's left is a crime scene, and we scrub those all the time."

Harvey takes a steadying breath, holds it, then nods. He wants to believe Yifei. "What could we even do, tell the cops a ghost ate them? We have to clean it up, we have no choice. No one will know." His words are quiet, mostly to himself. He swallows, then turns to Cora. "No one will know," he says, louder this time.

Cora's skin tingles, heartbeat punching her ribs. She never would have fed Delilah humans intentionally, and while she disliked Ryan and Paisley, she never meant for them to die.

But Harvey is right. Telling the police about it is a quick way to make sure all three of them end up in an asylum at best, or on trial for a double homicide at worst. The guilt can come later. For now, they need to make this crime scene disappear. Luckily, they're very good at cleaning.

"No one will know," Yifei says, nodding, turning to Cora.

"No one will know," Cora repeats, a promise.

The Return

On the last day of the seventh month, a door begins to close.

The dead cannot see their way back home, so they follow the lanterns down the river. The names of the dead are painted on the lanterns' paper skins, and the lost souls chase its light like children after fireflies as they wander back through the gates of hell.

When the last lantern is extinguished, the gates swing closed once more, and will not open until next year. No hands can pry the gate open. If you knock, no one will answer.

Auntie Z

NINETEEN

Cora wakes to darkness. She's done that more nights than not in the past week, something in her dreams whispering, *Open your eyes*, forcing her to claw her way up from sleep. She stares at the beige ceiling of her apartment cast gray in shadows, tiny oblong circles of light that pierce through the curtains cast on the ceiling.

Cora came down with COVID a few days after the dinner at Yifei's apartment, then so did Harvey and Yifei, who firmly blamed Paisley as if she hadn't already paid ten times over.

For the past five days, Cora sweat through her sheets and watched her ceiling in a haze, her body burning, breaths scraping in and out of her throat, chest crushed into her stiff mattress. She showers once, sitting down, slumped against the wall while cold water rains over her, but the fever scrubs away all her compulsions and she turns to hot butter, unable to care about anything but breathing. Briefly, she wonders if she's going to die and finds that she cares less and less by the hour but needs to know someone will find her body.

She texts Yifei to come find her if she doesn't text back within twenty-four hours, and Yifei promptly responds, *I couldn't leave my bed even if my apartment was on fire, tell someone else to find your corpse.* Followed quickly by: *That was a joke, you're not gonna die, dumbass.* Followed once more by: *But please call 911 if you actually think you might.*

But Yifei cannot know if Cora will die. Delilah didn't know she was going to die. It's not something people know ahead of time, for the most part. Yet Cora feels like she's tightrope-walking on the edge of *something*, especially when her breath comes tight and she sees shapes of light dancing in the corners of her eyes.

It becomes easy to pretend that the feast was the beginning of a fever dream.

Cora can imagine they never scrubbed the blood from Yifei's walls, never bleached her floors and threw out the shattered wall art and shoved couch cushions into biohazard bags, never practiced reciting the events of an evening that had nothing to do with Paisley and Ryan at all, bleaching their memories away the same as the blood—they never existed. That is the one mercy of sickness: Cora cannot bring herself to worry about being arrested when she's too busy worrying about breathing.

Cora and Yifei are thoroughly steamrolled by COVID, yet Harvey escapes with nothing but a stiff cough and has spent the last week playing video games and eating Doritos and whining about how his uncle wants him to go back to work, but he'd sooner die than clean up a crime scene all alone. He's keeping all of Officer Wang's papers at his house on the off chance that the police end up searching Yifei's apartment, and he's been going over them with a fevered intensity that Cora can't summon the energy for in her current state, even though it's *her* sister.

Harvey says he's been researching each of the men in the case files, digging up their public records, calling their past employers with a fake name. Cora wants to tell him that this isn't an episode of *Law & Order*, remind him that the last person who asked too many questions got machine-gunned down, that he needs to be careful. But words are hard to come by and Cora exists in a daze, unable to move much at all, her energy consumed by breathing. She knows that she should be the one researching, that Harvey is doing this for her, but there is no room in her mind for shame, for anything.

There's something peaceful about your worst fear coming true. Cora had hidden from the virus for the last half of a year, the fear of it chained to her at all times, the feeling of needing to cry but not being able to always lodged in her throat, choking her. Now that it's here, Cora can live through it one minute at a time. It's no longer the faceless entity of her nightmares. It's been defanged, as her therapist would say, because the not knowing and guessing is always worse than the knowing. And even when Cora thinks she's going to die, it's not as bad as the fear that came before, the fear that might have killed her anyway.

Through the worst of it, she swears someone is knocking on her door. It's rhythmic, like a heartbeat, not the way normal people knock. But no one visits Cora, especially not in the middle of the night, and when she unpeels herself from the sticky surface of sleep, the sound is always gone.

She texts Harvey to please find her corpse because Yifei won't and he texts back, *lol, want me to send you a pizza or something?*

As the days bleed together, Cora leaves her lights off at all times, as if daring Delilah to appear.

Show me, Cora thinks, in the deepest, quietest parts of night, when the fever makes her want to run, to strip off all her sheets and then her skin. *Show me that you're still here. I don't care how ugly you are now. I don't care what you've done. Just be here, however you are.*

But the darkness is just darkness now, and Delilah is gone.

When the fever breaks on the fifth day, Cora feels reborn. Her legs shake, but she drags herself to the shower anyway, strips her sheets, sweeps her floor, throws out the produce she hasn't been able to eat, has to sit down on the floor next to the fridge, head pressed against it, feeling electric whirring in her skull.

She decides that she is done being sick, but the CDC says she has to quarantine for ten days, so she orders groceries online and scrubs the dust from every surface, falls asleep halfway through. Her lungs feel full of tinfoil, crackling as she breathes, sharp on the exhale. But she can stand, she can shower, she can eat—she is fine. She has survived her worst fear, and there is a sad kind of confidence that comes from it, which she hopes will endure.

The last five days of quarantine count down, and her lungs unfold like flowers and the only thing that remains is the knocking in her dreams.

Yet, on the last day, she opens her eyes and the knocking is still there.

She jolts up in bed and waits, fingernails curling sharp into her palm, the pain grounding her. Yes, she's definitely awake.

Three knocks. Pause. Two knocks. Pause. Five knocks.

Cora slips out of bed, slides her feet into her slippers, moves silently across her apartment. She jolts back at the jagged shadow that her English ivy casts on the wall, large in the afternoon light. Her door is still double-bolted shut, yet somehow it feels like no protection at all against the rest of the world.

Three knocks again, and Cora stills as if she's been caught doing something wrong, as if the peephole in her door is an eye, watching her. The Instacart shopper is the only person who could maybe be knocking on her door, but the groceries aren't scheduled to come until nighttime. Yifei and Harvey are both quarantined and definitely shouldn't be at her apartment door. She's paid her rent on time and hasn't made any noise, so her landlord shouldn't be bothering her.

Maybe she heard someone knocking on her neighbors' doors in her dreams, and now the knocking on her door is just a coincidence.

Or maybe someone has been trying to get inside for the past ten days.

Delilah, she thinks, even though Delilah does not need doors, she knows this, but the thought carries her across her room as she gently presses her face against the door, lays her eye against the peephole.

The wide white walls of the hallway stare back at her. No one is there.

Her phone vibrates on the coffee table and she jolts back. It keeps buzzing and Cora sighs, crossing the room and picking up Harvey's call.

"Yo, can you come over?" he says.

Cora glances at the clock. It's day ten of quarantine, but she isn't sure when she's officially allowed outside. At midnight? At noon?

"I have a grocery delivery tonight," she says. "And I don't know if I can—"

"Cora, I think I know who Batman is."

Cora's whole body goes cold. Something stirs in her, something she hasn't felt since before she got sick. She grabs on to it, that kindling rage.

"Who?" she says.

"It's…a lot," Harvey says. "It's hard to explain. Come over and I'll show you. I already called Yifei. Text me when you're here and I'll unlock the shop for you."

Cora remembers that Harvey lives above his uncle's dry

cleaner. She has never actually visited Harvey's apartment, has only ever been to the dry cleaner on the day she interviewed for the job.

It feels foreign to put on shoes and tie them up, then throw on a jacket, pack a bag, grab her keys. For a hazy week her entire world has been her apartment. She puts on her masks and peers into the hallway, half expecting someone to be there waiting for her, hand poised, ready to knock. But the hallway is empty.

It's raining, and all at once Cora wants to go back into her apartment. She'd forgotten that there was a world beyond her home, loud and dirty. She's fairly certain she can't catch COVID again so soon, but that doesn't take the edge off the city's blaring horns and murky rainwater and greasy handrails. She boards the train, mind scraped raw, and considers that she might not want to know what Harvey has to say.

Giving the White Spider a face will defang him, Cora knows this.

But maybe she wants this monster to have teeth, wants it to be some intangible, hungry darkness that can swallow all her rage like a black hole. She doesn't want him to have a name, a job, a wife that he holds with the same hands he uses to gut Asian girls like fish. The thought sickens her, the idea that the kind of person who carves people like her open could smile at other people. That he could be loved by other people. Because what does that make Delilah and Yuxi and Zihan and Ai and Officer Wang? Subhuman, bat eaters, garbage to be taken out, people who don't deserve his humanness. Cora wants him to be a formless ephemeral ball of pure evil, but she knows that he's not. And she doesn't care about his redeeming traits but she knows that other people will, that the newspapers will highlight his accomplishments, that the courts will talk about him being a good father or diligent worker or a thousand other things he did that matter infinitely less than what he took from Cora.

And Cora doesn't know what she'll do when she knows his name, when she's seen his face.

Maybe Harvey will report it to the police, and the decision will be mercifully taken away from her. But maybe Harvey won't want to admit to all the dubiously legal digging he's been doing, maybe he'll drop an anonymous tip that gets ignored, or maybe the police will listen but there won't be enough evidence, and Cora will think about Delilah's shriveled face and know every day that Delilah had one last request and Cora was too scared to do anything about it.

She doesn't know what Delilah wants from her now.

Delilah never seemed the vengeful type. She drifted around life like she was riding a pool float, bumping into obstacles that gently nudged her to a new path but never overturned her into the water. There was nothing to be that angry about when you were Delilah Zeng.

Or maybe she just never showed Cora her anger.

There are many things Cora never showed Delilah either. She never told Delilah about the way she *knows* things, about the thoughts that leech onto her skin and drink her dry. So maybe there were worlds inside Delilah that Cora never saw, will never see.

The train doors open and Cora realizes, for the first time, that she never stopped to think about what *she* wants.

Because Delilah is dead and gone, she has no say in any of this anymore. Cora holds all the cards.

She walks up the wet stairs, out into the rain. Each step brings her closer to the answer Delilah wanted her to see, and each step she wants to know less and less. As long as Cora doesn't know, she can keep all the fear and rage trapped inside the cage of her heart, doesn't have to decide what to do with it. Because when it's gone, the last piece of Delilah will be gone too.

Yifei is already there when Cora arrives at the dry cleaner, frowning at the entrance. Her jawline looks sharper, her face a yellowish white, and the shadows darker under her eyes. With her hair wet and thin from the rain, she looks like a dungeon prisoner who only barely escaped.

"You look like shit," Yifei says. "Feeling better?"

"I'm fine," Cora says.

"Well, I'm not," Yifei says, turning and coughing into her elbow, deep and sharp, like something is trying to claw its way out of her. "I tested negative but this cough won't go away, and now Harvey is making me stand out in the rain."

Cora turns to the dry cleaner, the faded CLOSED sign in the doorway.

"You texted him?"

"I called him twice," Yifei says, already calling him again, scowling.

And that's when Cora *knows*, in the way she sometimes knows things she shouldn't, that something is very wrong.

"We have to get inside," Cora says, turning down the back alley.

"That's what I'm trying to do," Yifei says, coughing and hurrying after her.

Cora turns the handle to the side door and it isn't even locked. Cora expected resistance, so she falls halfway into the hall as the door swings open. She doesn't know how to get up to Harvey's apartment from here, only vaguely remembers the front door leading into the dry cleaner. She enters a dim hallway with a series of off-white doors, most of them locked and one of them a storage closet.

Cora's hands are pouring sweat. Her knees shake and maybe she isn't as recovered as she thought because she reaches for a doorknob but it slides past her fingers like silk and she hasn't really reached for it at all, has only brushed her hand against air.

"Are you okay?" Yifei says.

Cora reaches the last door at the end of the hallway. The doorknob is loose in her hand and the door pops open.

Something crashes against Cora and she hears a high ringing, a sound she's heard before but can't remember where, something sharp scraping across her cheek. Yifei screams and Cora swats a hand at her face and brushes against something soft and burning hot, falling to the floor.

A bat launches off Cora and crashes into the ceiling, spinning, one wing crooked, slamming against walls as it breaks for the open door and sails out into the street. Cora's face feels hot and she realizes she probably needs a tetanus shot or something after being scratched by a wild bat, but the thought sinks like a stone in a pond as she pulls herself back up and enters the dry cleaner.

She's entered from the back, a maze of plastic bags on hooks, the stinging scent of chemicals. Far away she hears the *thump thump thump* of the cleaning cylinder tossing clothes around, a steady heartbeat.

"Harvey?" Cora says, brushing aside coats. She hears Yifei enter behind her, coughing harder at the scent of chemicals. Cora leaves her, pressing deeper past the slick plastic, ducking under the hooks, carving her way through the darkness. She pulls out her phone, taps the flashlight on, and crouches down. Sweat rolls into her eyes, and she's unsure if she can even stand back up. She sweeps the light across the floor, but there are no bloodstains, no fallen bodies, no Harvey.

"Maybe he's upstairs?" Yifei says, moving to a door that says STAFF ONLY and finding the handle locked. She swears and tries calling Harvey again, and this time they both freeze at the sound of a ringtone somewhere distant. It comes out warped, as if his phone is broken.

They drift toward the sound, to the back of the dry cleaner, brushing the garments out of their path. The *thump thump thump* of the washing machines grows louder and Cora draws to a stop, Yifei bumping into her.

"What is it?" Yifei says sharply.

Cora swallows, wipes the sweat of her palms onto her pants. "It's after seven," she says quietly.

"Yeah?" Yifei says, swallowing to hold back another cough.

"They're closed," Cora says. "The lights are off."

"Yeah, I gathered that," Yifei says.

Cora tugs at a loose thread at the end of her sleeves. The heavy *thump thump thump* of the washing machines is now a pounding ache behind her eyes, air suddenly thin, her throat feeling needle-thin.

"So why are the washing cylinders running?" she says.

Yifei opens her mouth to respond, closes it. Her face goes slack, a grayness settling over her eyes. She pushes past Cora, shoving through the plastic bags, racing across the room.

"Yifei—"

But Yifei sucks in a sharp breath. Cora can't see what she's found, but she draws closer as she hears Yifei sink to the ground, a muffled sound like she's cupped a hand over her mouth.

The industrial washing cylinder is a great beast of a machine, twice as tall as Cora. It churns through suds that slosh against a tiny round window. Cora steps closer, shines her flashlight on the small portal.

The water is bright red.

It splashes against the window again and again and Cora realizes all at once that clothing should not make such a heavy *thump thump thumping* sound inside the machine. The water draws back as the machine churns, and the next thing that presses against the glass is not soap or blood or water, but the side of Harvey's face.

TWENTY

Yifei grabs the handle on the machine, pulls against it with all her weight, but it won't budge.

Cora grabs her arm, pulling her back. "Yifei—"

"Fuck off!" Yifei says, wrenching her arm back. But Cora is good at latching on to things, and Yifei only succeeds in dragging Cora to the ground, both of them crashing to the tiles. "We have to get Harvey out of there! What are you doing?"

"He's dead," Cora says. She knows, has known since she entered the room, that this was what they would find.

"He's drowning!"

"Yifei, it's not water in there, it's perc!" Cora says. This was one of the things she'd researched before applying to work at the dry cleaner. She'd been morbidly drawn to the powerful solvent, fantastic at stripping stains but even better at tearing through kidneys and livers, causing cancer, burning skin off. Cora never thought she'd actually put it on her skin, but she'd wanted to be close to it, smell its sharpness, appreciate its stark cleanliness.

Not anymore.

"It's poison," Cora said. "The machines won't just unlock and let you splash it all over the floor. You could probably pull the power but it would still need to be drained before the doors would open. And Harvey..." Cora shakes her head. "You can't just swim around in perc and live."

It's almost startlingly easy to rattle off the facts, to tell Yifei about chemicals instead of acknowledging what's in front of them. Cora thinks of Harvey sleeping on her floor, the strange familiarity of his breathing, imagining a life where both of them hadn't been broken before they met. She thinks of him catching her as she jumped onto the train tracks, her hands on his shoulders, and she has to close her eyes, turn away from the machine, can't comprehend that that person is gone. He'd done so much for her, because of her, and this is where it led him.

Yifei's face crumples and she hangs her head. She starts coughing and can't stop, throwing up on the floor. Cora sits beside her and doesn't move, staring at the washing cylinder, the hazy red foam. When she was little, she liked to watch her clothes spin in the machine, could have sat there and watched it all day.

Objectively, Cora thought watching someone she cares about die would be easier the second time.

But it feels exactly the same. This is the hot bath of blood over her face in the train station, the coldness that sinks all the way down to her bones, a lost sound trying to force its way up her throat, a dying animal's last cry. But now, Cora knows she's not dying. Dying doesn't hurt this much. Dying means there's an endpoint to the pain.

She might not be alive for much longer anyway. Because if whoever killed Harvey knew enough about him to have wanted to stop him, he probably knows where Harvey got his case files from. *Who* he got them from.

Cora is struck with the sudden urge to run, violent and primal, a deer who senses a whisper of a predator shuffling through distant tall grass.

But Yifei is still crying on the floor, and Cora can't just leave her here.

Yifei shivers, spits on the floor. "Harvey's a fucking idiot," she says. "He asks too many damn questions. I told him. *I told him*—"

"Yifei, I want to go," Cora says. Because this is all too close to Cora now, and it has been for ages. It was too close when someone on Cora's floor died. It was too close when someone was knocking on her door. Now Harvey is dead and there's a good chance that whoever did this knows her name. "I don't think we should be here."

"But…" Yifei jerks a trembling hand at the washing machine. "We can't just leave him until his uncle comes in on Monday."

"I don't want to call the cops," Cora says.

"I know, but—"

"If you call the cops, I'm leaving," Cora says, her voice rising, and she takes a breath to force it back down. Because Cora knows what happens when you see someone die and call the cops. They keep you there for hours, hours that she and Yifei really can't spare if they want to get out of here before a killer catches up to them. And you try to leave and they throw around phrases like "impeding an investigation" and you know it's bullshit but you're so hardwired to be a people pleaser, to cooperate, to cower at men with loud voices and guns, that you sit there and drink water from a Styrofoam cup even though it never feels like enough. You cry and they push tissue boxes at you and say nice things but you know there's a camera in the room, and they ask all sorts of *why didn't you* questions and you don't know the answers and they finally let you go after wringing you out, no water left in your body, no money to get home, all alone and made of tissue paper.

"Okay," Yifei says slowly. "What do you want to do?"

Cora presses her lips together, scans the machine for an off switch. She doesn't find it, but she does find a fire alarm panel in the wall. She yanks it down and the room bursts into red light, a thousand bells ringing overhead.

"That should bring the cops eventually, if no one shuts it off," Cora says, offering Yifei a hand. Yifei casts one last glance at the washing machine, which is more than Cora can do, then takes Cora's hand, lets herself be pulled outside.

Except now Cora doesn't know where to go.

She hesitates in the alleyway, begs Delilah to appear. She wants to reach her hand into the shadows and let Delilah pull the two of them somewhere. *Please*, she thinks. *Please, I need you*. But no one answers.

"We should get as far from here as we can," Cora says, because this sounds reasonable, and Yifei nods. "I have an aunt who lives in Staten Island in a building with cameras and stuff. We should go there."

Yifei sniffs, wipes her eyes, and nods. "Okay, yeah, let's do that. Do you have a gun?"

"Why would I have a gun?" Cora says.

"Don't most Americans have guns?"

"Not in Manhattan," Cora says.

"Can you get one fast?"

"Me?"

"Cora, I'm not American, I don't have the paperwork," Yifei says.

Cora lets out a sharp laugh. "I have paperwork explicitly stating that I can't buy a gun," she says. That's one of the many things that happens when you're involuntarily committed in New York. Cora had laughed when she first learned this, never imagining that she'd ever want a gun.

"Okay, okay," Yifei says, scrubbing her face with her sleeve. "Paisley's aunt gave her a car that she let me borrow sometimes. It's a piece of shit but it works. Let's go to my apartment, grab every knife I've got, and get the hell out of here?"

Now that they have a plan, it's easy for Cora to let the emotions pool in her feet and fingers like blood.

They hold each other up as they hurry into the subway. Everyone gives them dirty looks as Yifei coughs, but Cora holds her hand and for once it doesn't matter—she has bigger problems.

Cora worries that Yifei might actually faint before they make it to Paisley's car; she's so pale and Cora is all but holding her up. She hates the tight walls of the elevator in Yifei's apartment building but crams them both inside of it anyway because she doesn't think Yifei can take the stairs. Cora feels dizzy but is held upright by the singular goal of the car. Once they reach it, they can go anywhere. People don't get stabbed to death in moving cars.

The elevator doors open and they're stumbling into the hallway. Yifei is fumbling for her keys. She drops them twice until finally the right key *thunks* into the lock and the door swings in. Yifei falls inside onto her hands and knees while Cora slams the door shut behind them, bolting it.

She helps Yifei into a chair, grabs a mug to get her some water, but Yifei shakes her head and points with a trembling finger at her fridge. "Top shelf," she says, her throat raw. "Green bottle."

Cora fishes around for a moment until she pulls out a bottle of soju.

"Yeah, that one," Yifei says, reaching out for it.

Cora turns the bottle over in her hands. "You know I can't drive, right?" she says.

"I'm not a fucking lightweight like Harvey," Yifei says, scowling and gesturing for the bottle. She seems to realize what she said as soon as Cora passes her the bottle, her expression darkening. She twists off the cap, drinks half the bottle in one go.

Cora gets herself a glass of water in the first mug she can find, the tap water sloshing over her hands because they're shaking so hard. She drains the cup in one gulp, feels marginally more human once her throat isn't scraped dry.

She hasn't been back to Yifei's apartment since the night of the dinner, when they stripped it clean. The couch cushions are gone, the floor pale without the area rug they had to throw out, blinds torn down and folded into biohazard bags. Rain beats against the bare windows, gray light streaming in. It looks like no one lives here anymore.

Cora takes a steadying breath, turns to Yifei's knife block, starts filling her backpack with every sharp utensil she can find.

"I think there's another bottle in the fridge," Yifei says, her voice steadier now.

"I think you should have some water," Cora says, pawing through the silverware drawer, contemplating the sharpness of a meat tenderizer.

"Fucking hell, Cora," Yifei says, rubbing her face with her hand. "Spare me the church girl moralizing. I think today of all days I deserve a drink."

"Yifei, we need to go, not sit here and drink," Cora says, turning around. Fear is a flame prickling under her fingertips, not letting her stay still. How can Yifei not see that?

Yifei sighs, rises unsteadily to her feet, shoulders past Cora and starts digging through the fridge herself. "Where the fuck is it?" she says. "I'm sure I had two. It's not like I was drinking while dying of fucking COVID last week."

Cora goes very still, crammed against the corner of the kitchen counter behind the fridge door. Yifei is probably just misremembering, but something about missing food makes Cora break out in a sweat. It feels like reality is flaking apart.

Cora slides out from behind the fridge door, goes to the table by the entrance to look for Paisley's car keys, hoping that will get Yifei moving, but her hand freezes before she can touch the bowl of keys.

There are dirty footprints on the floor.

Cora lines her own foot up to it even though she's fairly certain they're not hers, and sure enough, the shoe is much bigger than Cora's, which means it's much bigger than Yifei's because Cora has her mom's big American feet. It can't be Harvey's, because they cleaned the apartment so thoroughly that night, even went over it with a UV light to be sure. The footsteps lead directly to the fridge, then taper off into a faint whisper of dirt somewhere in the living room. Cora might have noticed it when they first came in if it wasn't so dark, if Yifei hadn't fallen over in the entryway.

"Yifei," Cora says quietly. When Yifei keeps shoving bottles aside, she says it louder. "*Yifei*, has anyone been over here?"

"Who the fuck would come over when I had COVID?" Yifei says.

Something *thumps* inside the coat closet.

Cora cannot move, her hand suspended an inch from the bowl of keys. Whoever knew where Harvey lived probably knows where Yifei lives as well.

Cora thinks of a thousand ways the man will kill them both inside this apartment. Chopped apart by all the knives in Cora's backpack. Heads smashed in with picture frames, curb-stomped against the kitchen counter, faces held underwater in the bathtub. Cora has seen it all, cleaned up after all of those deaths before. Now it's her turn.

And she cannot call out for Yifei, or open the front door. Because as soon as she tries to leave, whoever is in the coat closet will come out. Cora knows she isn't strong enough to hold it shut. Calling the cops would definitely bring out whoever is inside, and even if Cora manages to give the police their location, they'll both be dead before help arrives.

"Yifei," Cora says, more of a whimper than a word. She clears her throat, heartbeat pulsing through her entire body, nausea dangerously close to her throat. She takes a deep breath. *"Yifei,"* she says, and this time she says her name in Mandarin—tries to, at least—not the toneless American inflection that she normally uses.

The clinking of bottles stops. Yifei pokes her head out above the fridge door, frowning.

Cora swallows, flounders for words she can say easily. "Please be quiet," she says in Mandarin, which isn't exactly the same as *don't panic*, but she can't remember how to say that. "I think there's someone in the closet."

Yifei blinks at her for a moment, then slowly closes the fridge.

"Are you sure?" she says in Mandarin.

Cora nods.

Yifei takes a deep breath, glances toward her window as if calculating whether she can survive the fall. "You have the car keys?" she says.

Cora glances down at the bowl, but there's only house keys and key chains, nothing that looks like it would unlock a car. "No."

"Fuck," Yifei says in English, turning her gaze to the coat closet, and Cora knows exactly where the car keys must be. Yifei grips the edge of the counter as if holding herself up.

"Okay," she says, switching back to Mandarin. "Subway it is, then. Make a run for it on three?"

Cora exhales, gripping her backpack straps. She half expected Yifei to smash her soju bottle on the edge of the sink and use it to try to gouge out the man's eyes and avenge Harvey. But she must know, just like Cora, that a man who can axe a woman to death is not the kind of person you want to fight if you don't have to.

Cora holds her breath as Yifei slowly holds up one finger, then two fingers. Cora turns her gaze to the door, only a few steps away. Can Yifei even run that fast? What if Cora makes it out the door but Yifei doesn't? Will she have to stab someone, *kill* someone, to help her? Or will she just keep running like a coward?

Before she can decide, the closet door opens.

A bat shoots out in a flurry of scarves and gloves, crashing into the opposite wall, heading straight for the windows and smashing into the glass. It lands on the windowsill and claws at the outside world a few more times before disappearing somewhere under what's left of the couch.

Cora jerks her gaze back to the coat closet, where the door is now hanging open.

It's empty. Nothing but winter coats and boots inside.

Cora should be relieved; her heartbeat should slow down now. But the murderer has clearly been here, looking for Yifei. It's only luck that she wasn't home when he came. Cora would bet anything that he's been to her apartment too.

"Jesus," Yifei says, storming into the coat closet, jamming her hands into a few coat pockets before she pulls out a set of car keys. "Let's get the fuck out of here."

They run through the lobby, down a side street to where Paisley's car is parked. They throw open the doors, slam them shut so hard the whole car quakes. Yifei locks the doors while Cora checks the back seat—she's seen videos of men strangling women with cables by hiding in the back. But no one has infiltrated Yifei's car, and once the doors lock, Cora allows herself to take a deep breath.

The car takes a moment too long to start up, and Yifei swears once it does.

"I need gas," she says. "You have any money?"

Cora feels her wallet just to be sure. "Yeah, let's just get out of here, get as far away as we can first."

Yifei peels out into the street while Cora pulls up directions. Yifei drives timidly, like every sudden movement is the end of the world, slamming on her brakes and making Cora nauseous, though the last thing she wants to do is criticize Yifei and make her even more nervous. Cora waits for her heartbeat to slow the farther they get from Chinatown, but it never does. Maybe COVID has permanently damaged her heart and it will just keep beating faster and faster until it bursts.

They make it over the bridge, onto 278, have just gotten off the expressway when Yifei says, "I think we're being followed."

"We're not," Cora says, unwilling to look around. They can't be. Cora cannot be in a car chase. She can barely stand to be in a car that drives normally without worrying about crashing.

"I… Okay, they turned, it's okay, it's okay."

Yifei takes the next exit but slows down too much and a car honks at her. She screams, swerving into the other lane. Cora grabs the wheel and jerks it straight, yelling at Yifei to *Pull over, pull over right now*, until Yifei manages to take the wheel back and pull off onto a quiet road while the other car sails by, middle finger out the window.

Yifei bursts into tears.

"Okay," Cora says, wiping the sweat of her palms onto her pants. Cora wants to offer to drive but she doesn't have a fucking license, never learned to drive because she was too much of a nervous wreck in high school to even ride a bike much less operate machinery and who needs a car in New York City?

They're out in the suburbs now, with houses spaced luxuriously far apart, pulled over next to a pile of dirt at a new dig. Another car rolls by and Yifei shields her face with her hands, trembling and hiding from its light.

Cora has never seen Yifei this undone. Cora is supposed to be the one who falls apart. She's very good at it. But she's so stupidly convinced that once she makes it to Auntie Lois, everything will be fine. All she has to do is drive there and her aunt will tell her what to do, how to handle this. White women are good at handling crimes, right? They call the cops, who listen to them. They get the bad guys thrown in jail. The cops will protect someone who looks like Auntie Lois, who lives in the kind of house she lives in.

All at once, Yifei stops crying.

"Yifei?" Cora says quietly, scared of the sudden stillness on her face.

Yifei shakes her head slowly. Another car rolls by, headlights brightening the tears on her face. "That's not my name," she says.

"I… What?"

"It's not my real name," she says, turning to Cora, eyes fever bright.

"Okay," Cora says. "Why are you telling me this now?"

"Harvey asked," she says. "Do you remember? When we were drinking on the train tracks and I said I needed to drink more before I'd tell you about my family. I would have told him eventually. I would have told *you* eventually. I worry that if I don't tell you now, no one will ever know. I've never told anyone else."

"You can tell me later," Cora says. "We're going to my aunt's place." Doesn't Yifei think they're going to make it there? She has to believe they will. Cora can't be the only one who believes. Because if Cora Zeng is the only one who believes in something, it's not real.

Yifei shakes her head. "My name—"

"Yifei, we have to—"

"I never had a name!" she says, louder this time, and Cora closes her mouth and sits back, knows that she has to hear this. "Liu Yifei is an actress I saw in a TV show when I was a kid. We already had the same last name, so I took her first name too because I didn't have my own. No one ever gave me one."

Cora stares, not recognizing this version of Yifei, but she won't look back at her. She's staring at her own warped reflection in the glass. "How can you not have a name?" Cora says at last.

Yifei sniffs, wiping her nose on her sleeve. "You know the one-child policy in China? When you're dirt poor, like my parents, and you can only have one kid, you want a boy. Sons take care of their parents when they're old. Sons can work the fields. When I came out as a girl, they didn't even give me a name. They just called me *girl*. My mom got pregnant a few times, but kept losing the baby. And I was always terrified of what would happen to me if their next baby was a son. They couldn't keep two of us or they'd get fined, so they'd get rid of one kid, and I always knew it would be me." She swallows, and the headlights of a passing car illuminate her papery complexion. "But my mom had another girl. What were they supposed to do then? No one wants to get fined for having two girls. I saw my dad take the baby and bring her down to the river. I knew what was happening, but I was just a fucking kid, Cora, what was I supposed to do? But something went wrong. I don't know if he got caught or what, but he came back with my uncle and the baby was still there, soaking wet. She was crying, but it wasn't the way she cried before. It was all wet, this strange sound, and it echoed like she was inside a seashell. He told my mom, *It didn't work*, and they put my sister down in a box. She cried all night and I couldn't sleep. They decided to just keep her a secret. She was always shut in this tiny closet, and I'd pass her grains of rice under the door. Sometimes all I saw for weeks was her tiny fingers reaching out from underneath the door. They only let her out at night, so she had such white skin, I could see all her veins through it. When she got older, I started to realize that my dad half-drowning her had done something to her. She didn't talk at all. But sometimes she opened her mouth and I could hear the river, like she was a conch shell held up to my ear. Her eyes were gray, and sometimes when I looked at them for too long, I felt like I was drowning too. I couldn't breathe at all. I was scared of her, Cora. And I know that makes me terrible, I know it wasn't her fault. But at night I heard her fingers scraping under my door like little spiders and I hated it.

"When I was ten, I came home from the market and put down all the bamboo and my parents weren't there. Neither was my sister. I checked every room, then walked around the backyard. My parents were floating in the river, face down. My mom's skirts were all spread out, and when my dad hit a rock and rolled over, his face was all swollen. And I hated my parents, Cora, I really did, but I was a kid. They were all I had. And my sister was just standing there, watching them like they were just ducks bobbing along, like it didn't matter that we'd have to go to an orphanage now, that the house I'd grown up in wasn't ours anymore. Her dress was all wet, and I knew she did it. I *knew.* Then she looked at me and her jaw hung open and I could hear the river and it was *so loud.* I'd never seen her outside in daylight before. Her skin was so bright, she didn't even look real, like she was already dead.

"Then she started running toward me.

"I ran back into the house, but I had no idea she was so fast. She grabbed my ankle and started dragging me, and at first I thought she was going to drown me too, but then I saw she was dragging me toward her closet. She would have left me there forever, Cora, I know she would have. I grabbed her hair—it was so long, my mom never cut it for her. I pulled it and I wrestled her down and I shoved her back in the closet and locked it, then pushed all the furniture I could find in front of it while she screamed and pounded on the door. She was still screaming when I grabbed the only money my parents had and ran away to the city. I left her there, Cora. Like a fucking coward, I told myself she deserved it, but I couldn't finish the job because even back then I knew I was wrong. And it's easy to say I was just a kid, I did the best I could, I was scared and abused and traumatized, and maybe for some people that's true. But I'm not a kid anymore, and I know I'm a terrible person because I don't regret it. I don't regret it because the only other option was that I would be the one in the closet. I'm so fucking scared of dying, Cora. I'm the kind of person who runs and lets other people die for her, and it doesn't matter how much they mean to me. It's not even like my life is worth all that much. I'm alone, I have no family, no friends, so it's not like I'd be losing that much if I died. But the idea of never waking up again scares me so fucking much. I don't even like going to sleep because I hate not being fully there in my dreams—I'm afraid I'll never resurface. I want to be here for you, Cora, but I almost pissed myself when we saw Harvey and I need you to know that if they come for you, I can't save you. I fucking love you, Cora, but I would still run away and let you die, and nothing in the world makes me sorrier than that. I don't care about anything else, just that you can forgive me for that."

Cora doesn't know what to say. Yifei had always alluded to being haunted by something, but Cora had never imagined this. Yifei is not supposed to be a scared little girl running away from a farm; she's supposed to be the tough one, the one who will get both of them out of this alive, because Cora can't do it. She's proven again and again that she can't.

"You're not going to die," Cora says, because she doesn't know what else to say.

Yifei shakes her head, lets out another sob. "Don't lie to me, Cora. Not after everything I just told you. Don't you fucking dare."

"We just need gas," Cora says, scratching at her arms. "Or if you can't drive anymore, we can call an Uber? Worst-case scenario, we can call my aunt. She'll be pissed but I'll just talk about repenting to God and she'll come, I know she will—"

"Cora!" Yifei says, gripping the steering wheel. "This asshole knows who we are! He knows where we live! *He drowned Harvey in a fucking washing machine!* You think he doesn't know where your aunt lives too?"

"I..." Cora trails off, voice wobbling. "I don't know where else to go," she says. "I don't know. Delilah would—"

"Delilah isn't exactly my go-to authority on how to not fucking die, Cora."

Cora swallows her next words, clutching her seat belt like a lifeline. She wants her hand sanitizer but the plastic holder snapped off her bag at some point. Her hands feel grimy, gummy with blood from her own arms, skin under her nails. She wipes the window with one hand, gathering the condensation and spreading it between her palms to break up the gumminess, and in a normal world she would never do something like this in front of someone else, but what does it matter now?

Yifei watches her, lips pressed together. "That's all you're going to do?" she says. "Clean your hands?"

"I'm thinking," Cora says, not looking at Yifei. It's only half-true, because her mind feels empty except for the sticky sensation on her palms, between her fingers.

"Jesus," Yifei says. She takes a steadying breath, then starts the car and pulls back onto the road, jerky and sharp. "Do I have to do everything?"

"I'm sorry," Cora says, even though she isn't sure what she's apologizing for, but she senses Yifei's disappointment. Cora knows she's not the best person to be stuck with when a serial killer comes after you, but it's not like Cora asked for this.

Yifei picks up speed, finally shedding her nervous twitchiness, racing down the roads. When she flies past a stop sign, Cora sinks deeper into her seat.

"Let's get gas," Cora says. "You're running on empty."

Yifei shakes her head. "We're getting out of here," she says. "We'll make it to your aunt's house. That's what you want, isn't it?"

"I don't think we'll make it without more gas," Cora says, and Yifei takes a left turn that throws Cora against the window. Her hands are wet, her cheek stinging from the cold glass. The streetlights are shooting stars racing by, bleeding tails of white light.

Cora wants to tell Yifei to slow down, but the words won't come. Cora knows that Yifei is no longer driving *to* somewhere, she's driving *away*, and she won't stop for anything, least of all Cora. If Cora is lucky, the car will run out of gas and roll to a stop somewhere close to her aunt's house and she'll have no choice but to call and have Auntie Lois pick them up.

But Cora Zeng is not lucky.

Yifei is driving too far over the dotted yellow line, the whole car thumping as the textured paint rumbles beneath them. They're zooming toward an underpass with low clearance and tight walls, and if Yifei doesn't correct, she's going to sideswipe an oncoming car.

"Yifei," Cora whispers, but in the end she's not sure if she ever says her name out loud or just thinks it.

Yifei corrects at the last second, as if snapping awake under the stark blast of headlights. The car leans on its horn, and the world explodes into a rush of black rain.

It thumps against every side of the car and the windshield is covered in a dense black blanket, chirping, scratching the glass, clawing. *Bats*, Cora realizes in the breathless second before Yifei crashes the car.

TWENTY-ONE

The car slams into *something*—Cora can't see through the panicked swarm of bats—and the car spins out. Cora's head hits the window and she can't peel her cheek from the glass, forced into it as the world reels. She catches glimpses of the underpass, tall trees, a flurry of bats, red eyes and white teeth.

Then the world tips and they're falling and Cora is crushed under a sudden blast of rubber that knocks her jaw off-center, a solid punch to the side of the face. Her stomach clenches as they flip over, the crunch of metal too loud in her ears, and the world slams back into its upright position.

Everything falls silent. The scent of rubber and blood knifes up Cora's nose, and something is tickling at her forehead. The headlights have gone out, so she can hardly see at all.

Cora swipes a hand into the dark and flinches back at the sharpness before she realizes that it's a tree branch, that a tree is now inside the car, stabbed through the shattered windshield. Something catches at her wrist and clatters down the side of the car door, her jade bracelet now in two pieces at her feet.

She feels around for Yifei, hands brushing the broken glass on her shoulders, the hot and slippery line of her throat.

"Yifei?" she whispers, and this time she's sure she says it out loud, even surer that Yifei doesn't answer. Cora feels around for her phone, pulls it out of her pocket, turns on the flashlight. She shines the light on Yifei and her hands go numb, phone falling to the floor as she sucks in a breath.

Yifei is crushed on her left side, pressed against the trunk of an oak tree. The car has folded around the tree, glass shattering to accommodate it, side airbag decimated. Yifei only has the right side of her face intact, the other half a slop of blood and shattered skull and eyeball jelly, jaw popped open, eye unseeing. Cora has seen so much brain matter at work, she recognizes the grayish pink mush oozing down the shattered windshield, crevices full of blood.

Cora's hands are reaching for the door before she even realizes it. She tries to jump out of the car, to get away, but the seat belt chokes her back. She slams her thumb on the button and finally it releases her, dumping her onto the grass where she curls up, halfway underneath the tilted car, and lets out a broken sound. Her fingers sink into the earth, soft with rain or tree sap or maybe even blood, and Cora tears up a handful, wishing she could dig a grave and bury herself, shove dirt into her eyes so she doesn't have to see this anymore, into her mouth so she can't breathe.

Everyone is gone, she thinks, the realization a violent tremor through her spine. Harvey and Yifei, who carried her home, who scoured the subway at night for her. She remembers Yifei feeding her dumplings, buying her food, texting her to make sure she was fine. They were never supposed to be her friends, but they didn't give Cora a choice.

You blast people to bits or hack them apart because you don't see them as human—you take away the shape of their body and then no one else can see them as human either, Yifei once said. But somehow, Harvey and Yifei feel more human now than ever before.

Harvey's body is a slurry of soap and blood, and Yifei is a crushed soda can, but those are not the images that sear into Cora's vision. The brightest, loudest memory is the two of them standing over Cora at Delilah's altar with their hands on her shoulders, when the spice in the air stung her eyes and Harvey was holding his mouth open for dumplings and Cora still had hope. A killer tried to unmake them, but he failed. Harvey and Yifei are still here.

Footsteps splash through the muck toward her and Cora hangs her head, breathes in the smell of dirt, folds herself down and tries to be small, even though there's no hiding now.

Cora is not so different from Yifei, she thinks. Because even when there's nothing left, when she's all alone and her life is worthless, she's so, so scared of dying.

The footsteps stop a few feet from her. A breeze rushes through the night but Cora doesn't feel cold at all anymore, bathed in the scalding splash of Yifei's blood over her left side. Yifei was right—someone was following them, after all.

"Go ahead," Cora whispers into the dirt. "There's nothing left to take from me."

Cora tenses up, ready for pain, but nothing happens. Cora does not want to see his face, but she can't help cracking her eyes open and catching a glimpse of tattered white sheets, bony feet.

Delilah.

Cora rushes to her feet. Her knees give out and she crawls the rest of the way. She wraps her arms around her sister's skeletal legs and sobs, fingers tangled up in her sheets. And it doesn't matter anymore that Delilah is dead, or what she looks like. She's *here.*

Delilah stands rigid and cold while Cora hugs her, legs sinking into the dirt. It's so like Delilah, who hated any emotion stronger than mild annoyance, who never hugged Cora but would scour Cora's face with a warm washcloth when she cried, slam a tall glass of water down in front of her and order her to drink the whole thing, and by the time Cora drained the glass, she wasn't crying anymore. Something about Delilah's stoicism always drained Cora dry, carved out all the sadness inside her and left nothing but a wind tunnel in place of her heart.

But this time, when the sadness soaks out of Cora and into the wet ground, there is something left inside her—it singes her ribs, forcing her fingers to clench around Delilah's sheet. She looks up until she's staring into Delilah's hollow eyes.

"Why are you here now?" Cora asks.

But Delilah doesn't answer. Of course she doesn't. Cora releases her legs, backs up.

"Why did you even bother coming at all?" she says, fingers clenching around sharp rocks and roots beneath the squishy entrails of the earth. "Everything is ruined. Everyone is dead. And you just hid in the shadows and *watched*?"

Cora tries to stand up, but the mud slips out from under her and she has to haul herself up onto the warped corpse of the car. Delilah's expression remains unchanged, eyes a spiraling chasm of black, and Cora doesn't know if she's truly unmoved or simply can't emote in death, but the cold response only enrages her more.

"I know you hated me just as much as I hated you," Cora says, arms trembling against what's left of the side mirror, holding her up. She will stand up when she tells Delilah this. She will look her in the eye. "I know you thought I was insane, that you thought all I could do was echo everything you did but quieter. I know you didn't want me to go to the same college as you, and that you only lived with me because you knew no one else would. I heard you talking to your friends, Delilah." Her voice cracks, and she remembers standing in the hallway while Delilah railed in Chinese to her friends about how awful Cora was, how she only let Cora stick around because their dad expected Delilah to look after her. Cora takes a steadying breath. "I knew exactly what you thought about me," she says. "I knew how much of a shitty person you were. Sometimes I hated you and hated myself even more because of you, but I still would have followed you anywhere, Delilah, because no matter how awful things got, I thought I'd survive because I'd always have you."

Tears run hot down Cora's face. She's shaking, maybe from the blood soaked through her clothes or the night breeze near the coast or what feels like an echo of fever still searing her blood. "You knew that, Delilah, I know you did," she says. "So how could you just go to China and leave me? How could you decide that for the both of us? *How can you keep leaving me when I need you? Did I matter to you at all?*"

The wind roars down the incline, ruffling Delilah's sheets, outlining the harsh grooves of her rib cage. Delilah takes a step closer, but Cora stays rooted in the mud. Delilah cannot hurt her now, she has already hurt her so much more than any kind of death.

She looms taller as she draws closer, and Cora remembers when she feared Delilah's ghostly face and spindly neck, but now all she feels is hate.

Delilah's grayed hand reaches forward, past Cora, into the car. She bends down, head disappearing inside the wreckage, before she stands up straight and moves to hand something to Cora.

Cora opens her palm without thinking, always trusting, even now.

Delilah sets Cora's phone in her hand.

She lets out a sharp laugh. "Who the hell am I supposed to call?" She taps the screen on her phone, but there's no service out here anyway.

Delilah shakes her head, the motion rocking her back and forth. She points up the muddy incline, at the road. Cora presses her mouth into a tight line.

Delilah wants her to keep walking.

Cora closes her eyes for a moment, not sure if she can even make it up the hill. But what choice does she have? Sit in the mud next to Yifei's corpse and wait for the killer to catch up to her?

So she pockets her phone, picks up her bag from the ground, then glances over her shoulder at Yifei and forces herself not to think of that last, terrible image of her. *I'll send someone for you*, she promises, and ascends the incline.

She slips down immediately, the slope wet as blood, but Cora digs her fingers into it, hauls herself up, fingers scratching against asphalt, pulling herself onto the shoulder of the road.

As she drags herself up, she comes face-to-face with Delilah's feet. She looks up, curses her under her breath, and rolls onto the road. Her lungs feel crushed, maybe from the car crash, maybe the lingering effects of COVID. Either way, her breath catches as she gets to her feet, shivering. There is a distant light farther down the road, and Cora shuffles toward it. She will call for help, she decides, once she's somewhere with light and people, where she can't get machine-gunned down in the dark.

Delilah stands in the distance, like a looming gray goalpost, as Cora trips and stumbles forward. There is blood in Cora's left eye making her vision pink, but as she draws closer, the hazy light converges into the pink Taco Bell logo. Cora wraps one hand around her stomach, feeling like her battered skin might unzip, spilling all her organs out. She doesn't think she's bleeding or cut open anywhere, but she knows that with adrenaline, you can't always tell.

She reaches the parking lot and some people smoking outside their cars give her weird looks but don't say anything. A couple carrying their order in paper bags walk past her like she's not even there. She looks down at herself as if to confirm that she really exists, is really coated in blood, then sits down on a bench leading up to the walkway. Someone pulls into the parking space a few feet from her and pointedly looks away, sidestepping her to get into the restaurant.

Cora thought the light would feel safe—no one gets stabbed to death in brightly lit, crowded areas, after all. But slowly, Cora begins to realize that it doesn't matter where she is. Cora isn't safe in her own apartment. She's not safe in a car. She's not safe in public. Anywhere she goes, she could be killed and no one would care. The police would never find her killer. The newspapers would never report on it. She peers at people's eyes over their masks and remembers the uneven black-and-white eyes on the case files that could belong to any of these men.

Cora thinks about a time, before the pandemic, when she truly thought the worst monsters were the ones inside her own head. When she thought people were mostly good, that they would save each other.

Cora hugs her knees, shivering as the neon sign far above her blinks on and off. Delilah hovers at a far corner of the parking lot, flickering as the headlights of a bus roll across her.

Cora shakes away the stray shards from her phone. She manages to make out her contacts through the spiderweb of her screen and calls Auntie Zeng. As the phone rings, Cora starts to wonder what she's going to do if she doesn't pick up. Because Auntie Lois sure as hell isn't going to understand the story about the serial killer.

The line clicks. "What?" Auntie Zeng says, sounding annoyed.

Tears gather in Cora's eyes and she lets out an ugly sound, so damn relieved at her aunt's voice. She's the only person Cora has left.

"Cora?" Auntie Zeng says. "Are you crying? What happened?"

Cora tells her everything. She babbles about throwing away the joss paper, rants about the bats in the vents, cries about Delilah eating Paisley and Ryan, her dead friends, everything ruined, her life amounting to nothing but being alone and blood-soaked in a Taco Bell parking lot.

When she runs out of words, her aunt is quiet. "I think you should come over," she says at last.

Cora nods quickly, even though her aunt can't see it. Maybe her aunt thinks she's crazy, maybe tomorrow she'll call her dad and lock her up, but for tonight, Cora wants to live.

"Once you're safe, we can talk about everything else," she says, "but, Cora, about Delilah… Did you say she *ate* your friends?"

"Not my friends," Cora says. "My friend's roommates."

"That doesn't sound like Delilah," Auntie Zeng says.

"Because Delilah is dead," Cora says, maybe for the first time. "I think that changes you."

"How do you know it's her?" Auntie Zeng says, and Cora wants to slam her face into the ground because this isn't why she called, she doesn't have time for this.

"Because of her bracelet," Cora says. "The one you gave her that says *hope*."

The line goes quiet. Cora doesn't know why *this*, of all things, surprises her aunt.

"Cora," her aunt says. But her voice is different now. There's a cold edge to it. Each word is careful, deliberate. "Are you with her right now?"

Cora glances across the parking lot. Delilah is still there, thin as the streetlight, the same gray shade, her needle-neck slowly swaying back and forth like seaweed waving with the gentle pull of the ocean.

"Yes."

Her aunt takes in a slow breath. "Run. Right now."

The words are deathly sharp. Cora feels them prickle across her skin. "Why?"

"Because," her aunt says, "that's not Delilah."

TWENTY-TWO

Cora's gaze settles on Delilah, whose form has gone oddly still, no longer swaying in the breeze.

"What do you mean?" Cora says. "How can you know that?"

"Because that's not Delilah's bracelet," Auntie Zeng says. "Hers said *strength*, not *hope*."

Cora lets out a dry laugh, wanting to cry but unable to draw in enough air. She'd always been ashamed of being illiterate in Chinese, but had never thought it was dangerous.

"Besides," Auntie Zeng continues, "I burned so much joss paper for her because I knew you wouldn't. Her ghost wouldn't be hungry, I made sure of that."

Cora feels rooted in place. The ghost is staring at her from across the parking lot, and Cora is sure that she knows.

If it's not Delilah, who has been following Cora around?

The thought feels worse than any dirt or germ or contamination Cora has ever imagined. The person she fed from her hand, let into her apartment, hugged and cried to, wasn't even her sister.

Cora jumps to her feet, dives into the circle of light from the neon sign five feet to her left. Something scrapes her foot, clamps around her ankle, but she rolls onto the pavement, and when she looks up, Not Delilah is looming over her, Cora's muddy shoe clutched in one hand. The darkness in her eyes blazes, but she stays outside Cora's circle of light. Her jaw unlatches, and she eats Cora's shoe whole.

Cora grabs her phone from the pavement, her aunt's tinny voice calling for her.

"I'm here," Cora whispers as the ghost's hair blows in the wind.

"Where are you?" Auntie Zeng says. "I'll come get you."

"Taco Bell," Cora whispers. "Near Auntie Lois's place."

"Why are you…of all places." Her aunt sighs. "Be there soon."

Then she hangs up, and Cora is left staring at the ghost. She flips on her phone flashlight and blasts it at the ghost, who cowers back.

"Fuck you," Cora says, her arms burning where she touched the ghost. "*Fuck you!* Go haunt someone else. I have enough problems without you!"

"Are you okay?"

Cora turns to a couple standing in the doorway of Taco Bell, light bleeding across the walkway as they hold the door open.

"Is that blood?" the girl says.

"I'm fine," Cora says, scrambling to her feet and all but throwing herself inside the restaurant, grateful for once for its glaring lights. She presses herself to the window and waits for her aunt, prays that Not Delilah doesn't get to her first. The ghost is across the lot again, near the bus stop, waiting.

Cora should have told her aunt to keep her cabin lights on. What if Not Delilah bites her head off the moment Cora rushes to her car?

It turns out she shouldn't have worried.

Cora spots Auntie Zeng as soon as she turns the corner because her high beams are blasting, all cabin lights on, some sort of multicolored light flashing around her. As she races into the parking lot, Cora sees that it's one of those Christmas sweaters that flashes rainbow lights. Auntie Zeng turns and peers through the window, a headlamp squeezed around her forehead like she's going hiking. She pulls into the closest spot and bends down, digging around in front of the passenger seat, reappears with a camping lantern in each hand. She hops out, waving the lanterns like she's signaling a plane to land, as if Cora could possibly have missed her.

When Cora opens the door, her aunt runs to meet her, the circle of light from the lanterns following her. She hands one to Cora and waves for her to get in the car.

"Come on, it's safer back home," she says. "Batteries won't last forever."

Cora slides into the passenger seat, lantern clutched in her lap.

"Is that your blood?" Auntie Zeng says, not sounding particularly worried, like she already knows the answer.

"No," Cora says. "How did you know how to keep the ghost away?"

Auntie Zeng laughs sharply. "You think this is my first time dealing with hungry ghosts?" she says.

Cora hugs the lantern against her chest. "We'll have to do this forever?"

"Of course not," Auntie Zeng says, peeling out of the parking lot. "Just until the end of ghost month. We'll send some lanterns down the river to help guide the spirits back and they won't bother us again. Until next year."

"Next year?" Cora says, throat tight.

"Yes, next year, when we'll burn a hell of a lot more joss paper."

The rest of the drive is silent. Cora feels sick with adrenaline, spends the ride with her head back trying not to puke in Auntie Zeng's car. Not Delilah is standing next to every telephone pole they flash past, a willowy silhouette in the dark, hand reaching out for their car, repeating itself every fifty feet like an endless loop of film. Cora sinks deeper into her seat and hugs her lantern.

They finally pull up to Auntie Zeng's apartment and have to cross the dark sidewalk to reach the lobby, but the lantern light forms a protective circle. Cora doesn't see the ghost anymore and prays she's given up, that she knows she can't mess with someone like Auntie Zeng.

Auntie Zeng punches on the lights to her apartment, then flicks off the lanterns and starts unpacking boxes of Christmas lights.

"Go shower," she says to Cora. "I'll find you some jade, then we're going to pray."

Cora thinks it's far too late for prayers, but she can hardly argue with her savior, so she nods and drops her bag and lantern by the door, kicks her shoes off, trudges to the bathroom.

The bathroom lights are sterile bright, a harsh judgment on Cora's bloodstained face, tangled hair. She takes off her clothes, which stick to her skin, glued from blood and sweat. She doesn't want the shadows from the shower curtain but also doesn't want to make a mess on Auntie Zeng's floor, so she shoves the curtain aside and starts to take a bath. She sets the water as hot as it will go and climbs in as soon as it's a shallow pool, scalding her feet, relishing in the sting. The water rises and Cora dumps half the shower gel into it until it bubbles up, the water already pink from blood.

Here, in the quiet safety of her aunt's apartment, she thinks about her friends and grips her hair and wants so badly to cry, but all she can do is stare at her own reflection swirling with soapy water and feel like she's rotting inside. She remembers drinking with Harvey and Yifei on the train tracks, she remembers them helping her home, the three of them sleeping on Yifei's couch and waking up as the sun bled through her cheap blinds and feeling something close to human, close to the way normal people felt when they had friends who knew all their secrets and didn't run away. The memory of that morning feels so brilliantly clear that it sharpens to a point and aches between Cora's ribs.

She closes her eyes, holds her breath, and sinks down. And there, in the burning tomb beneath the water, she hears it.

Three knocks. Pause. Two knocks. Pause. Five knocks.

Cora resurfaces, her eyes stinging from soap, wet hair hanging in her eyes.

The knocking continues. Cora feels it coming from the wall to her left, the side of Auntie Zeng's apartment that shares a wall with the neighbors. Cora presses a hand to it, feeling the steady pulse from the other side.

Not Delilah must be taunting her, Cora thinks. Locked out of Auntie Zeng's apartment by the light, this is the only thing she can do to remind Cora of her existence.

Three knocks. Pause. Two knocks. Pause. Five knocks.

But why, Cora wonders, does she knock in exactly the same way? The same sound Cora heard in her dreams when she was sick. Even if the ghost isn't Delilah, she'd clearly been leading Cora toward something, and she can't help but wonder what the ghost wants her to know.

Cora steps out of the bath. She'll take another one soon,

but first she needs to check something. She wraps herself in a towel and wipes her feet and steps out into the hallway, pulling her shattered phone from her bag while Auntie Zeng makes dinner. She looks up a Morse code key but isn't sure whether the knocks she heard were long or short, and can only come up with a nonsensical scramble of letters. If the ghost is trying to tell her something, she's doing a shitty job of it. The low-battery sign flashes across the screen, and Cora sticks her hand back in her bag, fishing around for her spare charger.

Instead, her fingers close around something small. Cool, sleek plastic.

Officer Wang's USB.

Cora had nearly forgotten about it through the chaos that followed its discovery. But Not Delilah had given it to her, had wanted her to see it.

"Auntie, can I use your computer?" Cora says, already rushing to her aunt's room before she can answer, still in her towel, tangled wet hair leaving a trail of water behind her.

She jams the USB into her aunt's old computer, curses when she realizes it isn't even on, taps her foot waiting for the dinosaur laptop to start up.

When the computer finally recognizes the USB, Cora double-clicks on it, waits for the password box to pop up, and keys in the sequence that's been echoing in her dreams for weeks.

325.

The password box disappears, and the contents of BACKUP spill across the screen.

One last (and probably most important) reminder

Many people think that death is the end. The ending of pain, of hate, of love.

But these things are not so easy to erase. Any kind of wanting leaves a scar. The living are good at forgetting, the years smoothing out memories until all the days of their lives are nothing but rolling planes of sameness. But in Hell, it is always just yesterday that everything was lost.

The dead do not forget.

Auntie Z

TWENTY-THREE

Neat rows of tiny folders fill the screen. Cora remembers the hallway of doors in the crypt, feels that each little manila square is just another door, that each one will bring her to a place she doesn't want to go.

Maybe knowing will be worse than not knowing, but Cora is no stranger to awful things, not anymore.

She double-clicks on the first folder, then the first image, and a JPG titled "Emily_Lam_05_11_20" opens up, red filling the screen.

Cora chokes on a breath, clapping a hand over her mouth so she doesn't make a sound and alarm Auntie Zeng.

An Asian girl is naked on the screen, cut up into cross sections, flesh poking out between the slices, all of her pieces just barely lining up but slightly off-center, like a puzzle put back together badly. A bat is spilling out of her mouth, wings blooming down both of her cheeks.

Cora hits the *next* button because she doesn't want to see it anymore—she's never supposed to see the bodies, only supposed to clean up after them—but the next one is even worse.

Another Asian girl, speared through with what looks like a harpoon from her crotch up to her mouth, where the sharp end bursts out from between her teeth, a bat gored through on the tip. This one is titled "Zhu_Tingting_07_31_20."

Cora scans through the rest of the photos in a daze. Asian girls with chests blooming open from bullet wounds, Swiss-cheesed with machine guns that blasted away their faces, eyes gouged out with metal chopsticks, hands and feet and noses smashed in, bats tangled in their hair and clutched in broken hands and clenched between their teeth.

Cora closes her eyes for a moment, takes a steadying breath, and closes the image she has open. But all the icons have loaded now, and she can see small red squares in the thumbnails of Asian girls drowning in blood.

All 374 of them.

Cora thought she'd cleaned up after a lot of dead Asian girls recently, but she couldn't have been to more than twenty scenes. She never imagined that there were this many. Most of the cleanups had been for Chinese girls because the cases were funneled through Harvey's uncle from Shanghai and the people who knew him, but the names here are Chinese, Korean, Japanese, Vietnamese, Filipina.

She knows she should stop here. She feels like Harvey—poor Harvey—staring wide-eyed at snuff photos in sick fascination, and she has no idea how or why she made it to the end of the folder, only clicking through until she could convince herself that some of these had to be fake, even though a police officer wouldn't keep fake crime photos.

Cora clicks the back button and hovers the cursor over a folder titled "Correspondence," which seems safer.

The first few files are emails between Officer Wang and

other officers, requests for more people on his case, requests to hand off smaller cases to other officers, requests for overtime. Cora skims through them, doesn't like the more complete picture of Officer Wang that's building in her mind, doesn't want to know someone whose crime scene she cleaned up.

The last two files are MP4s. Cora can't imagine how this could be any worse than the photos, unless it's live recordings of Chinese girls screaming while they're murdered. Cora lowers the volume just in case, so she won't startle her aunt, and plays the first one.

"—my emails," a man says, the recording starting midsentence.

"Stop sending so many emails CC'ing the whole damn department, Wang," says another man. *"It makes you look like a rat."* Cora is sure she's heard his voice before, but she can't remember where.

"I just need more men on the Chang case," Officer Wang says, and Cora hates that now she knows what his voice sounds like, low and full and just a little bit sad. *"This guy is always a step ahead of us. He's already got three more women this week and we have no fucking clue where he is."*

"There are no more men," the other man says.

"I talked to some guys who—"

"Stop doing that."

"What—"

"Stop talking *to people. This is my fucking case, you're going behind my back, making it look like I can't do my job."*

A pause. *"I just think we're in over our heads,"* Officer Wang says. *"It's gonna look really bad for us if we wait until ten more women die."*

"What looks bad for us is you nosing around like I can't handle my own fucking case. Is that what you think, Wang?"

"No," Officer Wang says, after a pause that's just a second too long.

"Then get out of here and do your job, not mine."

There's another twenty seconds of staticky quiet, then the recording cuts off and Cora clicks to the next one. This time, the recording is muffled, like Cora has pressed her ear against a wall and is listening through layers of insulation.

"You want me to forget about it," Officer Wang says, his voice dull, empty.

"That's not what I said," another man—the same one from the first recording—says. *"I want you to file your report, business as usual. Then I want you to move on. This case has been deprioritized."*

"We're deprioritizing an active serial killer."

"Look, everyone in this city needs us, always. You're never going to have time to save everyone, Wang."

"I'm not trying to," Officer Wang says, voice rising, becoming clearer. *"Did you even read the report I sent you?"*

"Kevin," the other man says. *"What these guys want is attention. We're not gonna give that to him, and all of this will fizzle out."*

"But we can catch him!"

"No, we can't."

"But—"

"We can't. *Do you understand me? He doesn't want to throw any more money into this pit. It's gone on too fucking long and it's just making us look like idiots now. He just wants it gone from the papers. People die every day, and somehow the world keeps turning. You know how many people are dying from COVID? More than this guy can get, I can tell you that. This isn't any different."*

Who is "he"? Cora wonders. *Who wants it gone from the papers?* She can't make out what comes next, because both men lower their voices. Then a door opens on loud hinges.

"Leave your bag," the man says.

"Excuse me?" says Officer Wang.

"You're not bringing confidential items home, are you?"

"Are you gonna strip-search me like a fucking criminal?"

"Are you gonna run to the papers like a fucking pansy? I know your type, Wang. You think you're a hero, but you're just a snitch. None of us thinks it'll come down to this when we start, but soon you'll learn that this is how the world is. People die. If you want to stay here, you better learn that."

There's the sound of items hitting a table, a door slamming shut, static, then the recording cuts off.

Cora sits in the silence that follows, her mouth dry, shivering from her wet hair, wondering if she wants to keep going.

A dark part of her had always wondered if the police weren't actually searching for Delilah's killer, but the part of her brain that still believed in the goodness of strangers thought that surely they must be trying. Killers don't always get caught, even when people try their hardest to find them. This was just bad luck on top of bad luck.

She never thought investigations could just be shoved in the back of a filing cabinet, defunded, deprioritized, forgotten. Of course you can't solve every crime, but surely this one was important, surely Delilah mattered.

Officer Wang had tried, she'd give him that. But some nebulous "him" had stopped it.

And Cora wants to know his name.

She moves to the next folder, finds the same profiles she'd pieced together in Yifei's living room, titled "Copy1," "Copy2," "Copy3" under each one. Maybe Officer Wang kept multiple backup copies of his files?

It's strange to see the pieces of their faces lined up correctly, making them look whole and real and not like distorted monsters. The glare of the screen makes their eyes too bright, like all of them are staring at Cora through the thumbnails.

By the time I finish reading through these folders, I'll know which one of you killed my sister, Cora promises. She reserves all her hate for that moment, holds her breath, keeps it trapped safe inside of her as she backs out of the folder.

The next folder has only one file, a JPG titled MAYOR_WEBB, a photo of a blurry sheet of paper, like someone snapped a picture of it on their phone in a hurry, something they couldn't get caught reading.

At the top of the page, Cora can make out the crest of the mayor's letterhead, CITY OF NEW YORK, OFFICE OF THE MAYOR in all caps. Below it, a scrawled note, not even typed.

ANTONI—
REGARDING OUR LAST CONVERSATION—KEEP THIS QUIET, PLEASE. DO WHAT YOU NEED TO DO.
W

Antoni? Cora thinks for all of half a second before her mind fills in the rest, a gold plate on an office door at the police station, *Antoni Mezzasalma, 5th Precinct Captain.*

She sat across an exam room table from him for an hour on the day her sister was killed, recounting what happened again and again after it hadn't been enough for the other cops. *Someone pushed her, she got hit by a train, no I didn't see who did it, yes I'm sure I didn't push her myself, no she didn't slip.* By the hundredth time reciting it, Cora was so dissociated that the story didn't feel like hers anymore, and Antoni Mezzasalma didn't like how emotionless Cora looked when she talked about it. He found it odd, suspicious. Made her stay even longer, yelled at her until she cried, and only then did he let her go.

Cora will never forget someone like that.

And if a letter from the mayor is in Officer Wang's backup files, the secret evidence he'd been gathering behind his boss's back, Cora doesn't have to think twice about what, exactly, the mayor wanted the NYPD to "keep quiet."

She thinks about reporter McSomething, who wasn't "allowed" to print her story, who would have been arrested for it. Turns out it really had been out of his hands. Next year is an election year, after all, and nothing quite dampens enthusiasm for an aggressively pro-police candidate like months of headlines about a serial killer your officers can't catch. Not to mention the Korean mistress he'd all but blamed for ruining his reputation, and to white men there's no difference between Chinese and Koreans. Asian women are all just prized sex dolls until the moment they say no.

Cora wonders if it would have been the same if all the victims had blond hair, blue eyes, American names. If they hadn't been bat eaters, disease carriers, responsible for the deaths of New Yorkers and the refrigerated body trucks in the streets. Would Officer Wang have gotten his backup then? Would those people be worth saving? Clearly, Delilah Zeng wasn't worth the tax dollars. Not to anyone but Cora.

There's only one folder left, and Cora knows this must be the one where she finds out his name. Whoever this ghost is wanted her to uncover something, wouldn't have given her the flash drive otherwise. These are the last few moments she will ever not know who killed her sister, and she still doesn't know who she will be once she reads his name, what she'll do, but knowing changes everything, she is certain of this.

She double-clicks on the folder.

Screenshots spill across the finder, so many that the scroll bar shrinks into a tiny gray ball. She opens the first one.

It's some sort of chat forum that looks like it's from the '90s, basic HTML web design and gaudy blocks of gray and maroon. But it's not from the '90s—the posts begin in April of this year.

The header says *American Dreamers* and has a pixelated GIF

of a Confederate flag flapping in the wind. It takes Cora all of thirty seconds of scanning the text to realize what kind of America these people had dreamed of.

I don't have a problem with the chinese living here, I just think they should try harder to show some remorse for all the dead Americans.

They get so offended when I call it the china virus, as if it didn't start with some bat eater in China.

Chinese are fucking liars, look at the leader they worship like sheep. They ruin the world, they should have to pay for it.

Cora skips forward a few pages, skimming the text. This is so much easier to look at, this is just a thousand things she's heard before, so innocuous in comparison to the snuff photos that it's almost funny.

That is, until she scrolls forward to July 30.

A few minutes to midnight, a user named *yellowdeath* posted the photo of the harpooned girl Cora saw in the first folder—had Wang posted it online?—and captioned it with only four words.

I <3 lamb skewers.

Cora's mind draws to a halt. The photo was bad enough on its own, the blood so fresh and vivid that it feels like it's stained her even though she's not there—but the caption is so much worse. Cora imagines how much force it would take to shove a harpoon all the way through a human body. There's no way you could do it all at once; you'd probably hit some pelvic bones if you went in at the wrong angle. And it's not like slitting someone's throat or bashing their skull in, because this woman would have screamed the entire time. Whoever did this would have had to ignore those screams, if she was even still alive when it happened, but of course she was, you don't harpoon a woman unless you want to see her suffer, and Cora doesn't understand who could look at this and see a joke, see anything but the worst pain they've ever felt, would ever feel.

Then Cora's gaze jumps back up to the date.

July 30.

She grits her teeth and goes back to the first folder, scans the thumbnails for the same photo, which Officer Wang titled *Zhu_Tingting_07_31_20.* One day after it was posted in the forum.

Cora shrinks down the image until it fills half the screen, pulls up the chat forum beside it, lines up the photos, realizes with a wave of coldness that they're not the same.

The angle is similar, but the photo in the chat room is zoomed out more, the blood a crisper red. The woman is lying limp on the ground, but in Officer Wang's photo, she looks tensed, fingers curled, rigor mortis tightening her muscles.

This wasn't some sicko prowling the dark web for crime scene photos and posting them for shock value. This was a photo no one should have unless they were at the crime scene when it was fresh, before the police got there.

Cora scrolls down slowly, reading the comments.

lol

bitch got what she deserved

fucking bat eater

Cora bites back the urge to slam the laptop shut. It wouldn't help because the words are burned into her brain, worse than the picture itself, the people who look at a dead body and somehow don't see a person at all. *Maybe they don't know it's real*, Cora tells herself. She has to believe this.

She keeps reading through the forum and sees more and more of yellowdeath's snuff photos, some the same women as the ones in Officer Wang's folder, others new. As she scrolls on, the comments become less flippant, the posters start asking for details, sending GIFs of applauding hands and confetti cannons.

Cora thinks of the ten profiles she'd pieced together in Yifei's living room and knows that one of them is behind yellowdeath, that this must be what the ghost wanted to show her. This is what Officer Wang and Harvey died for, and the answer is somewhere in these files.

But as she reads on, other users start posting photos.

Some people say they only found the pictures online while others imply they took them themselves. *An homage to yellowdeath*, one says below a picture of a woman face down in a bathtub of blood, bats bobbing in the water beside her, seventy-two upvotes. *How'd I do?* says another, below a picture of an Asian woman cut into pieces, jammed inside a suitcase, the photographer making a thumbs-up in the corner of the photo. Fifteen downvotes because *you forgot the bat.*

Maybe Cora has seen too much, but the nausea has all but disappeared, a strange emptiness in her stomach, almost like hunger, but sharper, deeper. She isn't even surprised anymore, the words meaningless, painless as she takes them in. She knows that half the world sees Asian girls as pretty dolls, tiny trophies to parade around and fuck and then discard because you can't love someone who isn't a real person to you. She knows this, none of this is new, this is all just fingers running over scar tissue.

Cora is speed-reading and almost misses the most important post, almost clicks past it but can't because she's reached the end of the screenshots.

I have a friend in the NYPD. Keep this low key, yellowdeath's cases are getting swept under the rug, bad publicity considering how much $ they gave the police this year.

How do they know if it's yellowdeath or one of us?

They don't.

It's open season.

And that's it. Cora reaches the end of the folder and realizes she has read through everything in BACKUP.

She must have read too fast, missed something important. She clicks back to the profiles of all the suspects—Copy 1, Copy 2, Copies 3 through 10—and stares at their bored gray eyes.

Somewhere deep inside, Cora already knows the answer. The thought bobs near the surface of her mind but she shoves it down, drowns it, won't let it breathe because it's not the answer she wanted. The answer is supposed to be satisfying, conclusive, life-changing.

But Cora *knows*. She has known ever since she saw the first photo posted by someone besides yellowdeath in the forum.

She knows that Officer Wang didn't write *Copy* on the profiles because he copied and pasted the files from somewhere else. He wrote it because these are copycat killers.

She knows that maybe this started with one person, one man she could hate for everything he'd taken from her, one single villain she could channel all her rage into, turn over to the police, hunt down and kill if she worked up the courage.

But it wasn't just one person anymore. It was a movement.

Wang hadn't saved those ten profiles because one of them was the killer. He'd saved them because all of them were killers.

If she could speak, would Delilah even know who killed her? Cora wonders. He was wearing a mask, after all, his eyes and his hand the only things visible, and how much time did Delilah really have to look? Was she even facing in his direction, or did she see nothing but the incoming train?

But Delilah didn't give me the flash drive, Cora remembers.

A dangerous quiet settles inside of Cora, the stillness that is the prelude to something awful, though Cora isn't yet sure what that will be.

Slowly, Cora reaches to the wall and turns the lights off.

The ghost appears in the corner of the room immediately, as if waiting for her. Auntie Zeng's ceilings are low, so her neck curves at a ninety-degree angle, pressed to the ceiling, sticky hair hanging down across the dresser.

"Who are you?" Cora whispers, strangely unafraid, her whole body numb after absorbing so much pain. She turns the computer around, screen facing the ghost, and pushes it forward.

The ghost draws closer, and at first Cora thinks she might eat the computer whole, but she reaches out a bony finger, taps the trackpad several times, then straightens up. Cora pulls the computer back.

A photograph of a girl collapsed naked in a bathtub, face blasted away by a machine gun. Cora recognizes the bathroom even before her gaze drops down to the title: He_Yuxi_08_01_20.

The first crime scene where Cora found a bat.

Cora meets her gaze across the dark room, Yuxi's neck drooping like a wilted flower, and she wonders how Yuxi would look if she had a face left that could cry or scream or talk, if someone hadn't stripped away what made her a person. Everyone wants Asian girls to look pretty. No one wants them to talk.

Yuxi He moved to America to become a doctor, worked during a pandemic, got blasted to pieces in her bathtub, and Cora would bet that no one even contacted her family. No one knew to burn joss paper for her, leaving her ghost starving and suffering because there couldn't be peace even in death, not for someone like her.

"I'm sorry," Cora whispers, tears hitting the trackpad. "I'm so fucking sorry."

She turns away so she doesn't ruin Auntie Zeng's laptop with her tears, hunches over in the desk chair. It would be so damn easy for Yuxi to kill her right now if she wanted to, just walk over and pop her skull off her shoulders and eat it, and Cora wouldn't even fight it because Yuxi deserves her anger, should be allowed to raze the city to ashes if she wants to, rip Cora's life from her chest and take it for herself.

But the ghost just stands in the corner and watches her, and Cora feels truly pathetic crying in front of someone who understands suffering better than she ever will.

All this time, Cora thought Delilah was leading her to her killer. She thought she'd have her chance at vengeance, or closure, or *something* meaningful. That secret was supposed to arm Cora, give her a choice, let her be the kind of person who forgives or the kind of person who calls the fires of hell or *someone*, anyone besides just Cora Zeng.

But the White Spider in Cora's dreams was a million different people—the man who spit in Cora's face, the one who grabbed Yifei's arm, the ones who called Delilah a Chink and threw garbage at her, the quiet ones on buses who glared at Cora for wearing a mask, who crossed the street to avoid her like she was a living breathing virus even though she was cleaner than any of them, the words *China virus* like a poison promise, go back home, repent for killing Americans.

And Cora knows the name of Delilah's murderer now, realizes she has always known it.

It is two words born of hate, buried in wet soil that grew crooked roots and poison leaves and sharp flowers. They fed a thousand hungry souls that wanted to know the face of fear, wanted to escape the end of the world and didn't care what it cost, who it cost:

Bat eater.

Cora stands up, pulls her soiled clothes back on, crams her feet into a pair of Auntie Zeng's too-small sneakers, ties back her wet hair, and stomps into the kitchen, where her aunt is stirring soup.

"I'm going out," Cora says. "I need to finish something."

Auntie Zeng looks over at Cora, her expression even. She raises an eyebrow as she takes in her appearance, but she must see something in Cora's eyes that changes her mind, because she sets down her spoon, takes off her own jade necklace, and places it over Cora's head.

"Take this for protection," she says. "You need me?"

"No," Cora says. This is something she has to do—wants to do—herself.

Cora tosses her backpack over her shoulder, throws a flashlight inside, moves to leave, but hesitates as her gaze catches a lone packet of joss paper, a box of matches on top of it. She grabs the matches, stuffs them into her bag, and heads out into the night.

TWENTY-FOUR

Cora enters the darkness and doesn't bother to turn on her flashlight. Not yet. She's forgotten her mask, but the night air feels sharp and clean and she misses the days when COVID was her biggest fear.

Yuxi walks close behind her, wet footsteps slapping the pavement as she crosses the street. People pass Cora, but they feel even less real than the ghost trailing her, merely shapes and colors and dreams floating down the street. Maybe some of them still believe in a world where the good guys win, where the inherent kindness of people prevails, and Cora wishes she could be like them again, even for a single moment. To worry about toilet paper and rent and finding your dreams. Cora hated her life back then, but she would give anything to slip back into it, knowing what she knows now.

She clutches her keys in her right hand, one between each finger like claws as she walks until she can see a church steeple, a wooden cross in the sky, stained glass windows. She passes by the main building because her god is not in the cathedral, he is in the crypt.

Yuxi has already opened the first door for her, crouched under the low ceiling, and Cora walks through the curtain of her matted hair as she forces open the second door. When Cora stands in the crypt, bathed in red light, breathing in dust, she can almost picture the Delilah of her imagination standing before the center door, pointing.

New dust has fallen since Cora cleaned, and she leaves footprints in the soft gray floor as she goes to the door, wrenches it open.

There is no second world in white fire, no ghost, no Father Thomas. The same as before, there is only an old coal-burning furnace in a tiny closet, a couple of spare mops, an overturned bucket, and tiny white propane tanks.

Cora takes one tank in each hand, one in her backpack. They're heavier than expected, straining the weak seams of her backpack straps, stinging her fingers, pulling at her shoulder sockets, but she welcomes the pain and she heads back outside. Behind her, Yuxi follows silently, observing, her spindly shadow falling over Cora, never letting her forget that she's there.

When she reaches the street again, Yuxi is not the only one walking behind her.

"Hey, you need any help with those?" a man says.

Cora barely registers the words, casts a quick glance over her shoulder at a white man in jogging clothes.

"No," she says, turning back around.

"Where you going?" he says, walking beside her now as she heads for the next intersection. And when Cora doesn't answer, her mind too full of static, he stands in front of her. "A pretty girl like you shouldn't be out walking alone at night," he says.

Cora doesn't have time for this, tries to step around him, but he steps in front of her again.

"It's not nice to ignore someone who's talking to you," he says, and the change in his voice makes Cora's skin prickle, because she knows that tone. She can't run, because she needs the propane tanks, so she stands rooted on the sidewalk, the tanks growing loose in her sweaty hands. There are some people on the sidewalk across from her, but hardly anyone is passing the church this time of night.

"I'm not pretty," she says at last, "and I'm not talking to you."

She tries to step around him again, but this time he grabs her arm.

Cora's mind bursts into a thousand white spiders. His fingers clamp down and the propane tanks tumble to the sidewalk. He's pulling her toward him and a scream catches in her throat and all she can see is the open mouth of the train tracks, jaw cracking open wider to welcome her between its teeth, how Delilah's hair had blown behind her as she'd fallen, how it happened so fast that she hadn't even put a hand out to break her fall, a roar of a train and a great crack of Delilah's neck breaking off, the heavy sound of her body hitting the platform.

Cora wrenches her arm away and shoves the man into the street.

Brakes screech and horns blare and there's a sound of folding metal and a blinding wash of headlights bright in Cora's eyes. There's a crunch, but she can't see anything at all, can only hear people gasp, a woman's sharp scream.

I've killed him, Cora thinks, disbelieving at first. Her ears are ringing, hands stinging from holding the propane tanks, and Cora Zeng never thought she was the kind of person who murdered.

But maybe he would have killed her first. The only way she would know was if she was dead like Delilah. The only time she's allowed to fight back is when it's an abstract thought, when she's already dead and reporters can speculate on what she should have done differently. But Cora Zeng does not want to die today.

The headlights shut off and when Cora can see again, the man is standing in the intersection, a taxi stopped in the crosswalk, all traffic drawn to a halt, the driver already getting out to see if the man is still alive.

And he is. He's fine, standing pale-faced in the middle of the intersection, a breath away from the cab, staring in disbelief at Cora.

"You're crazy," he says quietly, frown carving across his brow. Then louder, *"You fucking crazy Chink!"* he says, jamming a finger at her. The driver turns to look at her, so do the pedestrians on the other side of the street, everyone on the block. "You tried to kill me! I tried to help you and you try to murder me? You fucking bat eater!"

Cora's hands tremble, and all around her she can hear the roar of the train tracks even though no train is coming, the loudness of her mind crescendoing with the man's yelling and the brakes and the crunch of bone and Yuxi is still standing behind her, her long hair blowing in her face and—

"That's right!" Cora shouts, her voice echoing across the frozen crosswalk, words grating up her throat. *"I am a fucking bat eater!"*

The words silence the man, a cork jammed into a bottle.

Cora Zeng decides in that moment, with the whole block staring at her and headlights searing her vision and a hungry ghost looming behind her, that this is the kind of person she will be. The dirty street urchin who eats dogs and cats and bats raw, the communist spy who wants to kill Americans, the virgin in a schoolgirl skirt that will seduce him and ruin his life—all of his crooked fantasies can be true for all she cares. Because a bat eater is the kind of person that white men want to hurt, the kind of person who tangles their fear and hate together and elicits their rage, the kind of person who scares them. And Cora knows all too well that you can't fear someone who has no power over you.

She picks up her propane tanks, stares back at him, dares him to try to grab her again with all these people watching. But the man is stunned, out of words to say. Sex dolls aren't supposed to talk back.

Yuxi's hair blows over her shoulders, and the man's eyes widen as he focuses on something behind Cora. He takes a step back, stumbling against the taxi, sliding down its hood. The driver is talking to him again but Cora is already walking away, Yuxi's wet footsteps slow and steady behind her.

She descends into the train station, but the lights are off and Cora's footsteps echo across the empty caverns and she doesn't quite process it until the turnstile jams and she realizes the station is closed. The hours must still be reduced in the fever dream of COVID, and it's deathly late at night.

Cora stares out across the platform, the empty mouth of the dark awaiting the train, and remembers standing there with Delilah a lifetime ago.

This is East Broadway, the station where everything ended and began.

Cora sets down the tanks, shoves them under the bar, and hops the turnstile.

Yuxi is waiting for her on the other side as Cora picks up the tanks again, palms sweaty, and moves to the very edge of the platform, a breath away from the darkness. She inhales the wet air, and she hears the roaring of the train even though she knows it isn't coming, remembers distantly the splash of hot blood on her face, the moment Delilah became a body and not a person, wonders if it will ever feel less real.

When Cora opens her eyes, there is another ghost on the tracks.

It stands beside Yuxi, a pair of gray dandelions blurred by darkness.

Cora sits down on the ledge, swings her legs for a moment into the open jaws of the dark, then jumps down.

It is farther than she expects, and her knees ache as she lands, palms pressing into gravel, no Harvey to catch her this time, tanks clunking down beside her. She rises to unsteady feet, and the two ghosts are already twenty feet down the tracks, looking over their shoulders at her, waiting. She adjusts her bag, grits her teeth, and follows them.

She walks unsteadily across the gravel, aware of the low buzz of the third rail to her side. Her ankle feels wrong after the jump, but she moves forward, eyes adjusting to the dark that stretches on forever. Behind her, another pair of footsteps crunches across the gravel. Cora looks over her shoulder at a third needle-neck ghost craned over her, teeth bared.

Instead of terror, she feels an ache bloom in her chest. Another person who was forgotten.

She turns away and trudges farther into the dark. More footsteps begin behind her, the ground suddenly alive, whispering with shifting gravel. Cora keeps walking, trudging forward.

A sharp pain twinges in her ankle and she spills forward onto her hands and knees, the top of the tank in her right hand punching her in the stomach as she falls over it. She pants for a moment, the tunnel still and silent.

Then a hand closes around her arm, sharp nails piercing through her shirt, and pulls her to her feet.

Cora turns around.

The tunnel, as far back as Cora can see, is filled with hungry ghosts.

Like a field of gray flowers, their heads gently bob and sway, their shapes growing hazy the farther back they go. Hundreds of them.

And for a single moment, Cora does not see their withered faces and empty eyes. She sees the faces in Officer Wang's photographs, back when they had skin and eyes. The hundreds of girls torn apart, stripped of their dreams and then their bodies, suffering even in death.

Cora wipes her face on her sleeve, then tightens her grip on the tanks and moves forward, the parade of footsteps shuffling behind her, an ocean of gravel scraping across the tracks. It's hard to breathe, but she keeps going, imagines that one of the ghosts is her sister, even though she'll never know because both life and death stripped her body from her.

She comes up to a ladder, where Yuxi stands and waits. Cora hauls the tanks over the lip and pulls herself onto the platform. The ghosts trail behind her even as she clambers over the turnstile, a sea of gray rolling after her. She climbs out onto the street and the ghosts don't disperse under the streetlights, their wet footsteps slapping on the pavement, the people in the streets passing through them like they don't exist.

Cora reaches the gates of Gracie Mansion, the mayor's residence.

A police car is parked outside, and the ghosts climb over it, swathing it in darkness as Cora breezes past it, past the iron fences with perfectly trimmed shrubbery, perfectly cultivated ivy, tiny garden lights in soft circles of white. A moon-white path opens up to a pale yellow house with a wraparound porch lined with pink flowers. The glass windows capture the streetlights, reflecting the trail of hungry eyes behind her as far as Cora can see.

Cora remembers Auntie Zeng's joss paper house burning, how the dead had grabbed at it.

But it wasn't enough. These ghosts are starving, with no one left to feed them.

No one but Cora. And she has something even better than joss paper to give them.

Cora stands in the flowerbed, petals crushed under her sneakers, feet sinking into fertile earth. She twists the valve of the first propane tank, sloshes it across the porch, the railings, the windows. Some of it splashes back across her shirt and the stench burns her eyes, but she empties the tank and tosses it away, crosses to the other side, and starts again with the next tank. She paints the first floor in chemicals while the ghosts watch her just beyond the flower bed.

She turns to them, stares into the darkness where their eyes should have been.

"It's for you," she says to them, then again in Chinese, just in case. Because Cora understands now that they can only take what is given to them.

She pulls the matchbox out of her pocket, strikes it once against the side, and tosses it into the flowerbed.

A bony hand pulls her back as the fire races along the trail of chemicals, flowers withering black, flames spinning in ribbons around the banister, licking up the walls. The ghosts keep pulling her back, but Cora wants to watch. They pull her just beyond the fence and finally let her go, and she stands on the sidewalk as the house falls away like a long-dead body breaking apart, old wood eaten through by angry fire.

The windows fog up with smoke, and a blonde woman bursts out the front door in a gray cloud, silk pajamas covered in soot. She calls out someone's name, but the house is swirling in black clouds toward heaven or hell or whatever awaits things devoured. Sirens scream in the distance and a crowd gathers behind Cora, peering over the fence.

The smoke stings Cora's eyes, so she closes them and feels the rumble of flames and the screams and the sirens and for the first time in her life, Cora prays and means it.

She prays that this is enough. That this will placate the suffering dead. Even if it only gives them a moment of peace, it's worth it. Cora can never give them everything they deserve, can never make up for what's been done. But she can see them, she can hear them, she can give them this much.

Cora arrives back at Auntie Zeng's apartment covered in soot. Her aunt is praying in the corner, lights still blaring. She looks over her shoulder at Cora, then glances at the clock.

"It's past midnight," she says. "It's the last day of ghost month."

Cora stares back at her, eyes full of smoke, ankles weak. Auntie Zeng's eyes soften.

"There's only one thing left to do," Auntie Zeng says. She grabs a bag that rustles and clanks, takes Cora's hand, and leads her back out. Cora follows in a daze, feeling like she's spiraled up into the sky with all the smoke.

Cora can't feel her legs as she walks, the city lights blurring together, the night ripped open. They walk to the East River, along the promenade until they reach a small beach where Auntie Zeng hops down from the concrete ledge, ankle-deep in the water, and pulls out paper lanterns shaped like tiny pink lotuses. Cora has many questions, but she has learned to do what her aunt says when it comes to ghosts.

"We need to guide them home," she says, handing one to Cora, striking a match, and lighting the tea candle inside. Cora sets it gently on the surface of the water that laps cold up her wrists, and for a moment it wobbles as if it's going to overturn. But the river pulls it out and it sails slowly toward the center, a tiny star in the black waters, floating to a distant, undetermined destination.

In silence, they light the lanterns, feed them into the river's mouth, watch them disappear into beyond. Cora's fingers tremble as she strikes the matches, her aunt's bag seemingly never-ending.

White sheets begin to bloom in the dark waters, like butterflies rising to the surface. The ghosts tear through the water, chasing after the lanterns, walking through the river like it's deep sand.

At last, there is only one lantern left. Cora holds it in both hands, looks across the river at a single ghost swaying along with the river's pull.

She wonders if Delilah can hear her from across whatever expanse she has crossed. If she has heard her this whole time, or if the doors between them are sealed shut.

Would you have come back for me? she wants to ask, face turned toward the sky. But she will never know the answer.

She presses the lantern close to her face, feels its paper petals scratch her cheek, inhales the scent of fire and river and city grease and secondhand smoke and blood still on her clothes. She sets the lantern down, takes a deep, trembling breath, and strikes the match.

TWENTY-FIVE

April 2021

The end of the world lasts longer than Cora expects.

It turns out the pandemic is like a dream in that people have many different interpretations. Months roll by and the herd of refrigerated body trucks in the streets starts to thin as one by one the bodies are buried or burned, and people grow tired and start to pretend the apocalypse is over. Truth be told, Cora never really thought there would be an After. She doesn't think of herself as the kind of person who makes it through the teeth of the end of the world and ends up on the other side.

Cora drops her rubber gloves in her bucket, breathes in a single, glorious breath of cleaning chemicals, glances at her reflection in the polished linoleum, and shuts off the light.

Cora has learned that deep cleaning for apartment turnovers can be just as satisfying as crime scene cleanups. She uses extra-strength degreaser to scrub linoleum, polishes watermarks out of bathtubs, scrubs grime from windowsills, strips nicotine stains from walls.

The owner is a woman named Yejide who lets Cora work

alone and pays her on time and gives her health insurance, and it is more than Cora thought she would get out of life for a long time. Cora's life is simple now. She has no friends, no dreams beyond the reach of her fingertips. Not yet.

For weeks after ghost month, Cora slept on Auntie Zeng's pull-out couch. When the lease was up on Cora's apartment, she moved her things into her aunt's place because she didn't have a job anymore. Harvey's uncle never formally fired her, but Cora saw a sign that the dry cleaner was closed indefinitely and a neighbor said the owner was moving back to China. Besides, Cora didn't think she could work with anyone but Harvey and Yifei.

It took two days for them to find Harvey's body. Cora feels badly about that. For a while, the story was in every paper and reporters swarmed the dry cleaner. Cora asked Auntie Zeng to write an email in Chinese to Harvey's uncle asking if there would be a service, but Cora has a feeling her email got lost in the slurry of reporters trying to contact him. In the end, after the caution tape came down, the store went dark and the lights never came on again and Cora doesn't know what happened to Harvey. She thinks his uncle probably cremated him and brought him back to China because there would be no point trying to reassemble what was left of him in a casket.

Sometimes Cora sits in the park where they summoned the ghosts and remembers when she thought that was the worst thing that could possibly happen. She can see Harvey sitting there beside her with the exact same clarity that she used to see the White Spider, except the ghost this time is not hands but Harvey clutching his custard bun and telling her, *It's not a joke to me, Cora.*

Cora's greatest regret is leaving Yifei by the side of the road. If she'd thought more about it, if she hadn't been trailed by a hungry ghost, she could have stopped what happened next.

Yifei was undocumented, and Yifei Liu wasn't even her real name, so she became a Jane Doe in a morgue. Cora, having no relation to her, no proof of who she was, wasn't allowed to identify her body much less do anything with it. Cora would have paid the ten grand or however much it cost just to hold a funeral for her, but she wasn't allowed to. She read that unclaimed corpses are usually dumped into communal graves on Hart Island, so maybe she'll go there one day, when she feels less ashamed.

Cora did manage to save Yifei's stuff, though. She knocked on the landlord's door, hoping he would take pity on her, and found out that he can't tell Asian women apart when he immediately assumed she was Yifei. Cora didn't feel bad when she pretended not to speak English and pantomimed needing a spare key until he gave it to her. Then she emptied Yifei's room out in boxes with Auntie Zeng and never went back.

Most of it went to charity shops—Cora is fairly certain at least 80 percent of the trinkets were stolen anyway, and there simply wasn't room in Auntie Zeng's apartment. Cora kept a single box of Yifei's things that she leaves in the corner with Delilah's box. The only thing she took out is a fork mobile—a sculpture made of twisted forks that's such an absurd and pointless thing to steal that it made Cora laugh until she was sobbing. She set it on the windowsill of the living room and the fork on top bobs and dips and sometimes catches the glare of the sunlight and reflects it in bouncing beams of light across the wall.

Last summer, on the last day of ghost month, the mayor died in an unexplained house fire, and a USB titled BACKUP appeared on the desk of a *New York Times* reporter. With the unofficial gag order lifted, the reporter published a ten-page spread on the NYPD cover-ups.

The city protested for days while Cora watched from Auntie Zeng's window. The protestors in Brooklyn stood behind police lines, while the protestors in Flushing and Sunset Park got maced back into their houses. But the stories spread across the country, and so did the protests. Wuhan was the epicenter of body bags, and New York City was the epicenter of anti-Asian hate crimes. The public advocate who took over for Mayor Webb promised that those responsible would be punished and compromised cases would be reopened, then promptly put half the police force on paid administrative leave. Cora doesn't hold her breath waiting for justice. She knows better now.

Last month, a Korean spa in Atlanta was gunned down by a white man. Asian women dead over their foot tubs and nail polish racks. The day after, Cora sat in the corner at church coffee hour and listened to her Auntie Lois and her friends talk about how "China virus" isn't an offensive term, just factual, and Cora decided she doesn't want to go to church anymore. It means Auntie Lois won't help with her student loans, but because of the federal payment pause, that's a problem for another day.

One week ago, Cora got her first dose of a COVID-19 vaccine. She left the Javits Center with a sore arm and a strange feeling in her chest, something akin to resurfacing from dark waters, gasping down a new breath of cold air. There's still the second dose to go, and Cora knows she's not in the clear yet, but every day leading up to her second appointment feels a bit safer, the worry growing smaller and quieter as Cora knows she's statistically less and less likely to contract COVID again as the vaccine starts to work.

Cora stands in the subway station on her way home, a careful distance from the open mouth of the train tracks. She carries pepper spray and a rape whistle that screams at 150 decibels if uncapped. She clutches it in her hand like a promise.

She is double-masked because she's so close to her second vaccine dose that it seems ridiculous to chance it now, but a man in a Yankees hat rolls his eyes at her and calls her a sheep, which is one of the least offensive things she's heard lately, but she can't help but notice how he doesn't say the same to the other masked people on the train, the people who aren't Chinese.

At night, Auntie Zeng makes her pray. Cora still isn't convinced that anyone hears her, but it becomes easier day by day to sink into the silence, to let the river of her thoughts run past her. She asks for the obligatory things—look after her sister and her friends, wherever their souls are. Then, when she runs out of benevolent things to think and her aunt is still praying beside her, she starts to think about what else she's supposed to ask for. Cora doesn't know what, not yet. But for the first time in a long time, she can start to see her life in terms of things she likes instead of things she hates.

She likes feeding Auntie Zeng's fish, watching it wiggle toward the flakes and gobble them down. She likes sitting in the park in autumn and letting the dead leaves blow around her and thinking she can maybe hear Harvey's voice. She likes when Auntie Zeng drives her to the beach and she sits on the sand and lets the cold water rush over her feet. None of those things are dreams, or even jobs. But they are pieces. Maybe Cora can use them to build something else, to start imagining what a dream might look like.

Cora and Auntie Zeng have made an altar for the dead out of an old bookshelf. That's where Cora keeps the photo of Officer Wang that the secretary gave her. Next to it is a picture of Harvey that she took from his Facebook page and printed out, next to a Newton's cradle that Yifei stole.

The lower shelf has a framed picture from Delilah's graduation, and Cora realizes as she polishes its glass surface that she hasn't thought of that version of Delilah's face in a very long time. The White Spider had stolen her sister's real face and its memory as well. Beside it, they place a paper lotus lantern that, somehow, has never once stopped burning.

★★★

In the late afternoon, Cora sits cross-legged on her bed and peels an orange as sunlight falls in stripes through her blinds, the room half in shadow, half in light. She lays the pieces of peel on her bed, the air fresh with citrus, her hands sticky in a way that she is slowly learning to tolerate for five minutes at a time before washing her hands. *It's only an orange*, she tells herself, defanging the fear.

She splits the fruit in half, laying one piece on her plate, holding the other in her right hand. With her left, she leans over, drawing the blinds. Darkness falls over her bed. Not night, just a pale gray blur.

She stares at the orange half cupped in her palm.

It's a very bad idea. Cora knows it from the way her hair stands on end, the way her blood is knife-cold, the way the sounds beyond her window fall to hushed murmurs as if waiting to see what happens next. It is a bad idea.

But it's Cora's idea, and no one else's.

She holds up the wet, sticky orange half.

"For you," she says.

No one answers. Dust settles on her windowsill. A car flashes past, engine revving, quieting. Cora holds her breath.

Then a hand grows from the darkness behind the blinds.

It winds around the plastic, reaching out, palm extended. Cora tosses the orange and the hand snatches it from the air. A jaw unhinges with a long crack, wet teeth gnashing through the fruit, juice falling like a sticky rain over the floor.

Cora breaks off a slice of orange from the half on her plate, slips it into her mouth, and eats.

★★★★

AUTHOR'S NOTE

The scariest part of this book, in my opinion, is the first chapter. Not because of the decapitation, but because Cora and Delilah have no idea what's about to come.

Back in March of 2020, I was working as a receptionist at a dental office. When the state ordered us to shut down, I made dozens of phone calls, clearing the calendar for the next two weeks. *Two weeks.* How optimistic we were back then.

It was strangely haunting to write about characters who say things like "when the pandemic blows over," who have hope that all of us know will be extinguished. Someone should tell Cora Zeng that four years later, she'll still be wearing a mask on the train.

For me, no needle-neck ghost can compare to the way the COVID-19 pandemic has changed the world—the way we sacrificed the elderly and disabled on the altar of capitalism, the way trust in the government and the CDC swiftly dissolved, and the way we proved we as a country still haven't learned not to scapegoat an entire race of people in times of fear. The

Japanese side of my family was in the US during the Japanese American internment, and I bet my great-grandparents would have been dismayed at how little has changed.

I dedicated this book to "everyone we lost in the pandemic," but "everyone" should also include "everything." The pieces of ourselves that died in 2020. The hope we had in others, the trust we had in our leaders, the dreams we once believed in. Everyone who reads this book (at least, in the year it debuts) has lived through 2020 and will compare the experiences of these characters to their own at that time. There was so much we couldn't predict.

But I need to remind myself that the future is not a booby-trapped temple in an Indiana Jones movie, full of nothing but unpredictable pain. In *The Anthropocene Reviewed*, John Green wrote: "You can't see the future coming—not the terrors, for sure, but you also can't see the wonders that are coming, the moments of light-soaked joy that await each of us." Even in *Bat Eater and Other Names for Cora Zeng*, which is arguably my most depressing book to date, there are moments of brightness and laughter.

I look back on 2020 and see a woman with a lot of pain she wouldn't see coming, but also someone who didn't know she would publish four books, get a master's degree, make new friends, and be incredibly proud of who she's become. I hope that there are more moments of light-soaked joy in all of our futures, even in the midst of what feels like unending horror.

Lastly, it is important to note that *Bat Eater and Other Names for Cora Zeng* focuses on the discrimination faced by a group of Chinese Americans because this is my personal experience (and the only one I feel comfortable profiting off of), but many other marginalized people in the US face even more violent systemic racism. There would be no Stop Asian Hate movement without the advances of the Civil Rights Movement or the hard work and suffering of Black, Latine, and Indigenous communities. There is no justice for Asian Americans without justice for all BIPOC.

So please do not pity Cora Zeng while condemning Trayvon Martin. Anti-Asian hate is real and deserves attention, but it is only one symptom of a deeply broken society, and we cannot understand or stop it without acknowledging the danger of white supremacy and all the other people it has hurt. Do not let your empathy stop at the borders of your own community.

ACKNOWLEDGMENTS

When I think back to when I first started writing this book, my most salient memories are not the six weeks I spent frantically typing out a first draft before my second job consumed all my free time. Instead, I remember the feeling of relief when I opened an email from my agent, who called the first chapter "brilliant." I remember my friend Joan taking me around New York to visit all the places I was writing about. I remember Yume teaching me what Duane Reade was and where unclaimed bodies are buried in New York (Hart Island, in case you were wondering). I remember Van beta-reading for me even though she knew this book would give her nightmares. Above all, I remember that despite how solitary writing a novel can be, it is what happens in the real world, after you close your laptop, that feeds your soul and fuels your creative mind. I'm so lucky to have so many people who support my writing career while also giving my life outside of it so much meaning and joy.

Thank you, as always, to my agent, Mary C. Moore, for

making all my dreams possible. I'm grateful every day that we found each other and can't wait to see what's next for us.

Thank you to my editor, Leah Mol, for believing in this book and championing it so fiercely. I knew from our first conversation that you understood this book and that it would be in good hands with you. Thank you as well to the whole team at MIRA for your dedication to this story and all the hard work you've put into publishing it.

Thank you to Natasha Qureshi and the Hodderscape team for championing this book in the UK, alongside my YA work.

Thank you to my amazing and talented beta readers—Van Hoang, Yume Kitasei, Karen Bao, and Chelsea Catherine—whose feedback improved this book immensely.

I'm especially thankful to my dear friends Joan and Yume for taking me around New York at night to check out all the spooky places I wrote about in this book. Thank you as well to my friends Kin, Lina, and Jialu for helping me with Chinese.

Thank you to my friends who are too scared to even say the word *ghost* at night but have been endlessly supportive of this gruesome story. Thank you to my family, who is probably a little scared of me now but still buys my books and proudly tells everyone about them.

I am forever grateful to all the booksellers who have supported my previous work and made my career possible. Thank you as well to the librarians and teachers who have introduced your communities to my books. Thank you to all the creators on BookTok, Bookstagram, and BookTube for telling people about my work (whether you liked it or not!) and keeping the book community thriving.

And of course, thank you to my parents, whose love and support made all of this possible.